LARGE TYPE BALDWIN

Baldwin, Faith, 19——

Innocent

IN
W9-APM-412

Innocent Bystander

Also by Faith Baldwin
in Thorndike Large Print

And New Stars Burn
Give Love the Air
Enchanted Oasis
Beauty
Make-Believe
No Private Heaven
"Something Special"
For Richer for Poorer
The Lonely Man
The Heart Has Wings
He Married a Doctor

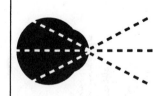

This Large Print Book carries the
Seal of Approval of N.A.V.H.

Innocent Bystander

Faith Baldwin

Thomas Jefferson Library System
214 Adams Street
JEFFERSON CITY, MISSOURI 65101

INTERBORO PUBLIC LIBRARY
802 MAIN STREET
PECKVILLE, PA 18452

Thorndike Press • Thorndike, Maine

SP

Library of Congress Cataloging in Publication Data:

Baldwin, Faith, 1893-
  Innocent bystander / Faith Baldwin.
    p. cm.
  ISBN 1-56054-272-1 (alk. paper : lg. print)
  1. Large type books. I. Title.
[PS3505.U97I5   1992]   92-17513
813'.52—dc20   CIP

Copyright 1934, © 1962 by Faith Baldwin Cuthrell.
All rights reserved.

Thorndike Press Americana Series Large Print edition
published in 1992 by arrangement with Henry Holt and
Company.

Large Print edition available in the British Commonwealth
by arrangement with Harold Ober Associates.

INTERBORO PUBLIC LIBRARY
802 MAIN STREET
PECKVILLE, PA 18452

Cover design by Ralph Lizotte.

The tree indicium is a trademark of Thorndike Press.

This book is printed on acid-free, high opacity paper. ∞

To my friends
IDA and GEORGE CURRIE

Foreword

This is the story of the whispering gallery; the Greek chorus; the destructive force of gossip, idle and casual or malicious; conscious or unconscious.

It is the story of the people who cannot endure to look on the happiness of others; who cannot leave well enough alone; who cannot see others normal, successful and content.

In the jungle the great drums are beaten in their intimate rhythm, and thus, through darkness and across miles of stifling secret space, the news is carried: of a war, an attack, a death . . .

In the world called civilized there are the drums which beat in the mind and find echo on the tongue. There is the grapevine means of communication. From the casual, the laughing, the bitter word spoken across a bridge table, in a locker room, at a dance, in a theater lobby, a missile is evolved which may ruin a business, close a bank or wreck a marriage, or force into a hothouse sort of bloom an equivocal relationship.

In a day when gossip columns flourish as

a symbol of the times, there is little immunity save for those who have learned to erect their barriers. It is a fallacy to argue a lack of character in the persons who permit their lives to be shaped by outside influence.

There are always the innocent bystanders.

CHAPTER I

Sherry and Jimmy Maxwell, standing side by side on the great veranda of Skytop Lodge, looked out one June morning upon an entirely new world.

It was their world; for them created. For them the mountains rose, darkly green, softly blue, into the incredibly clear air. For them the arched sky brooded in limitless tenderness, offering for their sole pleasure its steadfast miracles in a changing panorama: the sun, the storm, the downward-dropping dusk, the lucent silver of the moon, the bright astonishment of stars. For them the laurel surrendered its rosy bloom, the gardeners worked among their flower beds, and the lake lay radiant in the early light. For them the trees put forth an innocence of leaves, were patterned with the living fabric of delicate wings and vocal with bird-song.

Such a world, they thought, was discoverable only by themselves. And beyond this little world of Skytop, beyond the mountains' curving rim, the larger world in all its manifestations waited, and this, too, was their own. Each had lived in the world for a term of years, Sherry for twenty-two, and Jimmy for five more. For five years, for twenty seasons Jimmy Maxwell had inhabited an earth which did not, somewhere, contain Sheridan Nevins. Sometimes this amazed him when he thought of it. And in the last year only had each of them become aware of the world as something personal, offering to sight and sound and touch secret and unimaginable doors into a land of pure enchantment. These doors had become visible to each separately but were, as each had learned through fluctuant hope and despair, delight and melancholy, doors which opened only to their united hands, seeking, and gaining, admittance, with courage and belief and a wild wonder tinctured with humility.

It was the first week in June. For five days Sheridan Nevins and Jimmy Maxwell had been married.

They left the veranda and walked down the steps and took the path which leads eventually to the golf links. They walked close together, and held hands as children do. "I'm afraid," said Sherry, laughing, "that we do act too terribly bridal. We should have borrowed a couple of babies or something," she added, looking at the place set aside for children's amusements, with its slides and swings and sandboxes.

10

"Nothing," replied Jimmy firmly, "would have bored me more."

They sat down on a wooden bench beneath an old tree and looked out, across the lake, at the magic of hill and valley and the clear shining of water. "Funny thing," said Jimmy contentedly, hunting for his pipe, "I've been here a dozen times but I never knew it was as swell as this."

Sherry put her hand over his own. "You mustn't," she said seriously, "smoke before breakfast."

"Why not?" asked her husband, astonished.

"It's very bad for you," she told him gravely; "the one pipe or cigarette you smoke before breakfast does you more harm than the twenty you smoke afterwards, during the day."

"Let's," suggested Jimmy, brilliantly compromising — "let's have breakfast then, I could eat the side of a house."

"The doors weren't open when we came out," Sherry reminded him.

"They will be now — think of the starving early golfers," argued Jimmy.

He rose and pulled her to her feet, kissed her, despite her not very desperate efforts to defend herself, and set a smart pace toward the Lodge. The dining-room doors were open when they reached there. They went through the great, superbly paneled lounge into the dining room where their waitress greeted them with a smile reserved especially for them, and for such as they patently were, charming and bemused pair of honeymooners.

Their table was in the high arch of a window, and from it they could look past flower beds and fields, across golf links and lake to the Water Gap, many miles away.

"Orange juice?" asked Jimmy, writing industriously.

"Give me that," Sherry demanded, and took the order pad and pencil from him. "No one on earth can read your writing."

"You can," said Jimmy.

"What has that to do with it?" she inquired. "Want bacon and eggs, or ham and eggs — Oh, here's waffles," said Sherry, much pleased and secure in the possession of a figure which neither lost nor gained weight no matter what she ate or did not eat.

Early golfers came in, separately and in groups. Middle-aged men for the most part, talking, laughing, plus-foured. One group of eight sat at a nearby big table and presently a woman appeared and joined them. Seven men rose.

"It's easy to see," said Sherry, watching, "which one's her husband." She looked at Jimmy with severity, but her eyes danced.

"If I ever catch you — " she threatened.

"But you won't," Jimmy assured her hastily; "always courteous, that's me. If I ever come to hate you, Mrs. Maxwell, I will still totter to my dogs when you enter a room, with, I might add, your matchless grace."

"Idiot!" said Sherry lovingly.

At the table next to them a group of bottles and boxes proclaimed that one fellow guest was dyspeptic. He appeared finally, a wizened old man with his equally wizened wife. They had a smile for the young Maxwells, and a good morning.

"Swell people," said Jimmy. Everyone was swell today, so far as Jimmy was concerned.

When they left the dining room it was almost half filled and people turned to follow their progress to the door. Sherry stopped a moment to speak to the captain. A woman spoke smilingly to her husband. "That's the bride and groom who came yesterday," she said.

Her husband grunted into his grapefruit and his wife turned to hear her nine-year-old offspring requesting steak and fried potatoes in a plaintive tone. She took a pencil and wrote with decision, "Cereal and one boiled egg."

As they went through the lounge Sherry went to the desk to speak to the tall, attractive, red-headed girl presiding there. Jimmy lighted a cigarette and wandered over to the bulletin board. There'd be a tournament, he noted, qualifying rounds to be played today. There'd be motion pictures in the recreation room tonight, be noted further. As he stood there two men came out of the dining room, and passed him. One stopped and spoke.

"It's Maxwell, isn't it?" he asked, smiling.

Jimmy admitted it. The older man went on.

"My name's Peters. I met you at the last convention." He turned to his companion and made the introductions. "Maxwell, here," he said, laughing, "is one of the brightest young men in the insurance field. Expect to hear any day that you've joined the million dollar Round Table," he told Jimmy, grinning.

"Give me time," said Jimmy modestly.

"Here for a vacation?" Peters asked.

"Oh, for a week or two," said Jimmy; and, then, "Excuse me," he added, "my wife's waiting for me."

He stammered a little, he wasn't accustomed to saying, so casually . . . my *wife*. Sherry was beckoning to him. She stood at the desk, with maps in her hand, and Sam Packer, from behind the desk, was regarding

14

her with tolerance and pleasure.

"Mr. Packer's given me maps," said Sherry. "We can walk — or take the car — I'd like to see something of the country."

"We'll walk," decided Jimmy. "Good for the waistline."

They turned from the desk and went out again to the veranda, passing as they did so the man called Peters and his companion. Jimmy, holding a door open for his wife, stooped to pick up the handkerchief she had dropped. When he rejoined Sherry he was grinning.

"What is it?" she asked instantly.

"The secret's out," he told her gravely. "Peters — that's the man who spoke to me while you were at the desk, he's with the National — said to the other guy just now — Dr. Something-or-other — 'Oh, now I remember, he was married recently,' and *then* he said, 'Did pretty well for himself, young Maxwell.'"

Sherry giggled. "What do you think?" she asked.

"Me? Oh, fair enough for a starter," Jimmy said, pulling her hand through his arm. "As a mere lad," he went on rapidly, "I always aimed to marry money."

They both laughed, and still laughing went down the steps. People looked after them, wistfully, enviously, curiously, according to age, sex and circumstances.

They were well worth looking at. When Mrs. Reginald Nevins, born a Sheridan, sister of that lovely Sheridan girl who afterwards married the Count de Cassagnac, and herself a beauty, had given her only child her family name she did not foresee that Sherry would have hair the color of that conservative wine and eyes that were hyacinthine blue. Blue eyes (or violet, as the case might be) and brows a little darker than the sherry-colored hair. But she had seen to it, had Mrs. Nevins, that Sherry's skin had retained all the faint flush and fine texture of her babyhood, and that her small white teeth were straight and even, and that her figure was given an opportunity to develop naturally and beautifully, and a further opportunity to display itself, as Sherry grew out of her charming, long-limbed adolescence, in the frocks that for line and cut and color were perfectly her own.

Sherry Maxwell was a head shorter than her husband. Jimmy was undistinguished save for height and breadth of shoulder and a direct and sunny smile. Nothing of the cinema hero about him. Commonplace features and nondescript coloring, a look of health about him, of eagerness, of excellent disposition.

"You aren't," Sherry had told him when they first became engaged, a situation which had caused Mrs. Nevins to retire to her room with hysterics, "you aren't a bit good-looking, really. And *am* I glad!"

"Now why?" he had inquired.

"I loathe competition," she had said serenely and regarded him with an interest she strove to keep detached. But couldn't. Nondescript features and coloring were all very well, but there was something which made young Mr. Maxwell peculiarly Jimmy-ish and peculiarly her own. She sighed, after a moment.

"At that," she had admitted, "you have charm."

He had plenty of charm. It had made him exceedingly popular, in an unspectacular way, at preparatory school and at his university. Together with his excellent social connections, it had placed him in the rather high-hat offices of a beetle-browed, intensely go-getting, comparatively young man who underwrote life insurance for one of the largest companies in the world. It had caused many a hitherto faltering hand to sign on the dotted line, that charm of Jimmy Maxwell's. And, during a casual meeting at a football game, it had caused irremediable havoc in Sheridan Nevins' heart.

She had asked him casually, "I suppose you made the usual number of touchdowns for dear old Yale during your four years' rest cure?" and he had replied with considerable gayety, "I warmed a bench for several seasons, if that's what you mean."

She had liked him enormously and, with her round chin cuddled into the great fur collar of her tweed coat, had considered him, at first questioningly and then seriously. And she had continued to consider him seriously, despite her mother's almost theatrical opposition, for a subsequent number of months. "With your opportunities," her mother had wailed, "to say nothing of the opportunities abroad offered you by your Aunt Anna!"

But in the end she had married Jimmy Maxwell, at St. Thomas's, with all the trappings, and if, as her mother still contended, she had thrown herself away, she was sublimely unaware of it.

They walked toward the golf links, crossed the road and the little bridge over the lake and took the solitary way through the trees by the side of a hilarious brook which led to the falls.

Lady-slippers grew here in profusion, little pink galleons, and the long-stemmed violets were in patches about their feet. Sherry turned from the wood path to walk along the flat brown stones, some of them harboring little pools of sky-reflecting water, there at the edge of the brook. Once she sat down, her back against a tall tree, and listened to a silence broken only by the sound of the brook and the clamor of birds. The sun poured hot and golden through the branches, and across the brook the land rose steeply, thick with trees.

"It's marvelous," she said inadequately; and after a minute the true, the inevitable cry broke from her, "If it could always be — this way!"

Jimmy, sitting beside her, put his arm around her. He laid down his pipe on a rock and tilted her face to his own. "It *will* always be this way," he said, and it was promise and reassurance. "You know it, Sherry."

When they had kissed, deeply, with tenderness, with an inexhaustible delight, she leaned her wine-brown head, bright in the sunshine, against his shoulder and sighed.

"I'm sorry for everyone who isn't us," said Sherry, with a happy disregard for syntax.

Jimmy nodded. "Do you know," he inquired, "I came damned near bolting at the altar?"

"If you had — " She drew away to regard

him with immense eyes in which laughter was secret and proud, while the tilted corners of her generous, pretty mouth remained grave. "If you had," she said, "I'd have picked up my train and chased you screaming through the streets of New York."

"No, I'm serious," he protested.

"You are?" She looked at him tolerantly, with a strange, deep, maternal questioning. "But why, Jimmy?" she asked.

"Oh, I don't know. When I saw you, tall and a little strange, and very lovely — coming toward me . . . I felt frightened. The church, crowded, and the flowers — and all the people. I could hear them whispering — and the organ . . . I tell you I was terrified. It seemed too much, too much everything. Too much beauty, too much responsibility, too much happiness. I was weak in the knees. I'm sure Pete knew how I felt . . . he gave me a dirty look and hissed, 'Buck up, you unmitigated ass,' in my ear."

Pete was Jimmy's brother-in-law, two decades Jimmy's senior. Sherry laughed, thinking of how solemn Pete had been, how portly, as Jimmy's best man. Jimmy went on, after a moment.

"I think Pete was remembering his own wedding. I was about seven at the time, and carried the ring on a cushion. I bolted. That was once I *did* bolt, and Jenny never forgave me. It was just like her brat of a kid brother, she said, to ruin her wedding!"

"Just so long as you didn't ruin mine, twenty years later," murmured Sherry. She gave him a long, wise look. "I expect most men feel that way," she murmured, "and some girls. *I* didn't. I wasn't even nervous, Jimmy. Mother said it was indecent, I was so placid. She expected a few flutters. But I didn't give her any satisfaction. I was just — oh, dreaming, wide-awake, walking to where you were waiting for me. And I kept thinking, silly old march, it's too darned *slow!*"

He said, watching the bright flight of a red-winged bird, "Your mother will never forgive me. She's told me a thousand times I should appreciate my luck."

"So you should," Sherry told him, laughing, "*our* luck."

He looked at her a moment, as she drew away a little to put her curly head against the tree-trunk and laugh at him, her gaze consciously sidelong. There was color in her cheeks and gay bright lipstick . . . "Jimmy, it's really indelible after all; can you beat it?" . . . on her lips. Her lashes were dark and long and her small head was nobly set upon her shoulders. She was beautifully made,

21

not an ounce of superfluous flesh upon her bones. She would have been the despair of the ready-made gown department and the delight of a sculptor. Broad in the shoulders, the slender neck curving into the deep breast, the beautiful line from underarm to waist, the slim, modeled hips and thighs, the slender legs and narrow feet.

Jimmy regarded all this, silently aware of her, of the very color and texture of her flesh, the tracings of the veins, blue and faint, at wrist and arm and eyelids. He said merely, not attuned to articulate the sheer poetry of his mood, "You're a knock-out in that outfit. I wish you'd always wear blue."

He had told her the night before that she should always wear green. Her eyes danced. She said: "I can't say the same for you. That's a terrible tie, Jim. Hereafter, I'll buy your ties. At Charvet's, I think."

"I'll buy my own," he said in some alarm; "women have the damnedest ideas about ties."

"Have we found," she asked him, "something to quarrel about at last?"

"I hope so," he told her, lighting his pipe. He set it in the corner of his mouth, clasped his hands about his knees and looked across the tumbling water. "We must have some difference of opinion," he told her seriously, "or else we're too good to be true and we'll split up on compatibility."

"Oh, but there are some," she said instantly. "Riding. You don't like it. I do."

"That's right," he agreed, with a pleased alacrity. "I can think of other ways to spend one's time. The horse always knows so much more than you do."

"Then," said Sherry, "there's the theater."

"But I like the theater," Jimmy told her sadly, "so that's no go."

"You don't like it as I do, goof!"

"Oh, you mean that amateur stuff? Well, no," he acknowledged, grinning, "that's a complete washout so far as I'm concerned."

"There's bridge," said Sherry, ticking off the items on her fingers. "I loathe it. You're good at it, so I suppose you like it."

"Yes. The same goes for dancing, with you."

"You dance very well, Jimmy," she told him reproachfully.

"I was well brought up. I detest dancing — except with you. And even with you it's a waste of time."

"Jimmy!"

"Well," said Jimmy gracelessly, "after all, I can't kiss you to soft music, surrounded by the public unless we, and everyone else, are very tight."

Thomas Jefferson Library System
214 Adams Street
, MISSOURI 63

23

Sherry ignored this. She went on.

"Books. They bore you, all but detective fiction. I love 'em."

"Anything else?"

They looked at each other soberly. Sherry shook her head.

"I'm afraid not," she said apologetically. "We both like the country, and dogs and kittens and side-cars and sunsets and fast motoring and musical comedies and silly cartoons and trick advertising and lobsters and roast beef, rare, and hashed in cream potatoes and strawberry sodas and caviar and furniture that's a little shabby, and etchings of skylines and — "

"And each other," supplied Jimmy, as she stopped for lack of breath.

She nodded. "So," she concluded, "we haven't many grounds for quarrels, have we?" She shivered a little although her jacket suit, soft and knitted, was warm and the sunlight unseasonably so. "I can't bear people who nag and pick and hate each other with their eyes and poison each other with the things they say," she said. "Jimmy, promise me we'll never be like that."

"Of course not," he said; and added, with a pathos he could not realize, "Why should we? We love each other!"

"Maybe they did, once," she said, low.

Thomas Jefferson Library System
214 Adams Street
JEFFERSON CITY, MISSOURI 65101

She looked up at him, her eyes bright. "I — I'm not afraid of the big things," she told him. "I think we could work them out, compromise, find an answer. We're civilized people, Jimmy. But the little, petty, everyday things. Marriages go on the rocks, the jagged small rocks, somehow. They can avoid the big ones, or sail around them."

He could not as yet talk to her in anything even remotely resembling abstractions. He asked anxiously, "See here, Sherry, is anything wrong? You're not — *sorry*, are you?"

She came to her feet in one lithe, lovely movement. She said, as he still sat there looking up at her, his brows drawn, his pipe clamped between his teeth and his hands clasped about his knees, "You *are* an idiot, Jimmy. Sorry?" She flung out her arms in a wide, embracing gesture. "I didn't know there was so much happiness in the world," she cried exultantly.

He rose and stood beside her, not touching her. "Neither did I," he said.

This moment went too deep for touch, for the too-bewildering evidence of the senses. This was a golden moment, one which neither of them would forget. Love had as many facets as a fine-cut gem. If the bread on which it was now nourished was of the body, it was wine to the spirit. They looked

3 1331 00329 5237

at each other with laughter and with gravity.

Jimmy said, after a moment, "I love you, Sherry Maxwell. Shall we get going?"

They walked on together, matched in their step. They went down little hills and through tangled trails, turned from the brook and reached at last the rustic bench upon which two may sit and look at the ceaseless fall of white water over rock ledges, the fine spray tossing, and, the last ledge reached, at the quiet eventual pool under the little bridge.

It was green dusk here, little light came through. The trees were tall, reaching for the sun. Across the falls they grew thick and entangled, while among them were the strong, thrusting branches, the green, shining leaves of the hundreds of rhododendron bushes which later in the season would be an incredible sea of color.

Here by the falls the shining wet rocks were emerald with moss, the great violets sprang, purple, open-hearted. And somewhere, far among the tall trees, above the melodic, eternal noise of the water, a cuckoo called.

Sherry slipped her hand into Jimmy's. She said, and he had to bend his head to hear her:

"All my life I'll remember . . . Jimmy,

we can't stay here forever, we wouldn't want to, really. It isn't living. . . . Oh, I know it's living, intensely, just the two of us. But the people we see and speak to, they aren't really people at all, they're shadows, figures on a screen. It's as if we were the only two who mattered. Nothing touches us. We have to go back, to people who will matter whether we want them to or not, to a routine of living, to work, and . . . and all the rest. I — want to go back. But I dread it, too. This time here, together, is so terribly precious. It can't last — "

She was almost crying, Sherry who never cried. But emotions were easily disturbed these days. Jimmy said, holding her close, in that strange little solitude, green dusk and bird calling and waters falling on the polished rocks:

"It will last. We'll have it always to remember . . . sort — sort of *part* of us, Sherry."

She nodded, after a moment. And they were silent, sitting there, very near each other, not speaking.

After a while she looked at the watch on her wrist. She said: "Do you know it's been ages since we left? Let's go back the other way; look, across the bridge down there and up the hill. I thought we were going to play nine holes before lunch."

"Maybe we can make it," said Jimmy, not caring; "if we can't, there's always tomorrow."

They looked at each other, briefly. Always tomorrow, for them both, always tomorrow for them, together. Sherry rose and laughed down at him.

"Don't," she complained, "sit there all sprawled out and comfortable. You look like a pussy cat. Why aren't you on your feet, brushing obstacles from my path? You act," she accused him, "like a husband already."

"Do you mind?" he asked, not stirring.

"I love it," said Sherry; and turned and was off, moving among the trees, fleeing down the rocky little path before he could move to follow her.

CHAPTER II

Shortly after the middle of June, Sherry and Jimmy Maxwell said good-by to Skytop. The day before they left they had walked all around the lake, surprising a tight-coiled, harmless snake which left Sherry breathless and frightened, watching a flock of wild ducks drift to the surface of the still water, hearing birds sing in the woods, and picking their careful way along the twisted path which sometimes ran directly at the water's edge and sometimes took them back among the trees. They had bidden good-by, too, to the other lake, the falls, the golf links and the high, curving shapes of the mountains. And had seen a deer leap across the road on their last drive around the countryside.

This morning they stopped at the desk to shake hands with Sam Packer, amused and immaculate in plus-fours and sincerely sorry to see them go. They had spoken to the few people they had come to know during their stay; had assured the tall, red-headed girl that, yes, some day they'd be back; and now were standing on the front veranda, which gave on the drive, waiting for their car to be brought up.

Sherry, surrounded by shiny new luggage, looked out quietly over the lovely peaceful vista, her eyes deep, while Jimmy strolled over to the elaborate barometer on the porch wall and tapped it with an idle finger. "Looks," he commented, returning to her side, "as if the weather would hold."

It was in her heart to cry out to him that it must hold, this clear and sunny weather, with its crystal days and cool, dark nights, this June weather of their love. But someone had joined them, a man with whom they had struck up something of a friendship and with whom they had played golf and who now stood beside them, smiling at the array of luggage, and wished them a good trip home.

"Come and see me some time," he told Jimmy. "I'll be back in town in a few days. This is my only vacation, except for week-ends."

Jimmy nodded, flipping over the pages of a notebook to enter a name and an address. The car drove up, the gay, sleek roadster which had been Sherry's extravagant wedding present to her husband. The bell-boys leaped to attention. And presently waving to the pleasant Mr. Simpson, who stood there regarding their departure, Sherry and Jimmy drove off, down the road, past the early golfers and across the bridge.

There are two roads into Skytop, equally lovely, equally unspoiled by gas stations, billboards and the like. They chose the one that led them by a brown, tumbling river, through the trees and the great clumps of rosy laurel. It was very still, they met no cars, and the road was checkered with light and shadow.

Jimmy, driving fairly fast, was checked by a touch on his arm. He turned a little, smiling down at the hyacinthine eyes lifted to his own. Sherry's face was tanned, it was a golden face, and her eyes shone. She said: "Don't go so fast, Jimmy; let's be lazy along this road. It's so beautiful."

He slowed down at once, the car obeying him with precision. "What a car!" sighed Jimmy, well content.

Sherry said, "I wonder if we'll ever come here again."

"Well, of course. Why not? Lots . . . As often as we can," he added in astonishment.

Sherry nodded. She pulled her little beret from her short curly hair and lifted her round, firm chin, feeling the light breeze in her face, savoring the sun and the silence. She said, after a moment:

"I didn't mean that exactly. I — I can't

31

explain. It's just that we're driving away from something so absolutely perfect. I wonder if we'll ever find it again, just as it was?"

He said, "It will always be the same, Sherry."

A little later, driving out of the woods and away from the little river, they reached an open field with a few old apple trees, graceful, low and spreading, standing sentinel, and a tumble-down farmhouse, back of a rickety fence. There were also great lilac bushes, some of which had not yet lost entirely their scented purple blossoms. A bird the color of the sky rose from among the trees and flew away.

"It's a bluebird!" cried Sherry, radiant.

"A bunting, I think," argued Jimmy; "see, it's brighter than a bluebird."

"What does it matter?" she interrupted. "It's blue, isn't it? Bluebirds mean happiness."

He laughed down at her.

"Now you're talking like a greeting card."

"Perhaps. But somehow the bird's an omen. Or I'd like to think so," she said stubbornly.

"Sherry, I didn't know you were superstitious. How many times have I seen you spill the salt and walk under ladders and light three on one match. By the way, have you any cigarettes? Light me one, will you? There's a good girl," said Jimmy, taking the cigarette from her hand.

"I didn't know I was superstitious either," she told him, "but I suppose I am. Being happy makes you so, doesn't it?"

Later, driving through Stroudsburg and stopping farther on to look over the magnificent view on the top of a very high hill, Jimmy asked, "How about stopping at Pete and Jenny's overnight?"

"Let's," replied Sherry instantly. She added: "You know, Jimmy, I like them — awfully. And Jocelyn is the dearest kid I ever knew."

"She's only four years younger than you," he remarked, amused; and added, "At that she's a swell person, even if she is my niece."

"She's crazy about you," said Sherry, "and she likes me, too. I sometimes feel we have a lot to live up to — so far as Jocelyn's opinion of us is concerned."

"We must have her down to visit us, a lot," said Jimmy. "Poor kid, she doesn't get much excitement. Specially since Jenny hasn't been so well."

Sherry nodded.

"We can give her a good time," she promised. She was silent a moment and then she

33

INTERBORO PUBLIC LIBRARY
802 MAIN STREET
PECKVILLE, PA 18452

said, "If they hadn't liked me — your people — I would have *died!*"

"They couldn't very well have helped themselves," Jimmy told her mildly; "and if they hadn't — which was impossible, so consider this a hypothetical something-or-other — it wouldn't have made any difference. After all, you married me and not my sister and her family."

"Oh, that's all very well," Sherry told him, "but it would have made some difference, it's bound to, really. And then Jenny's all the next of kin you have and she brought you up — and did, I must say," said Sherry with her seductive, sidelong glance, "a darned good job of it."

"Thanks," said Jimmy, grinning. The smile died. He asked gravely: "Do you really think it makes so much difference, Sherry? You know I don't stand exactly ace-high with your mother."

Sherry flushed, faintly. She replied evenly.

"Mother's — oh, you'll get to know her after a while. You see, she's always had her own way — ever since Father died, and before, I guess, although I don't remember that part much. She married Aunt Anna off, I must say happily, and she thought she'd see me in Debrett, too."

MIFFLINBURG PUBLIC LIBRARY
402 MAIN STREET
MIFFLINBURG, PA. 1842

"Or Bradstreet," suggested Jimmy, smiling again. "Never mind, some day you'll get there. I'm out to make money and plenty of it." He added, "I have to keep my end up, you know."

"But you do," said Sherry, astonished, remembering the lavish entertainments of their courtship, the flowers, the theater tickets, the dinners, the books. She looked down at her engagement ring and the platinum circle which guarded it, and added slowly, "I thought we agreed that my — my having money didn't matter."

"Of course, it doesn't. And I'm glad you have," he said instantly, "because it means things will be easier for you, all around, until I can tell you, go chuck your little silly old income in Rye Lake, I've enough for two of us — or even five or six," he said soberly.

Sherry tilted her chin.

"Do you really count on — five or six?" she asked seriously.

"Well," replied Jimmy, driving carefully around a curve, "it would be sort of darned nice, wouldn't it? I've always been a family man at heart," he announced in a very deep voice, while Sherry giggled — it was really a giggle, that little chuckle of hers, "and I've always had a yen to play Santa

Claus under a tall tree and to set up a flock of electric trains."

"I pity your sons, Jimmy Maxwell," she said severely; "they'd never have a chance at electric trains or any other gadgets with you around."

Jimmy said, low, "Don't say things like that on a main road in public."

Sherry caught her lower lip in her even white teeth. She said, after a moment:

"We — we talked about this before. Babies, I mean, lots of 'em. You know how I feel. But not yet, Jimmy, I mean, not for a long time. We're pretty young," she admitted, "and I love this aloneness — this being together — just the two of us."

"So do I," he said briefly. "Here, give me your hand, will you? As a good insurance man I can't disobey all the commandments and start one-armed driving."

She slid her hand under his on the wheel. They drove along in silence and after a while went through Hackettstown, lying like an inverted cup at the foot of hills, and past Budd Lake, crowded with people in bathing suits, walking across the road.

"I'll stop after a while," Jimmy said, "and telephone Jenny."

He did so at the next town. Sherry stayed in the car. She snapped open her new vanity

36

case and powdered her slightly tip-tilted nose, she reddened her lips again and waited. Presently Jimmy came back, beaming.

"They're killing the fatted calf," he told her, "but I told 'em we'd stop somewhere for lunch. Okay?"

"Okay," agreed Sherry.

"If only," sighed Jimmy, climbing in beside her and driving on, "if only you'd always be so docile!"

When they reached Upper Montclair and the pretty house in which Jenny, her husband Peter Lee and their daughter Jocelyn lived it was late afternoon. They had lingered over luncheon at a wayside inn, they had gone exploring all sorts of odd and attractive roads, they had been lost, they had stopped for gas, they had stopped to buy popcorn and ginger ale and cigarettes.

Pete and Jocelyn came hurrying out on the porch to greet them. Pete was rather heavy through the middle and his rubicund face shone. Jocelyn stood beside her father, small and slight and fragile in appearance, an entrancingly pretty girl, fair, with an incredible delicacy of skin and feature.

The car drove up with a flourish and stopped dead. Jimmy and Sherry sat still, laughing. "Boy," ordered Jimmy, "give us a hand with the luggage, and make it snappy.

Have you a room for two in your hotel?
Where's the tourist welcome sign?"

Sherry opened the door and got out. Jocelyn
put her arms about her and kissed her.
"We've been waiting," she said shyly, "the
time just *crawled* by. Mother was sure you'd
had an accident."

"Where is she?" asked Sherry, going up
the steps, her arm about the shoulders of
the younger girl, while the men followed
more slowly with the bags.

"She was in the living room, lying down.
Oh, here she is, now."

Pete's wife came to the door, to draw
Sherry inside with gentle hands. She was as
tiny as her daughter and her hair was nearly
white. A pretty woman, in a faded and fine-
drawn way, with lovely, youthful eyes, on
her thin cheeks the bright flush of the heart
condition which kept them all so anxious
about her.

"Well, you two children," she said contentedly. "Welcome home!"

Later, in the big chintz-bright bedroom
assigned them, Jimmy, wrenching off a collar,
looked at Sherry, frowning.

"I don't like the look of Jenny at all," he
grumbled. "She's lost weight. Did you hear
Pete say he'd turned the little library and
lavatory downstairs into a bedroom and bath

for her? She can't take the stairs any more."

"Yes, I heard," said Sherry. She went to him and put her arms around him. "I know you worry a lot about Jenny. I wish I could help — "

"You do help." He caught her to him in an enormous boyish hug. "Just having you around is all I need to make me feel optimistic. But Pete's frightened," he said, releasing her reluctantly. "He doesn't say much, but he's sick with it. You see, they've been through a lot together. Pete built up one pretty solid fortune and then it crashed. Now he's back on his feet again. Jenny's stuck, through everything. I remember when I was a kid things weren't too easy for them. All Jenny's money from Mom and Pop went into Pete's business. She never so much as touched mine, although she could have done so if she'd wanted to, she was my guardian. She sent me through prep school and college and saw to it that I had a decent allowance; and all the time she scrimped pretty much for herself and Pete and Jocelyn, too. It would be — a damned shame," said Jimmy, his voice breaking on the inadequate words, "if anything happened, now, just when they're all set again, comparatively speaking, and she can have a little comfort and luxury."

"I know," murmured Sherry.

Just then Jocelyn knocked on the door and cried, "Aren't you two coming down? Father has cocktails ready."

"Baby, is that welcome news?" said Jimmy. "We'll be right along, Jocelyn — tell Pete to see that they don't go diluted on him, standing."

Sherry, in the bathroom, splashed cold water on her wind-burned face, ran a fingertipful of vanishing cream around her cheeks and eyes and fluffed on the powder. She dotted the lipstick on the curves of her lips and smoothed it evenly with the tip of her little finger. Emerging, she dropped her negligee on the floor, stood up straight and slender, in decidedly inconsequential garments, and, going to the bed where a bag lay open in wild confusion, plucked forth a little chiffon dress and slipped it over her head and tied the belt.

Jimmy commented, picking up the negligee, "This is what comes of marrying a woman who has always had a personal maid."

Sherry, running a comb through her hair, laughed.

"Poor Jimmy! I promise I'll try. You see," she said ruefully, "I've always been so untidy — and Jenny brought you up so well!"

Jimmy laid the negligee over the back of a chair and tweaked his tie into place. "Ready,

Mrs. Maxwell?" he asked, smiling at her.

She crossed to him and laid her arms about his neck and her lips on his mouth. "Did any come off?" asked Jimmy, later, looking for a handkerchief.

"Not a bit; and if it had, would it matter?"

"Well, no," he agreed after due thought.

Laughing, they left the room together. Jocelyn Lee, waiting on the landing, smiled to herself. She adored them, she thought tenderly, they were the dearest people in the world, except her mother and father. She had loved Jimmy ever since her babyhood, following him around with stumbling, uneven steps, the nine years between them seeming like forty-nine in those days. And when he had become engaged to Sheridan Nevins, Jocelyn had wept a whole night through, sure that she would loathe the stranger who was taking Jimmy from them. But she hadn't loathed Sherry; she had loved her on sight with all the intensity of a quiet nature, a nature which permitted itself but few attachments and those almost terrifyingly deep.

They were perfect, she thought, following them downstairs. Young, terribly attractive, beautifully in love.

After dinner Jenny lay on the living-room lounge; Sherry sat on a footstool beside her, talking and laughing. Jocelyn at the old-fashioned upright was running her slender hands across the yellowing keys in falling cadences, bright chords and dreaming melodies.

Sherry said: "Jocelyn has real talent. She should do something with it."

"What?" asked Jocelyn's mother. "We've given her the best training we could afford — when we could afford it. And her teachers all said as you do, real talent, a fine gift. But she's too shy to play for people, except for us, and then, without urging, she just sits down and plays. She has neither the brilliance nor the sure technique which makes the concert pianist — "

"She could have it, with study. She's awfully young."

"Yes. But she hasn't the temperament. People frighten her, criticism would wound her. She hasn't any *fight* in her," said Jenny, sighing. "I suppose I'm partly to blame; she worries so over me, and I'm so useless, such an old crock, most of the time."

"You!" said Sherry in affectionate disdain, and took Jenny's thin hand in her own vital young clasp and held it.

"Yes, me," said Jenny, laughing a little. She went on soberly: "We've spoiled Jocelyn. She always seemed so delicate. She isn't, really, she's strong, wiry, now that she's grown out of the ailments of childhood. The three of us have been very close. I sometimes wonder if it was wise; perhaps we should have let her stand more on her own feet. But she doesn't care for the things most youngsters like. She's a strange child and the most unsophisticated one I've ever met. I don't mean she's ignorant. She isn't, I've seen to that. But she's so dreadfully fastidious, so much an idealist, it terrifies me sometimes. And there's so little nowadays for her idealism to feed on — in people, and books, and plays, and movies. They all seem to present a viewpoint so diametrically opposed to her own that it bewilders and frightens and disgusts her."

"She has you and Pete," Sherry suggested, smiling. She added seriously: "I understand how she feels, I used to be a little that way myself. But — well, you know Mother's crowd and mine — I got a good deal of it knocked out of me, I suppose. For a while, when I was Jocelyn's age, I was the most hard-boiled specimen you ever saw. Then things sort of swung back to normal — and then," she said, her gaze deepening, "along came Jimmy."

"Lucky Jimmy," said Jimmy's sister. "And you two mean a lot to Jocelyn, too. She told me that she can't help believing in a world where people like you and Jimmy exist."

"That was sweet of her," said Sherry, moved.

"What on earth are the men doing?" asked Jenny presently.

Sherry laughed. "Oh, they're still in the dining room over that last bottle of famous port," she replied, "I can hear 'em arguing about something."

"Millie," sighed Mrs. Lee, who had considerable trouble with the here-today-gone-tomorrow, general houseworker, "Millie will be wild! She wants to get off and go to the movies."

In the dining room Jimmy and his brother-in-law were discussing the port and life in general.

"Old married man," mocked Pete, grinning.

"That's me," said Jimmy. He took out his notebook and turned over the pages. "Back on the job with three prospects, no less."

Pete regarded him solemnly. "Remember," he asked, "when you sold your first policy — and to me?"

"You bet," said Jimmy. "That twenty-five thousand policy looked pretty big to me, then. That was — let's see, almost five years ago; I'll be getting renewals for another four years," he said, smiling.

"It was one thing I held on to," his brother-in-law told him. He twirled the glass between his thick fingers. "You should do a lot of business in that Westchester crowd," he suggested.

Jimmy nodded.

"I mean to. At that most of them are anxious only to insure their liquor," he said soberly, "before it's drunk. After it's been lapped up it isn't so easy to insure *them*," he added thoughtfully. "Before I met Sherry," he went on, wondering if there could have been a time when Sherry did not exist for him, "I knew a bunch of that crowd — Westchester-Biltmore first, and then I got to going out to the Field and Tennis Club with Joe McKenzie. Funny I never ran into Sherry," he said; "it took a football game to bring us together, two out of seventy thousand — "

"You and Sherry discussed money yet?" asked Pete; and added quickly: "Don't answer if you don't want to, it's none of my business. But a word of quasi-paternal advice might come in handy if you haven't."

"Don't be an ass," said Jimmy affectionately. "No, we haven't talked much about it. When I asked her to marry me and live on my uncertain income, I was informed that she — and I — needn't live on it, that

45

she had her own. It's considerable," said Jimmy, "even with the cuts in dividends and all that. It figures up to around twenty thousand. Enough to keep her in shoes and horses, I suppose," he said, laughing. "I didn't have any wild notions of asking her to jump in the ocean with it. It's hers, her father left it to her, lock, stock and barrel — she came into the principal when she was twenty-one. Why should I amble along and tell her that she has to exist on what I make? That's silly. It goes all right in the books but not in real life, not any more. My point is, I've got to match her and double her, and that's that. I'll do it, too, before I'm through — and I don't mean maybe."

"You've decided, haven't you, to live in the tenant cottage of the Nevins place?" asked Pete after a while. "Permanently, I mean."

"Yes. There was some discussion about it, as you know. I wanted to take a house or an apartment. But Sherry seemed set on it. She's crazy about the cottage; and, of course, her mother wants her near. She's abroad a lot, too, and it means we can sort of keep an eye on things. . . . "I'm paying rent," said Jimmy after a moment.

"That's a good idea," Pete said casually.

"She didn't want it, or said she didn't, and, of course, it's a darned low rent; we couldn't get a room and bath for that any-where else in that district," Jimmy explained, "but I told Sherry before we were married that I'd foot the bills for rent and food and service and my clubs and insurance and the rest and she could do what she liked with her income."

"You've done well," Pete said after a time.

"I mean to do better. Of course, it's pre-carious. I get the jitters sometimes, think-ing — "

He looked up and laughed.

"Sherry thinks I pick it off trees, nice golden gobs of it," he admitted, "and I don't suppose I've disillusioned her — much. You know how people talk. She's heard Joe and a dozen others tell her what a bright young man I am — "

"I don't blame you," he said tolerantly, his small bright blue eyes wrinkled with amusement, "only some day you'd better sit down with a pad and pencil and do a little budgeting. You don't, after all, want to give Sherry the idea that every time you pull out a fountain pen some man grabs it from your paw and signs on the dotted line for a couple of hundred thousand."

"They're few and far between," Jimmy admitted, "but once in a while they come my way. I'm going out after the big annuities once we get back home, and, boy, you watch my smoke!"

"I'm watching it," replied Pete, regarding the blue ring evolving around Jimmy's head. He added, with a complete change of tone: "Jim — how does Jenny look to you? No baloney now. Straight from the old shoulder."

"She doesn't," said Jimmy, "look awfully well — "

They were silent, each with his own thoughts; Jimmy smoking, leaning back in his chair, his legs straight out ahead of him, and Pete, his big head sunk between his heavy shoulders, mutely brooding. Millie, the fat colored maid-of-all-work, put her woolly head in at the pantry door.

"Ain't you-all never going to let me clear away?" she asked plaintively.

Pete came to himself with a start. "I guess that's our cue," he told Jimmy, "and so — shall we join the ladies?" he inquired with the jocular pomposity which always made Millie — or the current general houseworker — giggle delightedly.

When the men reached the living room Sherry was exclaiming over an ancient album filled with photographs of Jimmy as a baby and as a small child, and Jocelyn had left the piano to hang over her shoulder and exclaim with her. Jenny was lying supine on the couch, her poor heart beating in its rapid, uneasy way, her lips smiling faintly. She reached up her hand to her husband as he came over to her.

"Tired, Jen?"

"No — just lazy," she answered inevitably.

"Jimmy," said Sherry. She laid a slim finger on the photograph of a fat, highly unintelligent-looking baby, clad simply in his own creased skin and a teething ring and tastefully arranged on a white bearskin rug. "Jimmy, say it isn't true!"

Jimmy looked at the likeness of his vanished self with horror.

"I'm afraid it is. Jen, you promised to throw that out!"

"I know I did, but I couldn't. You were an awfully cunning baby," she told him, laughing, "and such a good one."

"There!" said Jimmy proudly to his wife. "But I did think she'd keep her word. She used to threaten to show it to all my girls."

"And did she?" asked Sherry, her bright brown head cocked on one side.

"She did," replied Jimmy somberly, "all eighteen of them. The eighteen," he added hastily, "whom I dared bring to the house. The other thirty-six don't count."

"You can't make me jealous," said Sherry serenely, "I wouldn't be annoyed." She pon-

49

dered over the picture a little longer, her lips touched with laughter and her eyes with tenderness. "I'll have to show Angela this," she said.

"Angela! Holy jumping catfish, I'd never hear the last of it!" said Jimmy in alarm.

"Who's Angela?" said Jocelyn.

"You met her, dear," exclaimed Sherry, "the day we had the tea party at the Waldorf. She's my cousin, Angela Ward."

"The tall girl," asked Jocelyn slowly, "with the very black hair and the simply marvelous clothes?"

"I didn't know you cared about clothes, kitten," her father observed, laughing; and Jenny cried, "Why, that isn't a bit like you, Jocelyn. When I ask you what someone had on you always answer vaguely — 'Oh, blue — or perhaps pink. No, it was green!' "

Jocelyn laughed, her pale, pointed face flushing.

"You couldn't help noticing Miss Ward's clothes," she said, "they — well, she looked like all the *Vogue* illustrations you never see in real life."

"Doesn't she?" asked Sherry, delighted. "Yes, I'll show this to Angela, Jim," she told her husband gayly, "she'll love it."

"If you do," he threatened darkly, "I'll slay you."

"Angela," Sherry explained, ignoring him, "is an old girl of Jimmy's."

"Not very old," added Jimmy instantly; "thirty, at a venture."

"Thirty," agreed Sherry, "and how she'd hate you! She's been twenty-five for five years."

"That's the first catty thing I ever heard you say, Sherry."

"I'd say it to her face," Sherry defended herself. She turned to Jenny. "Haven't I told you about Angela? She met Jimmy before I did — and was quite crazy about him; she kept telling me, 'Wait till you meet my latest discovery. He's a lamb. Ugly as the dickens and more charm than Chevalier.' But she kept him all to herself — until that football game. Then she couldn't help our meeting. I bet she's been gnashing her teeth ever since," added Sherry lightly.

Jimmy thought, even while he muttered at her uncomfortably: Isn't she a darling? God, I'm shot with luck — Sherry, Sherry, just to look at you, never tiring, just to see you like this, not touching you, standing here, with people all around us, and to know you belong to me.

That had happened to him before, was always happening; had happened at Skytop, watching Sherry dance with someone else, sitting with her at a table, being with her surrounded by others, regarding her as she drove off, her lithe lovely body supple and effortless in the using. It would always happen to him, he thought, this amazement catching at his heart, this bright flash of knowledge seizing his mind, the awareness of her tingling through his nerves.

Sherry was talking.

"Angela's grand, when you know her. She lives alone, in New York, in a funny little penthouse with a swell studio."

"Does she paint or something?" asked Jocelyn, interested.

"Sometimes. Takes courses in things, she does, and then drops them. Then she goes abroad and is gone ages. She'd just come back when you met her, Jocelyn, that's why you didn't see her before and why Jenny didn't meet her at the family dinner — that *was* pretty awful, wasn't it?" asked Sherry, "all starchy and stodgy."

"But she wasn't at your wedding, was she?" asked Jocelyn, who had been maid of honor.

"No. She took a notion to fly somewhere. She owns a plane, you know, and has a pilot's license. No, she said she hated weddings, couldn't bear to see two people starting off in happiness and expectancy, like that. Worse than funerals, she says, because at a funeral, you know what's going to happen to the star performer."

No one laughed; Sherry, looking around, encountered Pete's drawn brows and Jocelyn's instant pallor. She went on quickly: "Angela hasn't much use for us, out Rye way. She has a big circle of friends in town, theatrical people, writers, artists."

"Bum risks, all of them," said Jimmy. "I used to try and sign 'em up when I went to Angela's shindigs, and of all the obstinate put-it-off-till-tomorrow, broke today and rich next week, improvident gang I ever met."

"Jimmy," cried Sherry in pleased astonishment, "what gorgeous adjectives!"

"I'm glad you didn't marry her," said Jocelyn, suddenly and sharply.

"Who?" Her uncle looked at her in amazement.

"Sherry's cousin — "

Jimmy burst into laughter, and Sherry, closing the album, clasped her slim hands about her knees and laughed with him. Jocelyn flushed. She was really, thought Sherry, watching her, dreadfully and unfortunately sensitive.

"She didn't ask me, Jocelyn," he said.

"She didn't ask you. Did Sherry?" inquired Jocelyn, beginning to smile.

"Well, practically," answered Jimmy solemnly; "she said, 'Jimmy, you're the nicest boy I've ever met. Marry me and live on East — no, Purchase — Street for the rest of your natural life!'"

"Liar," said Sherry, without moving.

"That's always the way," Pete commented, stuffing the tobacco into his pipe with a big thumb. "Now I know you're really married. I never knew a man yet who would admit that he had proposed to his wife."

"Just the same," said Jocelyn unexpectedly, "I bet Sherry would have asked him, if he hadn't asked her. She's honest enough . . . I mean," she went on as they all fell upon her with shrieks of delighted laughter, "if she were sure — of both of them — "

"I was sure," said Sherry, rather low, "but I didn't have to ask." She put her hand in Jimmy's and smiled at the others.

Her hand hurt, he held it so hard. But he just said, lightly, "Wish I'd waited then; I'd have been spared a lot of mental anguish, Mrs. Maxwell."

It still sounded strange to her. Strange and lovely. By what alchemy had Sheridan Nevins become Mrs. James Maxwell? By some magic that had nothing to do with churches and flowers and honeymoons. Some people, she thought, who'd been married

54

twenty years weren't married, not really, even though they lived side by side, in intimacy, even though their children grew up around them. Pete and Jenny were married, she reflected. Jocelyn would be some day if ever she surrendered that deep, shrinking heart of hers. She thought, Angela'll never be married, not if she has a dozen names on her calling cards before she's through. Mother and Father weren't married, not really. We are. *We are.*

She returned the pressure of Jimmy's hand. She thought: It's insane to be so happy, can it last? it must last, oh, it won't always be like this. I'm not a fool, I know that, we'll get used to each other, and take things for granted. But if we just won't let life come between us, if we're always honest — she thought of Jocelyn's word — something will come of it, even better, even finer. Aloud, she said, amazed to find her eyes wet and her breathing troubled, "Play for us, Jocelyn, will you? There's a dear."

CHAPTER III

The old Nevins place on Purchase Street, in Rye, has the privacy bestowed by plenty of acreage, a high brick wall, and the sort of landscaping which intrigues and, at the same time, defeats the eye. The gates stand open and the passer-by, on foot or in a car, may see the avenue of trees and the graceful groupings of shrubs, may catch a glimpse of colorful flowers in their season and, especially in autumn and winter, a fleeting view of the house.

This property to which Kenneth Nevins had brought his bride was named Quaker Hill because of the rolling land and the fact that all these manicured acres had once belonged to the old Quaker families whose meetinghouses still stood on Purchase Street. The house itself was a remodeled farmhouse. That is to say, the long, low, lean-to lines had been preserved and the shingles — hand-hewn on the old, main part of the house — were painted white. The blinds were a mellow blue-green and the chimneys of no less than five fireplaces were of a weathered brick. Back of the house, to the right as you entered, was the glorified tenant cottage, a miniature replica of the house itself, in which Sheridan and Jimmy Maxwell were to live.

As they approached it on the day following their stopover in Jersey, it was covered with early roses. Sherry squeezed Jimmy's arm and a little choking sensation came to her throat. "Isn't it — ?" she began; but he interrupted her, smiling, "It certainly is!"

He liked the little house a lot. Mrs. Nevins had refurnished it, complete to a new mechanical ice box and all the trimmings, as a wedding gift. It would have been more fun, Jimmy had thought, dutifully wandering in Sherry and her mother's wake through furniture departments and sitting on the side lines during discussions with decorators, if he and Sherry had furnished it themselves. Oh, perhaps haphazardly at first, with a few good things and quite a lot of bad ones. Getting a new piece now and then with which to live for a time, laughing at the contrast between it and the furniture which was not as good, until little by little they could have afforded replacements, as surprises, as gifts, from one to the other. But Sherry had been as pleased as a child with a doll's house. And, after all, he reflected, she was accustomed to walking through a shop or picking up a telephone and placing an order, and that was that. A new dining room — certainly, madam, walnut, mahogany, maple? She had missed, he thought, a lot of fun, the sort of fun Jenny and Pete had had in their earlier days together.

Mrs. Nevins and Mrs. Nevins' invaluable, dour housekeeper, Harrington, had briskly seen to everything. Sherry had kept in touch with her mother from Skytop, and had telephoned her from the Lees'. Now, the door to the tenant cottage stood open, there was movement and activity going on inside. Sherry jumped out of the car as Jimmy, turning up the little private drive, stopped in the circle outside the house. He heard her clear, happy call and himself got out of the roadster a little slowly, smiling a bit ruefully to himself, aware that he was not, and never had been, at ease with Sheila Nevins.

"Jimmy!" Sherry was calling, tapping her foot on the polished floor of the little square hall, "Jimmy, you old slowpoke!"

Jimmy went into his house. It *was* his house. He paid rent for it. The first month had been paid in advance despite Mrs. Nevins' laughing and lifted-eyebrow disdain. He would have liked very much to go into it alone, with Sherry. But Sherry was dancing

58

around the living room now, her arms about the stiff, unyielding form of Mrs. Harrington, and on Mrs. Harrington's face, like that of a suspicious horse, there was the faint shadow of a smile.

"Hello, Jimmy," said his mother-in-law.

She was standing by the long table, smoking rapidly. Jimmy went over to her and with a curious sensation of unreality bent to kiss her smooth cheek. She was an extraordinarily handsome woman, he thought for the hundredth time, but much of the sincere and astonished admiration which had assailed him upon their first meeting had evaporated.

Sheila Nevins was forty-five. When she was angry, she looked her age; when she was ill, she looked fifty; when she had had too much to drink, she looked sixty. When she was rested, amiable, and herself, she looked ten years her own junior.

She was darker than Sherry, taller. Her figure was intended to be a bit on the ample side but by excellent corseting and a usually temperate diet, considerable exercise and tri-weekly massage, she had restrained its natural curves. She had a bland and tended face, oval as an egg. Her coiffure was Antoine at his best, her frocks a miracle of custom-dressmaking, her shoes were bench-made, and her make-up was impeccable. There were those who said that, every so often, she had her face lifted by a man in Vienna — "or is it glands, my dear?" They lied in their excellent teeth. Sheila Nevins had yet to resort to these difficult means. Her skin was cared for, she generally managed to get a requisite amount of sleep, and, as she was entirely selfish, emotions had neither made nor marred her. Once upon a time she had been as much in love as it was possible for her to be; not, however, with her husband. But she had always been clever and cautious and had remembered that indulgence in grief and tears is ruinous to beauty. Since then about the only emotion that stirred her was directly due to a miserably bad temper which, on the advice of her doctor, she controlled as well as possible.

She was talking to Sherry, regarding her with eyes almost as blue as Sherry's own, and which saw her daughter as an asset which, since her marriage to Jimmy Maxwell, Sheila had been forced to write off her books. Still, in her way, she was fond of Sherry.

"You're tanned," she said accusingly.

"It's fashionable," Sherry reminded her, wandering around the room. "Oh, it's marvelous," she cried, "all you've done."

Harrington beamed, with restraint, and Mrs. Nevins permitted herself an expression of serene complacency.

Books, magazines, flowers; cigarette boxes open and filled; the house, if the living room was any example, keeping the "spirit," as the decorator had said, of the tenant cottage. But what a spirit! "Simple" curtains, at heaven knew what a yard, and careless, comfortable furniture, with just the right amount of period and no-period. A genuine butterfly table, a genuine ladder-back, a genuine Duncan Phyfe, and flower-painted cornices; an Adam mantel and then the thick, solid-upholstered chairs into which a man might sink and be at his ease.

"You shouldn't tan," Sheila went on, "you'll get that weather-beaten look — I can't understand the craze for it," fretfully. "I have to go into town in half an hour. Suppose we go through the house? Mary will take the bags."

Mary arrived, in a pale green daytime uniform, flushing a little, a pretty, well-trained Irish girl, anxious to please. Since this was the tenant cottage and butlers were not in the "spirit," Jimmy and Sherry would have to get along with the services of two maids. Mary was chambermaid and waitress, and Katie, older, fatter, more temperamental, was in the kitchen over which she presided.

The living room had a windowed corner

in which one might dine with comfort. The kitchen and tiny butler's pantry were miracles of perfection and neatness. The stairs went up from the square hall, and there were three bedrooms and two baths, and a dressing room for Sherry. The maids slept in a small wing adjoining the kitchen and storage shed.

The bedroom which Sherry and Jimmy would share was lovely. It was distinctly a woman's room, French blue, pale mauve, with little highlights of flowerlike yellow and green. Mrs. Nevins had insisted that it was "barbarous." "Why not two rooms?" she had inquired. "You won't need more than one guest room." But Sherry had shaken her shining head.

The twin beds were gay with candlewick spreads, there was a bedside table for each, and a reading lamp, glazed chintz draperies, two deep chairs, a little, ancient desk, and old hooked rugs scattered on the floor. The big closet was for Sherry, Mrs. Nevins explained; she would need all the space as the other closet had been turned into her dressing room. Jimmy, suggested his mother-in-law negligently, could keep his clothes in one of the other rooms. Surely two would not be in use all the time. Besides, they could send any overflow of guests to the main house — provided she was in residence, she added.

Sherry's clothes closet was already filled with her frocks, on padded, scented hangers and in bags. There were built-in shelves for her shoes and built-in drawers for her lingerie, and curious fixtures for her hats. The closet smelled of cedar and lavender. And the dressing room had a tiny latticed window, ample lighting arrangements and a table of heavy black glass and steel, on which the jars and bottles stood.

"Some bathroom!" Jimmy was announcing, wandering about its spaciousness and regarding the glassed-in shower, the various gadgets and the wild, washable wall paper which portrayed mermaids and lobsters and deep-sea fish. He had, of course, been at the house innumerable times since his engagement to Sherry and their decision — her decision — to settle there; but these final and almost finicking touches had not been completed when he and Sherry had left for their motor trip, go-and-stay-as-you-please honeymoon.

Sherry and her mother, having toured the two pretty guest rooms, returned to the bedroom. Mrs. Nevins was talking absently about the oil burner that had been installed. "I'll lend you Perkins for odd job work and general looking after," she was saying; "heaven knows he costs me enough and hasn't enough to do. Sherry, you're not listening!"

Sherry threw her arms about her mother and hugged her. Mrs. Nevins endured it, and then drew away a little. "I wish you'd get over it," she murmured. She reflected, She's just like her father, demonstrative, impulsive —

Sheila could be, she had often announced, devoted to her daughter and her friends without demonstration.

"Sorry, did I muss you, Sheila?" asked Sherry, a little amused but not much. She thought, she might unbend, once . . . On my wedding day, I thought— But she had thought erroneously. Sheila had come into her room, at the St. Regis where they were staying for the wedding, and had regarded her daughter, surrounded by a head fitter and Mrs. Nevins' own maid. She had pulled at a curling tendril of hair, had remarked that the scent of orange blooms made her ill, and that she thought Sherry's heels a little low. She sighed, then said, "You look very lovely."

The fitter and the maid had vanished. Sherry and her mother had been alone. And Sheila had said, smiling a very little: "I fancy I need give you no advice. Girls nowadays know more than their mothers ever knew." She had kissed Sherry's scented cheek; she had added, without conviction, "I hope you'll be very happy, Sherry; and have no regrets."

No, not a demonstrative person. Since that unfortunate betrayal of the heart she did not know she had, and which had occurred during her engagement to the eminently eligible Kenneth Nevins, she had discarded loving as upsetting and unnecessary. But she adored being loved. There were always half a dozen men, most of them considerably her junior, in the offing — or nearing. She treated them all alike, a little patronizingly, tolerantly, charmingly. "It takes a really frigid woman," one had said, washing his scorched hands of her, "to be a competent coquette."

Sherry called the young men her mother's troupe. They amused her. Now and then one had made the mistake of falling out of love with Sheila and in love with Sherry. That was regrettable and generally occurred when Sherry, tender-hearted, decided that her mother had overstepped the legitimate bounds of cavalier treatment.

She had never called Sheila mother; not, that is, since her babyhood.

"Mrs. Nevins," began Jimmy, entering the room, and both women looked at him a little blankly. Then Sherry laughed.

"Jimmy, you can't call her Mrs. Nevins!" she remonstrated.

He could hardly, he thought, call her mother. He didn't want to, moreover. He stammered a little, as he did when he was embarrassed. And Mrs. Nevins, fitting a cigarette into a long holder of black onyx and jade, asked coolly, with some amusement, "How about Belle-Mere?"

"Belle-Mere?" Jimmy repeated it reflectively, with an accent which made Sherry shout with laughter and Sheila shudder. Then he shook his head. His eyes laughed, too, but his strong young jaw was outthrust, just a little.

"No good," he said, after a moment, "I can't manage it. Besides, it sounds like a horse!"

No, thought Sheila, this entirely commonplace young man — oh, to be sure, he had charm, everyone said so, but it was not a charm to which she responded — would never use the graceful term with ease. She said, after a moment, "Then, Sheila?"

"Of course," cried Sherry delighted, "and it's a lovely name, isn't it, Jimmy?" She repeated "Sheila Sheridan," and added, "How on earth could you bear to change it?"

Mrs. Nevins shrugged. Her face was the perfect and tinted mask of youth she intended it to be. She had not borne changing it, for a little while. Ridiculous, she thought, remembering that she had even considered breaking her engagement to Kenneth Nevins, who was all that was attractive, gentle, eligible — the catch of her season — and marrying a footloose, crazy, impoverished engineer named Brown. Hiram Brown, no less!

"I must go now," she told them. "I told Conners to bring the car here. I want you to dine with me tomorrow night. I've asked a few people — "

"Oh, Sheila, so soon!" cried Sherry, in dismay.

"Why not? You can't keep yourself mewed up in a rose-covered cottage solitude forever," said her mother sharply; "it's absurd and a little indecent. I'm asking some people who might be of use to Jimmy," she went on, "among them Lorrimer Welles and his wife. It won't hurt Jimmy at all to know the right people, and as soon as possible."

Mary came softly up the stairs. Mrs. Nevins' car was waiting, she announced. Jimmy went down with his mother-in-law, handed her into the car and had a word for Conners whom he knew and liked. Then he went back into the house.

Sherry was still in the bedroom looking out the windows, at the fields and the lawns, the gardens, and the little pool in the heart of the rose garden. From a chimney of the main house smoke rose. The country was green and rolling, magnificent with trees, with glimpses of water. Sherry loved Quaker Hill as if the place had been a person. Next to Jimmy, she thought she loved Quaker Hill best. After that came Jenny and Pete and Jocelyn, and of course, her mother, she thought dutifully, guiltily. It wasn't so much emotional love she bore her mother as a sense of blood kinship, a sense of dependence upon her, upon her cool, un-hurried decisions, and a sense, too, of fear. . . .

When Jimmy came up quietly, she did not hear him. When he touched her shoulder, she started slightly and turned. Her eyes were wet and he murmured in distress and question, and kissed the broad, white lids, and held her there in his arms, silent, for a moment.

"It's just getting home. I do love it," she said, "I want you to, also. It's yours, Jimmy, as well as mine."

He thought, It will never be mine. But it must be, he argued with himself, between us we'll make this our own, this little house. Love in it, laugh in it, quarrel a little, make up, be happy, always be happy.

"I'm crazy about it," he said.

"Are you, darling? Look, let's have Mary

unpack the bags and things and go walking — "

"I'll take the car to the garage," he agreed,
"and meet you downstairs." He turned and
walked toward the door. Then he stopped
and came back to her. "If — if your mother
hadn't been here," he told her, "I would
have — carried you over the doorsill. I
wanted to. But she would have thought I'd
lost my mind."

"That's dear of you," Sherry told him.
"Can't you do it now?"

No, he couldn't, he informed her. It had
to be the first time, as a bride.

"And you say I'm superstitious!" she
mocked him tenderly.

After he had gone to take the car to the
small outbuilding that had been converted
to its use, Sherry went in search of the maids,
to give her first orders and to make friends.
Mary and Katie liked her on sight. They
had been engaged by Mrs. Nevins and had
been a little doubtful, at least Katie, older
and more experienced, had been. But Mrs.
Nevins had said, after terms had been settled
and duties explained, "You'll find Mrs. Maxwell very easy to work for, provided you
do not skimp your work and are reliable."

Grapevine communication from the servants' hall of Quaker Hill had informed Mary

and Katie that Mrs. Nevins was a good mistress. "Hard, works you to the limit, sees everything is done, she does, she and that old cat of a Harrington, but pays good wages, never complains if you do well, sees that you are taken care of when you're sick, gives a bonus at Christmas time." In short, a real lady, one who could command respect. But Mary, in the kitchen as Sherry entered, was confiding to Katie that you couldn't never get fond of the old one but the young one was "Sweet like" . . . and she liked the husband.

Mrs. Harrington had gone back to the main house. Sherry waited for Jimmy on the front steps. She came down presently and walked around regarding window boxes and bushes and the lavish bounty of climbing roses. The sun porch looked jolly from the outside, all chintz and reed furniture. Some day she'd want another wing to balance it, on the other side, an open porch. She liked open porches.

Jimmy appeared, dogtrotting up the road, the box bordered path. Sherry took his arm, and they walked away from the house together. Sherry was talking — about the open porch.

"Hey, go slow," said Jimmy mildly, "we've only just come, you know. You don't want to tear the house down and build it up yet

70

a while, do you?"

No, she admitted, she could wait a little. Still holding his arm, she gave an excited skip, like a child at a birthday party. She said, "Let's go to the stables."

They walked down the back road and into the stables, greeted by the head groom, who had been with the Nevins ever since Sherry could remember. In her stall Sherry's lovely chestnut mare greeted her with a toss of her beautiful head and a low whinny. Sherry stroked the satin skin and looked into the deep eyes. "Isn't she lovely?" she asked Jimmy, who was regarding the horse, and the other horses, at a rather respectful distance. Tomorrow, decided Sherry aloud, she'd ride. After Jimmy went to work. Would he drive in? No? Then she'd drive him to the station and come back and change and ride.

The kennels were near the stables. Mrs. Nevins had three fine police dogs. Her own favorite Pekinese, a pair of them, lived in the house with her. But at the kennels Sherry stopped suddenly.

"Where's McTab?" she asked. "I'd forgotten all about him!"

McTab was her very own, a wire-haired pup, not too well-bred, which Jimmy had given her shortly before they became engaged. "I was so excited," she told her husband, "I didn't think of him. But on the way home, remember, we said he'd be waiting for us?"

Clarke, the younger groom who "kept an eye on the dogs," hurried out of the stables when she called him. "Where's McTab?" she asked, without preliminary. Clarke was confounded, much embarrassed. It was like this, explained Clarke, there'd been a fight, see, with Nero — "always an ugly brute," said Clarke balefully, "and the little pup, he was just trying to make friends like, he'd got clawed up some. They'd had the vet for him, but — "

"But what?" cried Sherry impatiently.

It was simple enough, a lamed dog, a misfit. Mrs. Nevins had had him put away. "He didn't feel nothing, Miss — I mean Mrs. Maxwell," Clarke assured her eagerly.

Sherry turned away. She walked rapidly and in silence. Jimmy, striding beside her, said gently, "Don't feel so badly, Sherry, we'll get another pup."

But she turned on him, eyes blazing, lips shaken.

"Never like McTab! He was the first thing you ever gave me, Jimmy, and I loved him a lot." She was silent and then she said: "What did it matter if he was lame, I'd have loved him that much more. I — I can't understand Sheila. Why didn't she tell me?"

Jimmy thought, Yes, why? She could have written, have told us over the telephone, have asked us what to do, and we could have said, get him well, we'll look after the little chap. . . .

When he did not answer Sherry said, more evenly, "I suppose she didn't want to spoil anything for me, and that's why she didn't let us know."

"That's it," agreed Jimmy, relieved. But there was no conviction in his mind. Lame dog, put him out of misery, and forget it. Sherry's dog, any dog, except perhaps her dish-faced asthmatic Pekes, wasn't important enough to Sheila Nevins.

"I'll get a dog tomorrow," Jimmy promised. "I'll bring him home with me."

Sherry said: "No. Let's wait a while. Perhaps, after all, I don't want a dog."

She hadn't had McTab so very long, perhaps six months. He'd always been a nuisance, up at the main house. He liked to chew on furniture, he loved getting full of dirt and burrs and rolling on lounges and rugs. He hadn't been very well housebroken. And Mrs. Nevins had banished him to the cellar. "Of course, he can't sleep in your room, Sherry, what on earth's gotten into you?" But in the cellar he had made the nights hideous with his complaints and had finally come, with his basket, to Sherry's room. She'd loved him, she hadn't really forgotten him, ever. And she'd expected to have him waiting for them at the little house, half crazy with joy, his square, bewhiskered face beaming. Only in the excitement she'd forgotten, for a moment.

She thought, going up to the greenhouses with Jimmy, that perhaps they'd wait a while. Some day they'd be together and they'd see a pup who took both their fancies, whom they couldn't quite live without and then they'd buy him. But McTab had belonged to that waiting time, that time of expectancy and hope and wild delight, when you went to bed, every night, tremulous and wondering and so happy you cried and so unhappy you cried harder, and awoke a brand-new person, every day, wondering what the next hours would bring, sight, touch, sound — a letter — a telephone call. . . .

She touched Jimmy's arm.

"It hasn't been quite as we planned, has it?" she asked. "I mean — you couldn't carry me over the threshold — and there wasn't any McTab."

"Is anyone looking?" inquired Jimmy; "not that I give a damn." He kissed her, in full sight of Clarke and his superior, who grinned and turned their eyes away and went about their business smiling a little.

"If it's been spoiled for you, coming home — " he began.

"Of course, it hasn't." At the touch of his mouth on her own she was unthinkingly happy again. McTab's little ghost would often come to trouble her but for the moment it was dispelled, its hoarsely barking, insanely tail-wagging spirit laid. "It's been perfect," she said.

When they reached the little house again, Katie and Mary had tea ready. "Tea," Mrs. Harrington had said firmly.

Thin sandwiches, the fragrance of jasmine, and the silver service, very beautiful, which her mother's friends, the Lorrimer Welles, had given Sherry on her marriage, and the delicate cups and saucers, Spode, another gift. Jimmy said, sitting on a window seat and swinging his long legs, "Couldn't we stock up with five and ten, when we haven't company? I *do* drop things, you know, Sherry."

Mary came in with cup cakes. Cook hoped Mrs. Maxwell would like them. Sherry seized on one, fat and still warm and chocolate iced, and bit into it with a hungry exclamation. Mary was to tell Katie that she liked it very much.

And what time would dinner be? Katie wanted to know.

It was nearly five. "How would eight be, Jimmy?" Jimmy said eight would suit him nicely. Sherry, a little flushed and overcome with her own dignity, dissolved into laughter as Mary departed. "I suppose Mother — or Harrington — ordered dinner," she exclaimed, "I know we didn't. I'm bound to forget. If you rely on me, darling, we'll starve."

Jimmy was reading a morning newspaper, between bites of the cake he held in one strong brown hand. "What's the news?" asked Sherry, curled up in a big chair before the tea table.

"Nothing much. Nice, decent paper your mother reads," he commented. "We'll have to liven up the house with the tabloids. We can hide 'em if any of your high-hat friends come to call."

"They all read them," laughed Sherry, "with avidity — and apologies. And, of course, Angela's crowd just dotes on the columnists. They buy every paper in town which runs a column and read them all with shrieks of dismay if they are mentioned — or if they aren't mentioned, for that matter."

Jimmy threw the paper on the window seat and grinned at her cheerfully.

"No headlines," he said sadly; "beautiful Sheridan Nevins Maxwell, the recent, most dazzling bride of the season and her handsome husband returned today from an extended — and may we say successful? — honeymoon. They will reside at Little House, Quaker Hill, Purchase Street, Rye, New York. People will kindly stay away."

Sherry chuckled. "Not even an item?" she asked mournfully.

"Not an item. Nothing in the paper but a couple of murders, restrainedly reported, plenty of politics, and, of course, an innocent bystander."

"What on earth is that, darling? Do you put your umbrella in it?"

"No, dear," he told her kindly, "just any stray bullets you may have around. This one is average. Clerk in a shipping office decides to leave the subway and walk home for his health. Cop chases crook, radio cars and such flit about, innocent bystander gets a dose of lead, curtain, sorrowing family. Don't ever let me catch you walking on a Manhattan street," he added, "without a full guard and your second best armor."

"You're an idiot," she murmured lovingly. Then she looked up gravely. "Poor man hadn't done a soul any harm, had he?"

"No," replied Jimmy, "he hadn't. His number was up, I guess." He got down from the window seat, picked her up in his arms and sat down in her chair, still with her in his arms. "Forget him," he ordered.

"All right. But, look here, Mary will come in — "

"Let her come. If she's going to live with us, she'll have to get used to a lot of this," Jimmy said serenely. "One reason I married you was because I grew tired of holding hands behind Conners' sophisticated back, hopping up or away when that pie-faced butler up at the house came in, and of driving you on side roads in the old Ford, and of taking you to plays we didn't want to see and movies we didn't give a hoot for, just for some public privacy. I sez to myself, sez I, This engagement business is a flop. I'll marry the gal, I sez, and we'll have a house somewhere and a lot of doors we can shut —

Mary came in, blushed, stammered and started to back out. Sherry was speechless.

"You may clear away, Mary," said Jimmy grandly. He waved one hand. Otherwise he didn't stir.

Mary cleared away. And the pantry door swung behind her; they heard her laughter and Katie's muffled exclamation.

"Poor girl," said Sherry contentedly, "you'll put notions into her head. It's so awfully un-Emily-Postish, darling."

"I should worry," said Jimmy.

He sighed and tightened his clasp.

"Tomorrow," he said, "I go back to work, and tomorrow night we dine with Mrs. Kenneth Nevins, but tonight we'll be alone in our very own house, with, however, the inevitable exception of Katie and Mary. Maybe," he asked hopefully, "they'd like to go to the movies?"

Dinner at eight, candles flickering, and roses in a fat, silver bowl with little carved feet. Lace on the round, polished table, and crystal and porcelain. There they were, the two of them, regarding each other in the windowed corner of the big room, the shades, the curtains drawn. Lights glowed in the other part of the room, and here was candlelight to make a shining pattern of Sherry's hair, to flicker over the pyjamas she wore, the little black velvet jacket with its demure vest of white satin and a round satin collar, the plain heavy folds of black velvet falling to her feet, like a flowing skirt. And around her slim middle a coral-colored sash.

"What's that thing you've got on?" asked Jimmy.

It was new. She'd not worn it before. She

replied demurely, "Hostess pyjamas, they call 'em."

"Oh, word of ill omen," said Jimmy displeased, "and Mary dropped a fork — or was it a knife? — a little while ago. Mary," he ordered, as Mary, in that other black-and-white of her servitude, waited and endeavored to control her expression, "go out, pull up the drawbridge, poison the moat and bid the guards be on the alert against an unwelcome guest."

Mary left abruptly. They heard her soft laughter in the kitchen where Katie clucked at her in disapproval and amazement.

Coffee, at the cleared table, and liqueurs in silver thimbles. They'd had a cocktail before dinner. One for Sherry, two and a half for Jimmy. The little wine closet in the cellar was stocked. Angela had stocked it. It had been her wedding gift, and a characteristic one. Gin, in stone bottles, a dozen of champagne, a dozen of sauterne, a dozen of Burgundy, brandy, liqueurs, Scotch, rye, Irish, bourbon. A lavish gift.

"It won't last long," Angela had said, "not if I know your bunch. But save yourselves a bottle, now and then, hide it away. When you're very much first married and very much in love you won't need it, I suppose. But after a while it will help a lot."

Presently they left the table and, walking into the lighted places of the living room, found themselves a chair and a footstool; Jimmy in the chair, lighting his pipe; Sherry on the footstool, her head against his knees, a cigarette in her hand. "After a moment," said Jimmy sternly, "you're to get up and read to me. There's stacks of good books around, how about a thriller?"

A car drove up, two cars. They were very noisy. Someone put a finger on the bell and held it there, someone else seized and released the knocker. Mary, her expression shocked, thoughts of porticoes and drawbridges flitting through her mind, hurried to answer. She never asked her routine question. Suddenly, as Sherry, with a quick, dismayed look at Jimmy, came to her feet, as Jimmy, swearing audibly, rose to his, the room was full of people, young people, laughing, talking, exclaiming, welcoming, ribald . . .

Jimmy went out to instruct Mary. Ice cubes, whiskey, soda, ginger ale. In the living room Sherry greeted her guests. "We thought," said a red-headed girl, "you needed company. Or aren't you fed up with each other yet?"

Jimmy came back into the room. The red-headed girl had never met him, she had just returned from Corsica. Now she fell upon him with screams of delight and sorrow.

"Sherry, isn't he beautiful, he's grand," she shrieked. "Why didn't I see him before you did?"

Joe McKenzie, Jimmy's closest friend, took the bottles tenderly from his host's hand. "Run along, Nita," he said kindly; "if you had seen him, it wouldn't have done any good."

"But I like him," wailed Nita, "he's just my type."

Someone spoke from the door. It was Angela Ward. She had descended upon Quaker Hill in her usual unannounced fashion. She stood there, her arrival unnoticed in all the confusion, and smiled a little. She said, distinctly, "Never mind, Nita, he'll soon be back in circulation."

CHAPTER IV

Jimmy Maxwell, returning to Rye in the late afternoon of the following day, was conscious of something which was not quite a headache but which, if encouraged, might reach the full proportions of a stunner. It had been after two in the morning when he and Sherry had gone to bed. Not that their uninvited guests had shown signs of going home; Jimmy had gently but firmly put them out. It had been a rather gay evening, he reflected. Someone had turned on the radio, there had been alfresco dancing. Angela's lavish cellar-stocking wouldn't, he thought further, last long at that rate. Boy, could the crowd take punishment! It was by way of an impromptu housewarming, they informed him.

They certainly had warmed the house, if not ruined it, he concluded. They left in a whirl of expostulations. Sherry, wandering about the very disheveled living room, had raised one dark brow and permitted her mouth to droop a little at the corners. A smear of lipstick on the arm of a chair, a round ring left by a glass on the butterfly table, a cigarette burn in a rug . . . "Still," she defended her friends loyally when Jimmy made his trenchant remarks, "it was rather sweet of them, wasn't it? I mean, they're glad to have us home."

"It was like old times," Jimmy had commented somewhat grimly, recalling the occasions when he'd come out with McKenzie and dropped in on some party or other, and his frantic and generally futile efforts to get a minute alone with Sherry, recalling, too, the entertainment which had been proffered them both during their brief engagement, "I hardly saw you the entire evening."

Sherry had yawned before her dressing table. "Poor Jimmy," she'd said mockingly; "but that wasn't my fault, it was Nita's. She would pursue you into the pantry!"

"Nita *who,* for God's sake?" Jimmy had inquired crossly. He had never laid eyes on the girl before that night, and hadn't, even then, learned her surname.

All he knew about her was she was painted like a gas station, her hair was as red as an anarchist, her conversation a mixture of Boccaccio and revue black-outs, and that she had studio-couch eyes.

He said as much to Sherry.

"She's Nita Welles," Sherry informed him. "Her father's a big shot — president of the

Sloane National Bank. You'll see him — and his wife — and Nita at Mother's tomorrow night."

"That's something to look forward to," Jimmy had groaned.

Angela had been the last to go. She was staying with Sheila, she announced casually, not that Sheila knew it, as yet. She'd dropped her bag off there and come on over, expecting, she added, to have a quiet evening with Jimmy and Sherry. She had commandeered Jimmy to drive her up to the main house about a quarter of two and to take the car down to the garage. The last he saw of her she was inserting a key into the door and smiling at him over her shoulder.

She'd had the key for years. She got on extremely well with Sheila, none of this aunt and niece business there.

The train pulled into the station. There was Sherry, waiting in the roadster. She looked darned cute, thought Jimmy, tumbling down the steps. He was glad to get back to her. He had thought he'd come home this first day with a ceremonial sort of feeling, young bridegroom returns to bride after first day in the office. The office, in the Chrysler Building, of J. G. Gerard, General Agent, Gotham Life Insurance Company, had looked about as usual. The boss beetled his brows at him and growled genially, "Back on the job, eh? Well, we never missed you," and had at once plunged into a discussion of ways and means, prospects and what have you.

But his eyes had twinkled. He liked Jimmy and Jimmy liked him. The other men had slapped him on the back and made the usual comments.

"May I give you a lift, sir," asked Sherry, "or don't you ride with strange women?"

"And how!" said Jimmy thankfully, climbing in beside her.

There were cars by the dozens all about; and people: pretty girls in smart summer frocks, older women, men of all ages and descriptions, in station wagons, Chryslers, Cadillacs, Lincolns, Dusenbergs . . . Jimmy waved here and shouted there. It was all very friendly and pleasant; and cool after the heat of the city. He took off his hat and mopped his brow. "Was it very bad in town?" asked Sherry sympathetically.

"Bad enough. You look cool." He regarded her with delight. She had risen cheerfully and driven him down to the train. "Don't tell me you really rode. Bet you went back to bed until noon."

"Oh, I rode," answered Sherry skillfully guiding the roadster, "with Angela. And then we had lunch, at home — "

"Katie do you proud?"

"I meant — at Mother's. She wasn't there."

"I see," said Jimmy, a little disconcerted.

"Then," went on Sherry, "we went calling. I took Angela to see Nella Williams. She runs the newer of the little theater groups, you know. The Thespians. Angela," added Sherry, laughing, "had something to say about the name — "

"She would have," commented Jimmy. He didn't laugh, though. He asked, instead, "What for?"

"Oh, Angela's interested. She contributes, even if she doesn't live here. Most of the bunch do back Mrs. Williams, although the talent is drawn mostly from the town itself. I thought," said Sherry, "if she'd take me on — it would be fun."

"You're crazy," said Jimmy firmly. "If there's anything more upsetting than an amateur performance . . ."

"Well, I have to have something to do," she said. "I loathe bridge, I can't contemplate spending my days in town shopping and all that — except when I'm meeting you, darling — and really they do put on awfully good shows."

Jimmy, at the moment, didn't care. He lay back in the car and breathed deeply, letting the little wind from the water blow across his face. He roused himself to say, as they turned in at Quaker Hill, "I wish we weren't going up to your mother's tonight."

"We promised," Sherry reminded him with a quick look. "We won't stay late," she consoled him.

"I hope not," Jimmy told her earnestly. "I have one hell of a head!"

A little while later they dressed for dinner, Jimmy in the blue coat and white flannels indicated, save for very formal occasions, for summer dining-out. And Sherry in a funny little dress of cotton lace, the blue-violet of her eyes. Jimmy, stalking about the guest room and regarding his clothes in the ample spaces of the closet, decided that this marrying into the Nevins family had put a strain on his wardrobe. He'd have to find a good tailor — McKenzie would take him to his — and stock up.

Dinner at Quaker Hill was at eight. Jimmy and Sherry walked through the golden shadows of the evening, shadows scented with salt and the fragrance of flowers. It was a marvelous night. A night to sit in a rose garden and smoke your pipe and look through the dusk at the face of the person you loved best in all the world.

"It's just a small dinner," Sherry whispered comfortingly.

It was large enough. Lorrimer Welles was a crowd in himself, a big man, a little too fat, with cold, bright blue eyes and a clean-shaven, florid face and the thin tight lips of the reluctant Puritan. His wife was perfectly nondescript in a lovely gown; his daughter was Nita, red-headed, as usual, and not particularly abashed by the presence of a continuously disapproving father and an ornate washrag of a mother. Sheila was very much herself in manner and grooming, and there were three extra men, imports from town.

Mr. Welles did not drink. One made concessions to his peculiarity; at the same time one did not plunge one's other guests into gloom. There were tomato juice cocktails and cocktails which were not tomato juice. There was an excellent light wine served at the table, and coffee and liqueurs afterward. The Welles', mother and father, would leave early. One expected it of them, they always did.

"Where's Angela?" asked Sherry suddenly, as they went in to dinner.

"Heaven knows," replied her mother. She lifted her shoulders slightly. "She went off somewhere, said something vaguely about the

89

club. She had Meredith Post in tow. They'll be back later," she said. "I wanted her to stay for dinner, and Merry too. But you know how Angela is."

There was contract afterwards, which Sherry detested. It didn't last long, it broke up out of sheer ennui. Mr. Welles played "for the fun of it," which was no inducement to those at his table. And he played very badly, also, probably, for the fun of it.

Later he was standing with Jimmy in the corner of the modernish card room. He said, waving his hand at the array of bottles which had unobtrusively been set out, "Glad to see, my boy, that you don't drink everything you can lay your hands on."

"I don't like it, much — that is, not much of it," said Jimmy frankly, in his engaging manner, "and it seems sort of nitwittish to lap up everything in sight just because it's being done."

Lorrimer Welles beamed approvingly. He prided himself on being a judge of men, and he doubtless was. At all events, he had taken to this young man, who had married Sherry Nevins, at first sight.

"You're on the Street, aren't you?" he asked vaguely, and for one wild moment Jimmy wondered if the older man thought him a candidate for the bread-line or just a rich girl's husband.

"No," he said, recovering and understanding, "I'm in insurance. Life underwriting, we call it," he added, grinning amiably.

"Oh, I see," rumbled Mr. Welles, "with whom?"

Jimmy explained. Mr. Welles nodded. The Gotham, he intoned, was a good company, very sound. Third largest, he understood, in the country.

He went on to say that he believed in life insurance.

"There isn't," Jimmy agreed enthusiastically, "a better investment. Especially now." He checked himself, a little horrified. One didn't sign up the Lorrimer Welles' of the world at a dinner party. But one made a note of them, so to speak.

Nita flew in, all black lace and scarlet hair, and regarded her father with hostility. "I'm weighing anchor," she announced.

Mr. Welles looked at his old-fashioned watch. It was time for him to be going too, he decided, it was nearly eleven.

"I'm glad," he informed his daughter, "that you are thinking of getting a little sleep, for a change."

"Don't be dumb," she said lightly, "I've a date — "

When the Welles' had taken their depar-

91

ture, Sheila Nevins and her three young men sat down at the bridge table again and the bar wagon was wheeled up. "Now," said Sheila, "we can relax." She regarded her son-in-law, who was wandering about the room, looking at the distorted but strangely comfortable steel furniture. "Where's Sherry?" she asked him.

"She went downstairs, to talk, I think, to Mrs. Harrington," Jimmy answered.

Sherry came back, laughing. She linked her arm in her husband's. "We'll be going," she said, "if you don't mind, Sheila."

Sheila, knitting her brows for a moment over the cards, nodded absently. "Wait a moment, till we finish this hand," she said.

They watched while the hand was played. The three imported young men, each a replica of the others save for a difference in height and coloring, paid little attention to them. Sheila won, she usually did. She smiled lazily at her partner, and rose, and went to the door with her daughter and son-in-law.

"How did you get along with Lorrimer Welles, Jimmy?" she asked.

"Oh, all right," he replied, mildly astonished, "seems to be a nice old duffer."

"He's an unmitigated bore, a pompous old ass, and a very influential man," Sheila pronounced coolly, "and a good one for you to know, Jimmy. That's why I had him here. I noticed you had no difficulty in charming Nita," she added smoothly.

Presently Sherry and Jimmy walked back to the little house together. "That last remark of Sheila's," said Jimmy, "had all the earmarks of a dirty crack."

"She was looking for a rise," answered Sherry quickly, "and everyone knows that Nita's man-crazy. She certainly gave you a rush, darling," Sherry said, tilting her little head.

Jimmy was a perfectly sensible young man. This was no time to act astonished, grieved, confused or coy. He said, "Well, if she's really man-crazy, it's no compliment, is it?"

Laughing, they went into the house. The door was unlocked. Jimmy, putting his hand on the knob, sighed deeply. "Am I glad to get home!" he inquired rhetorically.

But Angela was waiting for them, perfectly at ease in the living room, Meredith Post in close attendance. Too close, thought Jimmy, watching the byplay between the two, and disliking it a lot. After all, Angela was older than Merry Post, whom Jimmy knew slightly, and a good deal wiser.

"I suppose you hate us for coming," murmured Angela. "We were at Round Hill. Then we got bored and came away. I couldn't face dear Sheila and her dinner party, so we came along down here. The door was unlocked — and your maids away; we could be arrested for housebreaking, you know."

Either that or something else, thought Jimmy, annoyed. Sherry explained cheerfully enough. "We gave the servants a night off. We want them to become very much attached to us, don't we, Jimmy?"

After all, thought Jimmy, as he lay back in a big chair and listened to the light talk going on all around him, after all, what did it matter? This wasn't a Victorian world, not a pre-war world; not even the world Jenny and Pete lived in. If Sheila Nevins wished to play contract with three young men, each of them at least fifteen years her junior, that was her business. Besides, in the little while he had known Sherry he had come to know Sheila, a little. At two or three in the morning, or at whatever time it suited her, she would dismiss her troupe and send them back to New York in their cars, if any of them had a car, or with the sleepy but overpaid chauffeur. Then she would go lightly to bed — alone.

Angela was different, however; and it struck Jimmy that if Angela expected to use his house very often for an intimate conversation with her latest enthusiasm, he would soon disabuse her of the idea. He didn't like it.

They left in an hour or so: Meredith Post to drive back to his home in Greenwich, Angela to go up to the main house where she might or might not kibitz the bridge game. She had a moment alone with Jimmy in the hall.

"You didn't like us — dropping in," she said reproachfully.

"Well," began Jimmy uncomfortably, "of course, we're glad at any time — "

"You mean, if you're here? And you're not glad! Well, I won't do it again," she said easily. "But what's come over you, Jimmy, you weren't quite so stuffy in the old days? You may cut it on his tombstone, you may write it on his card, but a young man married is a young man marred," she sang under her breath.

Sherry and young Post had come up to them. "What's the dirt?" asked Sherry.

"Nothing. I was just deploring the fact that people get married," replied Angela. She slanted her long blue eyes at her cousin. "I hope you and Jimmy recover, in due time," she said.

Sherry slipped her arm through Jimmy's. "We'll never recover," she announced gayly and confidently, "we're chronic cases."

"Sez you," murmured Angela. "Do you still believe in Santa Claus?" She smiled at Merry Post, who was regarding her with eyes of a doglike devotion but less than a dog-like trust. "I've been trying to persuade Merry for weeks and weeks," she went on, shrugging her shoulders under her tiny velvet jacket, "that marriage is an obstacle race and I don't like taking comic falls."

So Merry had asked Angela to marry him, thought Jimmy. Well, they all began that way —

"Oh, run along, idiot," said Sherry, yawning frankly. "I'm dead for sleep and you know. you don't mean half you say."

"That's true, but not in this case," said Angela. She thought, There is something very attractive about Jimmy Maxwell. She'd always liked him, when he was free, white and about twenty-five and a half. But then he'd been just one of her gang, not a constant member but a visitor, dropping in now and then, with his cheerful grin.

"I'll give you a year — no, I'll be generous," she said, "I'll give you two."

"That's decent of you," said Jimmy a little stiffly. "And if Sherry *doesn't* go to Reno, what then?"

Angela widened her eyes at him.

"I'm not betting on anything so crude,"

she expostulated. "Why, of course, you'll doubtless celebrate your golden wedding, and I'll come to it in a wheel chair. No. I'm going to give you two years to — well, just *to*. Remember what I said about being back in circulation?" She turned to Merry and said briskly, "Let's go." At the door she called, "Sherry, come into town next week, will you? I'm going back early tomorrow. I've someone I want you to meet."

"Who — ?"

"Holman Benson — he's the new producer," said Angela. Jimmy closed the door and locked it, carefully slipping the chain into place. Sherry watched him, smiling. "Jimmy, no one can possibly get in, not with the dogs and everything."

"I know, but it feels safer," he argued obstinately. He couldn't tell her that he wanted to lock her and himself away from all the world. "Katie and Mary have keys to the back door, haven't they?"

"Yes." Sherry had gone into the living room where she absently emptied an ash tray and plumped up a pillow or two and turned out the lights. Then she joined him and they went slowly up the stairs together.

"Angela leaves a bad taste in my mouth," said Jimmy abruptly, as they were undressing.

Sherry, in a wisp of a trousseau garment,

regarded him, astonished.

"You mustn't mind her," she soothed him, "she always talks like that. It's part of her line not to believe in anything or anybody. I never even listen to her," she declared, sitting down in a low slipper chair and kicking off her slippers.

"I know, but I hate it," Jimmy declared. He sat down on the edge of his bed, in his shirt-sleeves and braces, and lighted a cigarette.

"Then, too, she's envious," said Sherry serenely.

"Envious?" He stared at her.

"Of course. Of me. She was crazy about you, Jimmy."

"Not so you could notice it," he said bluntly and truthfully.

"You don't expect me to believe that? I know you've said, often, that you were only good friends. But she declares up and down, and black and blue, that she was insane about you and that the biggest mistake she ever made was to bring us together," Sherry said, laughing, but her eyes were a little troubled.

Jimmy ground out the fresh cigarette in an onyx ash tray and looked for a minute at the pert Airedale in porcelain which decorated it.

"She was pulling your leg," he said quietly.

Sherry, stripping off a gossamer stocking, twiddled her toes thoughtfully. Then she laughed. "Oh, what does it matter?" she said. "Perhaps she was — at lunch yesterday, and later, when she'd left, Mother asked me if there had really been anything in it."

She pulled a silken wrap about her and vanished into the bathroom. Jimmy still sat on the edge of the bed and stared at the great flowers on the hooked rug. Angela, he thought, was a damned fool. What was the idea of making trouble, or trying to make it? She hadn't given a thought to him before he married Sherry, and he hadn't cared in the least for her. Oh, she was good-looking and amusing and always had a gang around her. But that was all there was to it.

What the hell was the matter with people anyway, poking and prying, unwilling to see anyone happy? Even the men at the office, with their laughter and sly remarks. And the gang the night before. But especially Angela Ward.

He rose suddenly as Sherry came out of the bathroom, her face washed clean as a child's and her brushed hair shining. He took her by the shoulders; she felt his hard fingers bite through the silk and lace which veiled them.

"Why — darling?" she asked on a little

sharply-drawn breath.

He was staring down on her, not with passion, not with tenderness but with an agony of question and almost fear in his nice eyes. And he said roughly:

"Sherry, promise me that whatever happens you won't let outsiders come between us, ever. What we do with our life together is our own business and we'll manage somehow, loving each other as we do; but promise me that there won't be any side-line interference, that no one will matter, except you and me?"

"Why, of course," she answered, loyal, startled eyes on his own. "Why — as if you could dream — " she began indignantly.

But now he had swept her into his arms and was kissing her desperately and hungrily. It was a promise. He would keep it; she would keep it, he thought exultantly. Nothing not of their own making could ever hurt them or spoil the pattern of the life they would create together. Nothing.

Other lovers, in their moments of beautiful insanity, had promised "always together." Others had promised the impossible — "Promise me you'll never leave me, darling." These reckoned without death. Jimmy and Sherry in making their gallant and pitiful vows were reckoning without life.

CHAPTER V

Angela was throwing a cocktail party. There were at least twenty people in the long studio room, with its slanted glass roof and cockeyed decorations. All twenty were making a good deal of noise.

Someone was playing the piano. He was playing very well indeed, dreaming over the keys a little, remembering the wide acres and dark mountains of the place in which he was born, far away. Then he ceased to dream and rippled his long hands across the gleaming ivory with rebellion and resentment. He was a new "find" of Angela's; she had asked him especially this afternoon to play to her guests, many of whom, she assured him, were influential and all of whom were appreciative. Appreciative they may have been — but they never stopped talking. Now and then one of them screamed, "Angela, he plays *divinely*," and someone else muttered something about technique "hard and brilliant as a diamond." But none really cared.

This was a sensitive boy, and very poor. To have met Angela, to have been caught up by her in a whirl of excitement, to be with people once more, intelligent people, to feel that his shabbiness went unnoticed, and the glazed pallor of his semi-starvation, had been heaven. Angela had fed him, warmed him, pressed money on him. Coming here today in deep gratitude and tremulous expectancy, he had been happy. Now he was unhappy; no one really cared, he mattered not at all. But when he ceased to play Angela would call to him, "Go on playing, Serge, don't stop."

So he played, for his supper, dreaming, resentful, rebellious.

In a corner near the miniature bar stood Angela, in her scarlet gown, with a group around her. On the outskirts of the group Meredith Post hovered miserably. She was quite through with him, she had said so. "Darling, you *do* bore me," Angela had said. And when Angela was bored, she was finished. But he came to her parties, unable to stay away, waiting, wondering, hoping that perhaps she would change, that perhaps once more she would regard him with seeing eyes. He felt a curious kinship with the boy at the piano. He would have liked to go to him and say, "Here, you're wretched too . . . what can we do about it?" Never before aware of people under the conventionality of their formal gestures, living hitherto on the surface, a gay-hearted, not very intelligent person, loving Angela — with her permission, and then being requested to cease loving Angela, had made him sensitive and aware, as if his nerves were terribly vulnerable, as if they were raw, bleeding. Something in the youngster's music reached him . . . But hell, he thought, what's the use? He'd think I was crazy . . . And so poured himself another drink.

The group around Angela were talking of a man who had just written a great novel. "Swell," commented a girl who had met him, "a regular person." Everyone immediately chattered at once. Hadn't he a title? Was it authentic? Hadn't he been everything — cowboy — soldier — linguist? In ten minutes his reputation was made and ruined. Angela said lazily, "Bring him here some time, someone."

"He has a wife," said the girl gloomily.

"So what?" asked Angela carelessly, her imagination stirred.

"It's no use," the girl told her, pert blond head on one side, "he'd be bored to death with us — with all this. He's made the rounds, Park Avenue, Broadway — "

"I serve very good liquor," interrupted Angela.

"So does he, I believe," said the girl.

Jimmy Maxwell came in, from the office. There was melted snow on his overcoat. He stood in the doorway and looked over the people, most of whom he knew. Angela called, "So you came, after all. Where's Sherry?"

Jimmy shrugged himself out of his coat, dropped it on a chair near the door and came in. He brought with him a breath of cold January dusk. He answered, as Angela came forward to meet him:

"She met Jocelyn for lunch and matinée. They'll be along presently to pick me up, we're driving out home for dinner."

"Don't," said Angela. She came very close to him, breathing an aura of perfume, cigarette smoke, smooth, cared-for flesh. "Don't. Let them go out. You stay here, it will be amusing — later."

"Who's that?" inquired Jimmy. He shook his head and smiled.

"Who — ?" asked Angela.

"At the piano — "

"Oh, just a boy I found somewhere," she said vaguely, "he's really very gifted."

January, Jimmy and Sherry had been married six months, thought Angela, watching him cross the room to speak to Meredith Post. Jimmy, she thought, looked thinner, fine-drawn. He'd been working hard, Sherry told her. Sherry had been busy too; she had joined the little, new group known as the Thespians, she had rehearsed, helped to direct and planned costumes. The first performance had been given during the Christmas season, an entirely inadequate affair, a hint of mysticism, much gloom, tremendous dramatics. But Sherry had really been very sweet in it, thought Angela, smiling to herself. Sweet — and bewildered.

A tall, lean man standing near her asked, "Where's Maxwell's pretty wife?"

"Coming, so he says," Angela replied.

"That's good," said the tall man, clinking ice in his glass.

"No, it isn't," Angela told him; "she's in love with her husband."

"I like them to be in love with their husbands," said the tall man, "it's much more satisfactory. Then they always go back to them, a little remorseful and more in love than ever. A number of husbands owe me a lot," he said; and added proudly, "But I am perhaps the most despised man in town."

"You're a fool," said Angela casually. She heard through the chatter and the soft complaining sound of the piano, the distant doorbell. Perhaps that's Sherry now, she thought.

She did not move, watching Jimmy make

his way to the door. She heard him clatter down the short flight of stairs, as, contrary to the usual arrangement, entrance hall and bedrooms were below. She thought lazily about Jocelyn, whom she had met again once or twice since Sherry's marriage. The girl irritated her. It wasn't sensible, she thought, hunting for a phrase, to be so — so armored, so incorruptible, nowadays.

Jimmy came in, one arm around Sherry, rosy in her furs, the other around Jocelyn. There was crowding and talk and greetings, outthrust cigarette boxes, laughter, comments. Sherry, shedding her furs, accepted a cigarette and a cocktail but Jocelyn shook her head, smiling. It was her first experience as Angela's guest and she found it strange and exciting and a little disturbing.

The tall lean man who had been talking with Angela came up to Sherry and Jocelyn now. He said, with his impenetrable gloom, "You don't remember me of course. Rothman."

Sherry laughed up at him, and then looked around for Jimmy. But Angela had Jimmy in tow, had pressed him into service at the little bar and was tying a belaced, befrilled white apron about his slim waist.

"I remember you perfectly," she told Rothman. "You are the outrageous man who asked me last week, in this very room, why I didn't leave my husband."

"Well, why didn't you?" inquired Rothman glumly.

"You're impossible," she said lightly. Now Rothman was staring at Jocelyn. "What's she doing here?" he demanded.

Sherry put her arm around the girl. "Miss Lee — Mr. Rothman," she murmured; and added for Jocelyn's information, "Mr. Rothman writes those devastatingly realistic and unpleasant novels of the East Side, Jocelyn."

"Don't tell me," said Rothman, in horror, "that she hasn't read them!"

Jocelyn shook her fair head, flushing with embarrassment.

"I'm afraid not," she began, but Rothman interrupted, thrusting his dark, saturnine face within an inch of her own.

"That's quite all right," he said miserably "virgins shouldn't read my novels . . . you are a virgin, aren't you?" he said suddenly.

Jocelyn took a step backward, her eyes wide. Sherry said sharply, "Don't be ridiculous." To Jocelyn she added, "Don't bother to answer; that was a purely rhetorical question. Mr. Rothman delights in shocking the populace."

Jocelyn murmured something, anything. Rothman bent a little closer and whispered in Sherry's ear. Jocelyn slid away, her heart pounding in her breast, and looked about for Jimmy. Standing at the bar, agitating the big shaker, he waved at her and she started over to him.

At the piano the boy was still playing small defiant snatches of melody. Jocelyn veered and went across to him, leaning on the piano, watching the muscular, sensitive hands. Suddenly she felt at home. She didn't know who the shabby, thin boy was, she didn't care. Here was someone in this tower of Babel who spoke her language. Now he stopped and looked up at her inquiringly, his brows drawn and his rather weak, unhappy mouth set in a straight wretched line. Jocelyn said, softly, "Go on, please — it is lovely."

"You're the only one who thinks so," he said, but his eyes brightened and the drawn brows relaxed. Jocelyn came around the corner of the piano and sat down on the bench with him. "Mind?" she said. He shook his curly hair, as fair as her own. "Mind? No, I don't mind," he replied; and then he told her abruptly, "I'll play for you, really play."

He played.They sat there together entranced, under the same spell. It was Debussy he was playing, a silver pattern. Jocelyn sat with her hands clasped and her eyes clear and dreaming. Sherry, leaving Rothman abruptly, went over to Jimmy.

"We'll have to go soon," she reminded him. "Look, Jocelyn's perfectly happy."

Jimmy regarded the two fair heads close together over the keys. He said, really listening for the first time: "That lad's somebody, Angela. But it's a crime to ask him to play in here. No one's listening but Jocelyn."

"It makes a pleasant background," said Angela lightly.

Meredith Post, more than a little drunk, laughed aloud.

"Angela cares a lot for backgrounds," he said swiftly, "everything is just a background for Angela."

"I'll take him along with us," whispered Jimmy, and Angela nodded indifferently.

"Do," she said quite clearly. "Merry in his cups is about as boring as they come."

Young Post set down the glass he held, gently, with the exaggerated care of the drunken.

"You didn't always think that, Angela," he said dangerously.

"I may change my mind," she said, shrugging a slim shoulder, "it's my privilege, as I'm a woman."

Jimmy said uncomfortably, in answer to

Sherry's raised eyebrows: "Well, we'll be getting along now, Angela, if you don't mind. Merry, want to drive out home with us? you and I can sit in the rumble."

"I might as well," said Post, after a moment, "I'm wasting my time around here."

Angela smiled a little. Tomorrow, she thought, he'll be back. Not that it mattered.

She watched Jimmy cross the room to collect Jocelyn; saw the young man close the piano and rise as Jocelyn rose; heard him say, "I shan't play any more tonight," and frown. He hadn't, really, played for his supper.

Sherry and Jimmy, Jocelyn and Meredith Post left together. The musician went with them. Out on the sidewalk Jimmy asked, "Can we drop you somewhere — you won't mind squeezing in front with the girls?"

But the boy shook his head. "I'll walk," he said, "thanks just the same." He spoke with a fluent, accented English. He looked at Jocelyn with a strange and sexless yearning. "Thank you," he said to her, low.

They shook hands gravely. They would never see each other again. But it was worth leaving the warm rooms where there would be food and drink, wasteful food and drink, thought Serge, turning up the collar of his coat and walking rapidly away, very much

110

alone in the cold dark night, worth refusing the careless benevolence of his hostess in order to keep intact the memory of a small blond girl who had sat very still on the piano bench and listened with her heart and mind to the music which so greatly mattered to him.

"Poor devil," said Jimmy, staring after him, "another of Angela's proteges."

"He isn't poor," said Jocelyn softly.

Jimmy threw a careless arm around her shoulders and held her a moment.

"You're a good kid," he said, and it wasn't what he meant; what he meant was, You're a strange youngster and you're going to get hurt along the road, I'm afraid. Aloud he said, "How did you like Angela's?"

"Noisy," answered Jocelyn, smiling.

She climbed into the front with Sherry and Jimmy touched Meredith Post on the shoulder. "Us for the rumble, old man," he said cheerfully, "it's stopped snowing."

Merry was standing quite still looking down the street. He said, sobering in the cold, keen air, "That's what happens to Angela's men, isn't it? — they go on alone, around dark corners."

"Snap out of it," said Jimmy uneasily, "and sit your fanny down there, there's a rug for the old legs, turn up your overcoat collar, and we're off."

On the way out with Sherry, skillful and careful, at the wheel, Jimmy thought of the place he had just left. Angela's cocktail parties lasted very late. Some of those left would raid the kitchen for a scratch supper, or they'd go out. If they were out, they'd come back. What did it amount to, he thought, noise and smoke and gossip and wisecracks and the usual dirt dishing? No one liked any of the others very much, the women would fall on each other's necks with shrieks of "darling" and "dearest" and the men would watch each other warily and Angela would hold them all together for a while with the bright, strong thread of her personality. He wondered dimly why he had been there so much during the past month or so, why Sherry bothered to go.

They drove Post home and finally reached their own little house. Katie muttered in the kitchen and Mary was in a fever of fright lest dinner be spoiled. But it wasn't, although they sat down to it late enough, the three of them, the two girls rosy with the drive, their eyes bright. Jimmy looked at them contentedly. "Swell," he said, "to leave home — isn't it? — just so you can get back again."

After dinner they sat in the living room, Sherry and Jocelyn talking while Jimmy smoked a pipe and exclaimed over stock market reports. They turned the radio on, they turned it off, so that Jocelyn might play to them a little. And she played drowsily, dreamily until Sherry said, laughing: "You're asleep at the keys. Go up to bed, for heaven's sake. Mary took your little bag up, you'll find everything ready for you."

"My same room?" asked Jocelyn.

"Yes, of course. Shoo! I'll be up later."

"Come now," begged Jocelyn, "I'll be asleep later."

Sherry went up the stairs with her, and Jimmy, legs straight out before him, his substantial feet on a *petit-point* footstool, watched them ascend the steps and smiled to himself. Pretty darned nice girls, both of them, he thought lazily.

Sherry sat on the guest-room bed while Jocelyn undressed, wider awake now, talking, troubled, of her mother, of her increasing weakness, and of her father. "He has a chance," she said after a while, "to go abroad — there's some talk about a branch office in England and he's the one who should go. But he doesn't like to leave her — "

Sherry nodded. There was nothing she could say. The dread, felt so deeply by them both, was between them, unspoken.

A car drove up and stopped. "Who on

earth — " began Sherry. She added, after a moment, "We never have an evening alone, Jimmy and I — "

Then she looked at Jocelyn, at her quickly wounded face. She said instantly: "I didn't mean you, you crazy little nut. You're one of us, you belong."

Jocelyn was in bed. She reached up her long young arms and pulled Sherry's bright head close to her own and kissed her cheek. "You and Jimmy," whispered Jocelyn, "I don't know what I'd ever do without you — if you ever change — "

"Well, we won't," Sherry assured her, touched and laughing a little. "We'll always be the same, except that Jimmy will grow a long, white beard and I'll get fat . . . and cranky — and start running to fortune tellers and doctors as most middle-aged women do."

She kissed Jocelyn, opened the windows and turned out the light. She stood a minute in the doorway, listening. There were voices downstairs, yet she had not heard the bell ring. She asked, "Anything you want, Jocelyn?"

There was no answer. Jocelyn was asleep.

Sherry turned and went out, closing the door softly behind her. She found herself thinking, I'd like a daughter like Jocelyn. Absurd, there was but four years' difference in their ages. She was still smiling at herself when she entered the living room to find her mother there, a highball glass in one hand and a cigarette in the other.

"Hello, Sheila," Sherry greeted her, astonished.

"Hello," said Sheila. She looked at her daughter for a moment. "I don't like the way you're doing your hair," she remarked, dissatisfied.

"I'm letting it grow," explained Sherry. "I know it's all over ends, but Jimmy has a yen to see what I'd look like with long hair. Once it's all grown, I'll probably cut it off again."

But Sheila had already forgotten Sherry's hair. She sat on the edge of the table, in a smart black suit, with a tiny broad-tail jacket, an absurd smart hat cocked over one eye and announced abruptly, "Helen Post came to see me, this afternoon."

Jimmy back in his comfortable chair, looked up at his mother-in-law.

"We took Merry home before dinner," he said casually. "He had a bit of an edge."

"That's just it," said Sheila, "something has to be done about Angela. Helen's worried about Meredith. She's afraid he'll do something foolish — "

"What do you mean?" asked Sherry sharply.

115

Sheila shrugged.

"Oh, the usual thing, suicide, big game hunting, marry a streetwalker," she replied bluntly. "Something, anything. To cause a scandal. And she wants something done about it."

"What can we do?" asked Jimmy.

"You can talk to Angela," Sheila replied. "I've tried. Maybe you can do some good, I can't. But you have influence with her."

"I?" Jimmy sat bolt upright, astonished. He knocked the ashes from his pipe into a metal tray. "I — influence with Angela?"

"She says," repeated Sheila, smiling slightly, "that you're the only man she ever really cared for."

"Hooey!" commented Jimmy rudely. Sherry looked up, smiling, but her smile faded, as her mother went on.

"No, it isn't. Angela has always had what she wanted. She didn't, I take it, have you. That's the answer. Do reason with her. She amused herself with Merry as long as it suited her and then — "

Jimmy said, flushing: "It's none of my business. What does Mrs. Post want me to do? Persuade her to take Merry back again — or marry him?"

"No, don't be absurd. She wants Angela to stop seeing him altogether. It is this hanging on that is making things so difficult for him. If she'd be really through — once and for all. But she isn't. She likes to keep them — on ice," said Sheila coolly, "and whistle them back now and then to see if her training was thorough."

Sherry spoke violently, jumping up from the corner of the couch.

"Angela makes me sick," she said, "I don't know how we endure her. If she weren't a member of the family — "

"Well, she is," said Sheila calmly, "she happens to be my only sister's child and I have an interest in her. Her trouble is merely that she has too much money and no one to say a word as to what she shall do with it. So, if a scandal can be avoided — "

"Angela," said Jimmy, grinning, "isn't afraid of scandal. I did say something to her once . . . not about Merry, however. And she put me right in my place. She said, as nearly as I can remember, 'If you have money and a decent social background and are discreet, you can do anything and get away with it.' She pointed the moral by mentioning a lot of sacrosanct names — I was gaga with astonishment. People I'd never even dreamed had strayed from the straight and narrow — "

"That proves it, doesn't it?" cried Sherry.

"Proves what?" asked Jimmy.

"That you can't get away with it!" Sheila interrupted, slipping down from the table.

"It proves nothing. If Angela had been discreet — but she hasn't been. She made a tremendous mistake in character when she elected to favor Meredith Post with her attentions. She makes other mistakes. She doesn't always hunt on her own preserve. She travels with a very mixed crowd. I have to get back to the house, I have people coming in for bridge. But I thought I'd tell you what Helen said and ask you to try to do something, Jimmy. Go in some day, see her alone, use a little of that well-known charm — " She smiled briefly, a smile which did not reach her eyes. She added casually: "I'm shutting the house week after next and going down to Florida. The Garrods have offered me their villa at a very low rental." She looked at Sherry. "If you and Jimmy want to come down . . ."

"Love to, but can't," said Jimmy firmly. "I have to work. And how!" he added, under his breath.

"Sherry then, if she likes," said Sherry's mother carelessly, walking toward the door.

Sherry linked her arm through Jimmy's as they followed. "It can't be done," she said gayly, "the little woman's place is in the home."

"I expected that," admitted her mother serenely, "but in a year or two you may be very glad of a vacation."

When she had left, Jimmy and Sherry came back into the house and looked at each other. Jimmy said, ruffling her hair with his big hand, "Looks as if everyone has us headed for the rocks, infant."

"What do we care?" asked Sherry stoutly, and kissed him.

As they were going up to bed after Sherry, in the midst of reading aloud the most exciting chapter of the newest mystery-thriller, observed the practically comatose condition of her audience, the telephone rang furiously.

Jimmy leaped into their bedroom and took the call there. Sherry watching from the doorway, saw his face set and whiten. He said, merely, "Yes — yes — all right, I'll be over."

He replaced the receiver.

"It's Merry," he said. "The damned fool — !"

"Jimmy — he hasn't — " Sherry stopped, sickened.

"No, he hasn't," he said hastily, "but it's a close call. His mother wants me. Why, Lord knows. I suppose because we were with him today and because of — oh, Angela, everything — "

He came up to her like a minor hurricane,

119

pulled her close, kissed her hard and was gone, pounding down the stairs. She heard the door slam, as she stood there and the running feet on the frost-hard road to the garage. She thought, Poor Merry. She thought, We woke Jocelyn, as a sleepy call reached her from the room across the hall.

Sherry poked her head in at the door, trying to keep her voice steady.

"It's nothing. Jimmy had to go out — go back to sleep, Jocelyn," she said.

She went back into her room and undressed; impossible to sleep. She lay with the reading light on and a book open on the bed beside her. She picked it up, looked unseeingly at the print, put it down again. Impossible to concentrate. She put out her hand for the phone. She'd call Sheila. Her hand dropped. No, what was the use?

It was lonely in the little house without Jimmy. Lonely, thinking of Meredith Post, thinking of how they had driven him back home, how he'd sat there in the rumble seat, breathing deeply of the cold rush of air, scarcely answering when Jimmy spoke to him. What had been his thoughts?

She hated Angela, suddenly, and in a way, irrevocably. She thought, It won't mean anything to Angela so long as the papers don't get it. She won't care, she'll think it a —

120

a tribute, maybe. She was sick with disgust at herself, at all of them, for their careless acceptance of Angela Ward for what she was, simply because she "belonged," she was "family." She remembered the woman Sheila refused to receive . . . "Oh, impossible, my dear, she was his mistress for years before she married him. Yes, I know she did marry him, but one must draw the line somewhere — a manicurist, wasn't she?"

But one drew the line so very crookedly, thought Sherry.

She was hot with pitying anger against young Post for his weakness, his absurdity, his idiocy in believing Angela worth the sacrifice of himself. Couldn't he see, couldn't he know? Couldn't he laugh it off as most of the others had?

He was in love with her, Sherry supposed. She stirred uneasily on the high-piled pillows. Love —

Surely, it couldn't be love, this emotion which Angela inspired? Meredith was like a child deprived of a bright, dangerous toy, one which had given him excitement and pleasure. He couldn't endure losing it, couldn't endure seeing anyone else possess it, with the same excitement, the same pleasure —

Jimmy, thought Sherry, come home —

please, quickly. When Jimmy came home things would be right again, not so muddled, she would be herself again, not fretted by these fine distinctions.

But it was late when he came, and he was tired. He told her, snatchily, briefly, undressing, dropping his clothes anywhere. By that token Sherry knew how upset he was.

"No, no danger," said Jimmy wearily, "it was all over when I got there. Doc Ferris was around. He knows how to keep his mouth shut. The liquor Merry'd drunk helped matters. He took an overdose of — the other stuff anyway. I mean, it made him sick. The rest was — work. Stomach pump, all that miserable business. He's pretty well shot, and the place is like a madhouse. He left a letter — I mean, he intended to leave a letter. No one had seen it till I got there. I — I tore it up. That's a lot better, I think, though I suppose," he said, trying to grin, "I compounded a felony or whatever they call it. Mrs. Post is fit to be tied, she wanted in one breath to sue Angela — for what I haven't the least idea — and in the next to be certain that Angela would never know. She doesn't, of course, know what she's doing or saying. They're going to take Merry to some sort of sanitarium tomorrow,

122

where his nerves will get back in shape and then send him abroad. Lord," said Jimmy, "he's only a kid . . ."

From the vantage point of his twenty-seven years he regarded Meredith Post at twenty-four.

Sherry said, a little sharply, "He's old enough to know better. And Angela — when I think of Angela — !"

"Don't think of her," advised Jimmy, crawling into his bed with a tremendous sigh of relief. "Hey, come over here, will you," he requested, "and say good night properly!"

She went, to sit beside him, to kiss him. She said, "Angela oughtn't to go scot-free."

"She won't," said Jimmy grimly, thinking of the house he had just left, the distracted woman, the grave, slightly cynical doctor, the frightened servants holding their breaths. But they'll never hold their tongues, thought Jimmy, and bribing won't help either, it will only make matters worse. He thought of Dr. Ferris' office nurse whom the doctor had picked up on the way over to the Posts', a still middle-aged woman with strong, sure hands and sagacious eyes. He thought of something she had said, looking down on the boy who lay exhausted in bed, his darkened eyelids shut — what was it she'd said?

It eluded him now, perhaps he'd think of it later.

"I'll go to Angela's," Sherry was saying, "tomorrow."

"Keep out of it," ordered Jimmy. "And get back to bed. You're shivering — " He added, "I'll go myself."

Before he dropped off to sleep he roused himself to ask, anxiously, "Jocelyn doesn't know what's been going on, does she?"

"No, dear — "

"That's good," he said. "I'd rather she didn't, she's such a kid" — and slept profoundly, the sleep of deep fatigue.

CHAPTER VI

Jocelyn returned home in the morning and Sherry drove her and Jimmy to the train. Things seemed a little flat but much more normal in the brilliant light of the January sun, lying golden and dazzling on the slight snowfall of the afternoon before. Nothing had been said at breakfast because of Jocelyn's presence, and there was, moreover, nothing to be said. But Sherry had just a word with her husband at the station.

"You'll see Angela then?" she asked.

"I'll try. I don't know why, really," he added in some surprise, "unless it's to throw the fear of God into her. And I doubt if that can be done."

"Perhaps you'd better let it drop — "

"No. She should hear — if she hasn't already heard. These things get out — "

He kissed her hastily.

" 'By, darling — and don't worry. Come on, youngster." He seized Jocelyn by the hand and fled with her down the platform. Sherry stood watching them a moment, then she turned and walked slowly back to the car. She thought, driving toward home, that she had been unduly nervous the night before. Angela's studio, people, laughter, gossip, the tinkle of ice, the blue rising of cigarette smoke. Then her mother's sudden appearance at home; and afterward the telephone call and the unprecedented loneliness of the hours in which she waited for Jimmy to return and the dark reaches of her imagination. She wondered, turning in at the gates of Quaker Hill, if her mother had learned. She and Helen Post were close friends. That is to say, neither said anything memorable against the other in public and they were together a good deal. On an impulse she stopped at the main house and went in. Her mother, she was informed, was not yet up.

Sherry tossed her tweed coat with its soft beaver collar on to a chair in the hall and went lightly up the winding stairway. This was the old portion of the house, and it was very lovely. Her hand touched the polished wood of the beautifully turned handrail with affection. She had always loved the house; it spoke to her of past generations, of eras of dignified and simple living.

In the passageway outside her mother's door she met her mother's maid, Ella. Ella smiled at her, she liked Miss Sherry very much. Yes, Mrs. Nevins was awake and had breakfasted, she had just removed the tray.

Mrs. Harrington was with her.

Sherry knocked. "Come in," said her mother briskly.

Sheila was in bed, in the great swan bed which had replaced the heavy four-poster of her mother-in-law's time. She wore a little jacket of lace and sable over her sheer night-dress and her dark hair was caught close to her well-shaped head by a net cap. She was not made up, and, curiously, looked younger and less brittle. Letters and bills strewed the fine silk and lace of the blanket cover, the great rose-colored down puff was huddled about her feet. The shades were up, the draperies pulled back and the light streamed in. The room was large, gracious, and very feminine, but without unnecessary frills and ruffles.

Harrington, in her decent black, stood by the bed with a menu in her hand. Sheila said, "This is a surprise — " She tossed a bill to the foot of the bed and remarked petulantly, "The woman can wait." Then she looked up at Sherry. "Why so bright and early?" she inquired.

But she knew. Sherry knew that she knew. But with Harrington in the room it was impossible to speak of what had happened the previous night.

A visiting social secretary would come in

about eleven. The bills and letters would then be taken care of; meantime here was Harrington with her menu. "Artichokes," decided Sheila. She pondered a moment, one rose-tipped finger at her lips. "Fresh strawberries?" she said doubtfully, and then, "No, the price is absurd." She looked at Sherry and laughed, "Why," she complained, "people have come to consider that you don't really do them well unless all the food on the table is out of season, I don't know."

She gave Harrington brief, concluding instructions and dismissed her. The door closed softly. She turned on her pillows and regarded her daughter alertly. She said: "You needn't bother to tell me why you came. I know. I talked to Helen this morning."

Sherry sat down on the foot of the bed. She was slender and supple in the soft knitted dress of rabbit's hair, the pancake tam tipped over the bright waves of her hair. Her astonishing eyes were troubled. She said, helplessly, "It's all such a *mess* — "

"Meredith Post is an ass," said Sheila shortly, "like his mother. Still, it's unpleasant for Angela."

"Angela!"

"Oh, don't frown, and look at me as if I had committed the unforgivable sin. Of course, I agree with you, she is entirely to blame. I told her not six months ago that she wasn't handling Merry correctly. The boy's unintelligent and an idealist. It was bound to happen. Helen said Jimmy went over," she added, reaching for a cigarette.

"Yes, he was pretty upset — "

Sheila blew a long spiral of smoke, lying back among the pillows.

"Was there a suicide clause in the policy he sold Merry just before you were married?" she asked mockingly.

Sherry colored.

"I don't know. He wasn't thinking of life insurance policies," she said a little tartly, "he was thinking of Merry. We drove him out last night." She shivered. "He hardly spoke all the way home."

"We?"

"Jimmy, Jocelyn and I. Jocelyn and I had been to the theater, and we picked up Jimmy at Angela's. Merry was there," Sherry explained.

"Angela does get her way," said Sherry's mother with admiration.

"What do you mean?"

She was no fool. She met her mother's cool eyes directly. Sheila said evenly:

"Don't be absurd, my dear. It's perfectly patent, isn't it, that Angela has been playing for your precious husband ever since you two returned from your honeymoon? Merry was — a stop-gap — "

"I hate it when you talk like that," said Sherry passionately, "as if — as if — "

"As if what?"

"As if there were no decency in the world, no loyalty — " She stopped, feeling like a ridiculous child who had been drawn on only to encounter ridicule. Her mother's eyes narrowed slightly.

"My dear, *is* there?"

"Of course," replied Sherry slowly, with deep conviction.

"You're very young," said Sheila. She lay back and studied her daughter. It seemed absurd to think she had borne her. She had loathed it all, her pregnancy, her delivery. She laughed, soundlessly, delivery was so inadequate a word and yet it made sense. She had hated surrendering her body to that elemental necessity, that common usage. Sherry isn't at all like me, she thought, she's rather like her father; I suppose she'll get more so as the years go on —

Aloud, she said:

"You do dramatize life and yourself a great deal, don't you, Sherry? Get over it," advised Sheila, whose code was to live as well as possible and entirely on the surface. "It won't do any good and after the first, fine, careless rapture wears off it will bore Jimmy. And when Jimmy — or any other man — is bored — "

She permitted her warning to trail off into silence. She went on:

"Well, there's no use worrying over what has happened and what might have happened. Helen will get Meredith away — first to some sort of convalescent place and then abroad. She'd do better not to go with him. A shipboard romance will do a lot for his ego. But not with an anxious mother in the background hiding all the lethal weapons. Forget it," she said, and asked abruptly, "How's Jimmy's business?"

"Why, all right, I believe," replied Sherry, astonished.

"Don't you know? You should make it your business to know," her mother rejoined tartly.

"He doesn't discuss it very much. You know how it is; there are disappointments, of course. I know when those happen," she said, smiling; "he comes home pretty darned glum. And other days he comes in whistling, off-key. When he whistles, off-key, somebody has been persuaded."

"It's precarious," said her mother after a pause, "and Jimmy hasn't been entirely frank with you. Or me, for that matter. I couldn't, somehow, pin him down to figures. There were plenty of pleasant rumors. Joe McKenzie, of course, was the instigator of most of them. How well Jimmy was doing, what a name he'd make for himself. But in a depression of these proportions — "

"Jimmy says that it's just at such a time that sensible men realize the value of protection," began Sherry eagerly.

"Spare me the rubber stamp," Sheila said. She looked at the clock and frowned. "The Lawson place is sending a girl out to give me a facial and a finger-wave as I can't get to town — and there's my Swede for the massage, now — "

Her quick ear had heard the faint sound of the doorbell. Sherry rose. She looked down at her mother. She had come to talk out this business of Angela and Meredith Post, seriously, gravely, in all its implications. Nothing with any substance to it had been said. She bent and kissed her mother's smooth cheek, from habit, but added, pleased as a child on a voyage of discovery, "You have a gorgeous skin, Sheila."

Sheila nodded. "It's the upkeep," she said, laughing, "but this new shop has really sensible ideas. It wouldn't hurt you to take a few treatments," she told Sherry.

Sherry shrugged. "I haven't time."

"That's silly. You do nothing all day long. Oh, I know, your absurd Thespians." She laughed at Sherry's instantly resentful face. "You were really very sweet in that gaga performance," Sheila told her comfortingly. "I sometimes wonder if it wouldn't have been wise to have permitted you to go on the stage when you were so terribly keen on it . . ." She paused, but Sherry knew how the sentence was concluded in her mind . . . then you wouldn't have been in such a rush to marry.

She had reached the door when her mother called her sharply.

"Sherry?"

"Yes, Sheila?"

Sheila, oddly enough, flushed very faintly. She was a woman who enjoyed a "good" story and a "daring" play and a banned book. But it was almost impossible for her to speak of things that were real and intimate and of life. Sherry's pre-marital education along biological lines had been conducted by medical men, governesses, her small companions and, later, reading.

"You haven't — you aren't — I mean, there isn't — ?"

Sherry knew. She laughed frankly. "No, there isn't," she said. "Don't worry, I won't make you a grandmother, yet."

The door closed behind her. Sheila lay back, waiting for the rosy, slim little Swedish girl to come in and work over her well-preserved body. There had been absolutely no malice in Sherry's reply, but it had been a barbed shaft nevertheless. The thought of being pigeonholed as a grandmother was terrifying to Sheila. She did not like children, she had never liked them, she was frank enough about it. If Sheila had been a boy, thus gratifying Kenneth Nevins' deep-rooted instincts, there would have been no girl. One child was enough for any woman to produce. She knew that, currently, there was a trend back to the large family. It was considered rather smart. But so far as she was concerned a million babies could be born to rich and poor alike in the course of the next few years, as long as one was not born to Jimmy and Sherry Maxwell.

Sheila was a young woman. Since her husband's death, early in her married life, she had had innumerable offers of marriage. She had refused them all, principally because she enjoyed a widowhood free from any material worry and because she was determined never to bear another child. Lately, even, she had had offers, but they were lessening; the more unconventional suggestions predominated. She had no illusions about those, either. For perhaps five years, possibly more, with her appearance and her means, she might delude herself. But no longer. After that it would be simply another aging woman involving herself with a dissatisfied young man who found aging women a better source of caviar and champagne than hard work — what with jobs so difficult to procure.

She was not such an idiot, she thought, submitting herself to the steel-strong clever hands of the Swedish girl, watching the bright dew of perspiration on the clear youthful forehead, feeling her nerves relax, her blood tingle warmly through her veins and her muscles respond.

Sherry went home and garaged her car. She had several members of the amateur dramatic society, too amateur to be dignified by the Little Theater label, coming in for luncheon, and to discuss the new play. These were pleasant, talented young men and women she would enjoy herself, she thought, trying to follow her mother's advice and shake off the unpleasant memory of last night. How, she wondered, would Jimmy get along with Angela? She wished now that she had begged him not to see her, implored him to let well enough alone. Angela, she thought, sighing, leaving the kitchen, sitting down to the telephone to order, would feel so very important!

But Jimmy would tell her tonight what he had said and what Angela had replied and the chapter would be closed.

Jimmy saw Angela about four o'clock. He had telephoned her. Could he see her, he asked, alone? — it was extremely important.

Angela said that he could. Her laughter, rising on the scale, was gay over the wire. "What's wrong, Sherry eloped?"

"Don't be a nitwit," he said shortly; "shall I come to your place?"

"Yes. No. There are some people coming . . . they can get along without me," she decided indifferently, "as long as there are drinks and smokes about. Nita Welles is coming in, she can be acting-hostess. And how," said Angela, laughing.

They arranged to meet, therefore, at four; at, of course, a speakeasy which advertised tea and dancing. There was usually very little tea.

Jimmy was there at four promptly, wishing himself any other place. The room was small, and already crowded. He spoke to the captain, a corner table was arranged, a little apart from its fellows, away from the music. Lights were soft under the silk folded across the ceiling. Jimmy ordered a drink and waited.

She was only fifteen minutes late. She wore

136

a marvelous, slim suit and a great scarf of silver fox. When she was at the table she gave her order quickly, without consideration. She linked her hands under her chin and looked at Jimmy . . .

"This is an honor," she said. She laughed at him, her eyes deep and narrow. "There is something about you, Jimmy," she said, "which makes me feel so deliciously clandestine, even though I realize, of course, that Sherry knows where you are. Every minute, day and night."

This was not an opening gambit calculated to put him in good humor. He said, as the frosted drinks came and were set before them, and the little plates of biscuits and caviar and thin toast, "Yes, Sherry knows."

"She would," said Angela. She raised her glass to her lips. "Here's to crime," she said banally. "Or to the occasion when she doesn't know."

"Oh, stow it," said Jimmy crossly. He drank; set down his glass. He thought, Hell, what's the use? But he let her have it without warning.

"Merry Post tried to commit suicide last night," he said baldly.

She flushed astonishingly, a great rush of color; then she paled, and the delicate rouge stood out in patches. She whispered, with a slow, terrifying venom — *"The Goddamned fool — "*

Jimmy said evenly:

"I agree with you. But that doesn't get us anywhere. He didn't succeed, thanks to the fact he'd had too much to drink at your place, and to his doctor. He had written a letter — "

"To me," asked Angela quickly.

"Yes, to you — to whom else — Mahatma Gandhi?" said Jimmy.

"Give it to me," ordered Angela. Her hand, with its scarlet nails, was outspread like a claw. Jimmy said, "I destroyed it."

Her hand fell to her lap. She regarded him a moment. "Of all the consummate nerve," she began.

"Angela, snap out of it. The scandal's been avoided, we think. He's been shipped, or will be shipped, to a sanitarium. That's that. Then he goes abroad. The grand tour," said Jimmy sardonically, "and that's also that. You're out of the picture, for good. But you were bound to hear it, it will be whispered about, these things can't fail to happen. Now you know, you're warned. And there isn't any letter, see? It might have been temporary insanity, depression, anything, for an excuse — but I'm telling you — be careful — next time."

Angela asked softly, "You do despise me, don't you, darling?"

Jimmy beckoned a waiter and duplicated the order. When the man had gone he said slowly,

"No, Angela, I've always liked you. But — "

"*But . . . !*" she said. To his consternation her eyes filled. She said, low, "Jimmy, believe it wasn't all my fault."

He shrugged his broad shoulders. His pleasant intent face, which had not the slightest claim to masculine beauty, was clouded, grave.

"He's pretty young," he said, "and not — forgive me — very bright. He wasn't much like that talky, shouty, clever do-nothing gang you run with — They," said Jimmy, out of his brief experience with Angela's group, "leap lightly from bed to bed and it leaves no mark. But Merry — " he frowned and looked away — "he was weak," said Jimmy, "and a fool." He thought of the nurse that night. Now he remembered what she had said, her work done, looking down at the drained exhausted young face . . . "Such a pity," she said, "such utter futility, when there are people in the world strong enough to suffer — "

"Jimmy," said Angela, "I don't care what you think of me. That's a lie. I do care!" She looked at him with violence, with fury.

139

"You make me sick," she said, a little shrilly, so that the girl at the nearest table stopped talking to giggle, and stopped giggling to stare; and staring, recognized Angela Ward, and so whispered something to her escort.

"I?" asked Jimmy, mildly astonished.

"Yes, you! — smug, thoroughly middle class, the epitome of all the virtues. Merry was — all we called him, you and I. Is. Will always be. But he had the courage of his convictions even if it didn't even quite come off. You," she said mockingly, "you wouldn't kill yourself for anything — would you? — a dream, a woman — not even for Sherry."

"No, I wouldn't," Jimmy told her quietly, "but I'd live for — her. That's a damned sight more sensible."

Angela sighed. She said, pushing her glass away:

"I suppose so. . . . Forget it — I suppose, too, Sherry's upset about this — "

"Well, why not? You're her cousin."

"And Sheila?"

"I don't know about her. Mrs. Post went to see her yesterday, before it happened."

"And begged her to use her influence with me." Angela smiled wryly. "How quaint." She looked at Jimmy and her eyes were brilliant. She said:

140

"Can't you see that the things I do are because I'm so utterly bored, because I haven't anything to hold to, because I believe — yes, I'm that much of an idiot — in the things people tell me about myself — and then I find they're not so and no one ever meant them — and — " She broke off. "Men — " she said, again with that distilled fury, "all they want is something so easy in the main so worthless that it's easy to give. Now and then that isn't enough for one of them and you haven't anything more, then he — dies of it, I suppose. Or tries to." She dropped her eyes a moment. "I was never in love with Merry," she said very distinctly. "I was sorry for him, that's all. I thought, If that's all he wants . . . ? Well, it wasn't. He wanted more than was in me to give — *him.*"

She was silent. Jimmy was slightly embarrassed. If this was Angela with the mask off, he wished she would replace that mask. For he felt himself on the verge of pity and he didn't want to pity Angela Ward of all people in an incalculable world.

"I've always liked you," said Angela suddenly. "I thought, Jimmy really knows me, cares something about what makes me tick, sees through these crazy makeshifts and pretenses — then Sherry came along."

Jimmy felt exceedingly uncomfortable. He said, awkwardly, the easiest thing, in order to stop her from talking, from making further disturbing revelations.

"We've been good friends, Angela, and we still are. Sherry — she's upset, of course, but she'll get over it. She was pretty sore about the whole business, but not entirely at you. She's fair, that way."

"I don't care what Sherry thinks," said Angela. "No, that's not true. Try and make her see, Jimmy." She was silent again, then she said: "I'm not, of course, any good. I drift. I've too much money and no real talent. And I can't keep at anything long."

Jimmy looked at his watch. "Golly!" he ejaculated, staring. He called the waiter and paid the bill. "I've got to get back," he said, "and make it snappy."

Angela rose. "I'll drive you to the station," she told him. Presently he moved through the crowded room following her slightly sensational progress: heads turned, people spoke, women looked at her clothes, men at her bright lips . . .

In the tiny square hall, as a uniformed man went through the mechanical gesture of producing a key and unlocking a door, someone spoke to Angela . . . a dark man, rather young, rather good-looking, with an intense and eager face.

"Holman Benson," cried Angela, flashing into conventional life, "where on earth did you come from, when did you get back?"

"Today," replied the man called Holman Benson, smiling, "and it's good to see you. I'll drop around, if I may?"

"Any time," said Angela carelessly, "before two A.M." She made the introductions. She said, "This is the man I've been wanting Sherry to meet — "

"Sherry?" asked Benson, with a dark, raised eyebrow.

Angela explained, while Jimmy fidgeted, looking again at his watch. She added, ". . . adores the theater, very intelligent about it, too," and then, as Jimmy turned to get his hat and coat and Benson's face was expressive, she said, laughing, "Don't worry, she's awfully pretty — "

To Jimmy in the car, driving to the station, she explained further.

"He's going to be a big shot in the theater some day. Came out of the West with some money and a lot of executive talent and ideals and a belief in himself. He's been the soul of a really big Little Theater group out there for some time. He had a play here, last year. Did you see it? *Good-by to Love*. It was really good but it took more than he

143

had to ballyhoo it and it flopped, after a month or so. He left town right after you came back from your wedding trip, to do a directing stunt in San Francisco and to raise some money. I think Sherry would like him, he speaks her language."

Jimmy was irritated but there didn't seem much to say. "Don't I?" was not indicated. He left her at the station, taking her hand briefly in his. The chauffeur sat at the wheel of the little town car, his eyes straight ahead. This was one for the book, he thought. Too bad, this Maxwell was a nice guy and had a helluva pretty wife . . . he liked his employer's cousin.

"Good-by," she said slowly and then low, "please try not to judge me too harshly, Jimmy. If you really knew — "

He was late for dinner. Sherry, tired from her luncheon, a strenuous discussion, and an appointment for tea in Greenwich, flew at him with kisses and mild reproaches. He said, a little shortly, "I couldn't help it — Sherry, I got held up, Angela was late as usual."

Sherry had waited a couple of trains in anxiety. But now that he was here the anxiety fled and even the reproaches. She said, "Let's go home and eat, and then we'll talk."

After dinner she deluged him with questions. What did she say, how did she act, tell me all about it — !

His head ached. He wanted to forget Angela and her mistakes. Meredith Post was, he supposed, her worst error so far. He replied, after a moment, and found himself believing it.

"She was pretty cut up about it, Sherry."

"Do you think so?" Sherry frowned at him a moment, considering. Then she asked, "What really happened, I mean between you?"

"Nothing," he answered and did not know he lied. "I just told her. She was upset, as I said. She tried to explain things to me — "

"Explain!" cried Sherry, her eyes very wide.

"Oh, I don't suppose it was entirely her fault," he said uncomfortably, "after all he pestered her to death, and she was sorry for him — "

Sherry said primly, "I think that sleeping with a man because you're sorry for him is going to extremes."

"Sherry!" cried Jimmy, amazed beyond belief. Then he laughed up at her as she stood over him, and pulled her down on his lap. "Talk about mid-Victorian coarseness and prudery!" he remarked.

"I didn't mean it — either way," she said,

hurt, "but really, Jimmy — "

"Well, we don't know for a fact that she *did*, do we?"

"No," agreed Sherry after a moment, "we don't know. No one really knows those things unless they look through keyholes. But it seemed pretty obvious." She got up from his knee and walked to the table and lighted a cigarette. "What on earth's come over you, Jimmy?" she wanted to know. "It isn't like you to champion Angela — I've always done that, in a way, I suppose, because she's my cousin — but you — "

"Oh," said Jimmy, "don't let's talk about it. I did my duty, didn't I? I told her what happened. I said, in effect, Let this be a warning to you. She isn't such a bad sort," he argued, tamping the tobacco down in his pipe with a spread thumb, "she's just a little crazy . . . too much money, nothing to hold on to — "

"Well!" said Sherry.

She walked over to the radio and turned it on. An instant blare of raucous music which made Jimmy jump and mutter plaintively, "For Pete's sake!" greeted her. She adjusted the volume control. Now, the music was muted, gay, contagious. She tapped her foot to the rhythm. She said, over her shoulder;

"Men are all alike — I know Angela's

line. I didn't think *you'd* be taken in, Jimmy."

"Who said I was taken in?" he asked equably enough, around the corner of a newspaper. "I don't approve of Angela, I never have. I think she's unbalanced. But Merry's a sap. You've said so yourself."

"Yes, and meant it. But Angela's intelligent enough to have foreseen this. It will get out, Jimmy," said Sherry seriously, "and she won't be able to get away with it again. I hope you told her so — "

He was exasperated because he thought, or preferred to think, that she was concerned only with the scandal.

"I didn't have to tell her," he said, "naturally, she knows. She's not such a dimwit that she wouldn't know!"

"You *are* taking her part," said Sherry with unreason.

He threw down the paper.

"I am not!" He made a wild gesture with his hand. "Good Lord, she's nothing to me . . . she's your cousin, not mine — "

He had a grievance. As man of the family he had stepped into the arena to argue sense into the head of a woman who mattered not at all to him. Whereat Sherry, instead of being grateful and letting the matter drop, made childish accusations.

Sherry came over and perched on the arm

147

of the chair. She ruffled his hair with her hand and he grinned sheepishly and bore it, although he loathed having his hair ruffled. She said sweetly, "Never mind. We were almost quarreling, weren't we?" They regarded each other in childlike astonishment. Jimmy pulled her from her perch, she tumbled into his lap. He chuckled and kissed her. "We were — " he admitted; "that is — you were."

"Jimmy Maxwell!" she said, sitting erect.

"Don't shoot, colonel, I'll come down. To the devil with Angela," he said gayly. "I was trying, I suppose, to be — oh, just or fair or something. If," Jimmy said, floundering, "she weren't Angela Ward, just anybody, and bank-accountless, people would be giving her a lot of sympathy. Merry will get it in this case. Sort of reverse English stuff — "

But Sherry had had enough of Angela. She said merely:

"Oh, all right. Perhaps it wasn't all her fault. Maybe I'm unfair. I don't know. I only know that I won't ever feel quite the same toward her again."

"But you've always known about her, Sherry," he said gently.

"I suppose so. It's just that we're all such hypocrites we keep our eyes, well, half-shut, anyway, until we have to open them. Tell me what you did today, I mean before you saw her — ?"

"I went to call on Lorrimer Welles," he replied, "all intrenched behind a period desk in a very swell room, ancestors looking down from the walls. Someone's ancestors anyway. I went to sell him insurance. He has some already, a wad. He said, no, he couldn't see his way to it now. I asked, when? He said, 'Oh, possibly six months or a year.' I said, 'That's fine, if you're sure of being here then.' That didn't go over so big. However," added Jimmy, grinning, "I'm going to work out a plan for him which will knock his eye out — and which can't fail. Then went to see some more big shots. I was a little more successful — "

"You *are* smart," she said contentedly.

"I have to be. Living with you costs a lot of money, Cleopatra."

"There's mine," she reminded him.

"Nope. That's for you to spend as you want to. Then," he went on, "Pete came in and had lunch. Jen's about the same, he said. This English affair looks pretty good, would be, if he could handle it himself. But he's afraid to leave her — "

They were silent for a moment. Presently he asked, "Now, how about your report?"

Sherry told him of her little crowded day, the Thespians, the tea, Sheila.

"That reminds me," he said suddenly, "leaving the speakie — I told you Angela had people in at her place so didn't meet her there — we ran into some bozo she wants you to meet. Benson Something. No, Something Benson," he said with a yawn and a violent effort at memory.

"Not Holman Benson!" cried Sherry, bolt upright.

"The same. Who is he anyway, the archangel Gabriel or what?"

"They were talking about him at lunch. And I remember Angela knew him. He's a new voice in the theater, he really amounts to something — "

"White Hope, eh?" asked Jimmy sleepily. He yawned again. He said briskly, "Get the book, woman, and we'll find out who murdered the old miser in the back room of the Polo Club . . . that is, if I can keep awake."

CHAPTER VII

Toward the end of February, miraculously open, with more of spring than winter in its progress, Jenny Lee's life closed gently, reluctantly, quietly, as if Jenny herself, coming to the end of a beloved, incident-crowded book, had shut the covers, sorrowful that the tale must end but contentedly aware of how satisfactory it had been.

For the first time in Sherry's short married life she saw Jimmy as an entity, apart from herself. Her own grief was deep and sincere, she had grown so fond of Jenny in the brief time she had been permitted to know her. But Jimmy for a space was rudderless and incredulous, all his forebodings, all the warnings which he had known to be authentic, could not lessen the shock. One hopes, always, for a miracle. Sherry's love for him took on the brooding tenderness of maternity. She felt inadequate, she felt as if she were an intruder and yet, yearning over him, she had the victorious sense that without her he would have been more truly lost. After all, it was to her and her soft breast and shining eyes, her inarticulate murmurs of comfort, that he turned.

She thought she would never forget the hush which lay like the dark shadow of wings over the house in Jersey; would never forget Pete's stupefied face and blank, tired eyes, nor the face of Jocelyn, a small white flower, bruised and piteous.

When it was over, the plans were made, during the long hours of conference in the still house from which Jenny had departed for one more still. It was Jimmy, pulling himself out of the morass of amazement and rebellion which for a few days held him struggling but helpless, who made the plans. The house must be put on the market, Pete must go to England and conduct the important business which was still hanging fire, and Jocelyn must come to the little house to live. He made these suggestions with economy of phrase backed by common-sense arguments until they reached some cell of his brother-in-law's brain which responded. Pete agreed, after a time. Perhaps that was best; it might be, he thought dully, easier to orient himself in strange surroundings, and occupied with a matter which would need all his drive and fight and business acumen to see it through to a successful conclusion.

Jocelyn, while not difficult, was more

doubtful. Didn't her father want her with him? she wondered.

He did, he said, holding her cold, small hand in his own. He looked at her with a passion of pity, divorcing that pity from himself for a moment. Yet he didn't, really. Better to go away somewhere, work like a dog, get his feet on the ground, alone. He loved his child dearly but that which had been between him and his wife was something else again, something to which the child had most beautifully contributed but which even without her had been perfect in itself.

He would have to travel all over, he told her; he would be forced to leave her very much alone, among strangers. He would worry. It would be better if she went with Sherry and Jimmy until such time as he returned to the States. Then they could make a new life together.

Jocelyn nodded. Not a particularly articulate girl, she dreaded, secretly, the very things of which he warned her, strange faces, a new country, loneliness. Her father was not brought closer to her through their mutual grief. Such an intimacy, barriers down, complete understanding of each other's loss, does not always occur. She could not break through her own hard shell of sorrow, nor through his. He was somehow a stranger to her, be-

153

loved, but nevertheless alien. She was even a little envious, a little jealous, as if her own grief could not reign supreme, as if, in sense hidden from her, her father had a prior, and a deeper, right to sorrow.

So having made her offer, she was content to go with Jimmy and Sherry.

The house in Upper Montclair was closed. Pete took a room at a quiet hotel until time for sailing came, and Jimmy and Sherry brought Jocelyn home with them. The rose-and-green guest room was no longer a guest room, it was her very own. Her small belongings were about it, gave it an air of familiarity as if one had met an acquaintance who turned out to be an old friend.

She said to Sherry:

"I don't want you to bother about me. Let me fit in somehow. I mean, you mustn't feel responsible, as if you had to do things for me. When you're out, there are books and the piano. I — I don't want to interrupt your lives — "

Sherry caught her to her, hugged her, strong young arms holding the younger girl close.

"You know we love you, Jocelyn," she said, "of course we'll let you 'fit in.' You belong, that's all."

She thought, when the first shock had

passed, when the numbness wore off, things would be better for the child. When spring came, green and faint mauve on the Westchester hills, she would see that Jocelyn was assigned a horse from the Nevins' stable, that she learned to ride with Sherry, along the lovely roads, the trees feathered in green, the blue sky fallen to the dimensions of the little rainwater pools. She would help her, as imperceptibly as possible, out of herself, back to the normal gayety of her youth. There would be golf and later swimming. Later, too, she would persuade her to dance. Jenny would prefer it so, Jenny, whose last command had been, "Don't grieve, darling, don't hide yourself away — it's been so happy, all of it — "

She, Sherry, would buy this little niece by marriage the prettiest frocks, she would surround her, when she was ready, with young people, she would help her over this bad time. She said as much to Jimmy, lambent eyes on his own, feeling herself shine within because of her clear purpose.

"You're — swell," was all that Jimmy could say with extreme difficulty, but she understood; understood the hard pressure of his hand on her own and his broken — "If it weren't for you, Sherry — "

She felt that she had more confidence in

life with Jimmy — not that she had ever lacked it, merely that it had been driven home to her now — because she had met death with him. Their marriage had achieved something, had taken on a new importance. If she had not been able to share fully, still she had shared, and in something which was basically her husband's own. Sharing, hitherto, had been a mutual adventure, the sharing of passion, of tenderness and of strangeness. This new element which had entered into their beginning life together was in the nature of a mission.

Her mother wrote her petulantly from Palm Beach:

"Of course, I suppose there was nothing else for you to do, but it seems foolhardy to me. I have never approved of a third person in the home of a young married couple."

There was more, in that strain. Sherry crumpled the letter in her hand and said nothing about it to Jimmy. Later she reread it with a sort of futile distaste, and tearing it into small meticulous pieces, disposed of it. There was no sense in wasting good emotion on letter paper in an effort to make her mother understand that, aside from her own affection of Jocelyn, this sharing of Jimmy's burden mattered essentially to their

156

marriage. Her mother lacked all comprehension of certain basic things; had always lacked it, and would so continue to the very day of whatever death awaited her rebellious nature.

Sherry reported to Jimmy merely that her mother was well, was enjoying a rather restricted season and that Angela had flown down to join her. Jimmy nodded. He had had a conventional note of sympathy from his mother-in-law, correctly phrased, written on thick creamy paper in her large black penmanship. He had replied to it in sentences as stilted. "Angela!" — said Sherry, shrugging.

Meredith Post was quite out of the picture. He had sailed a week or so previously, he had dropped from their little circle. There had been whispers, comments, speculations, and then the circle had closed again, for most of them as if he had never been a part of it, as water closes when a stone is flung and the ripples have died away, leaving the smooth unblemished surface with no sign of its brief disruption.

Jimmy said nothing. Angela had telephoned him several times since their meeting after the Post incident. He'd seen her, of course, at her own place, at their own, with Sherry. But she had not referred to the telephone calls, mocking, provocative, in Sherry's presence. And Jimmy had made the mistake of believing in the "business" which had, shortly before Jenny's death, prompted the last.

"Come and see me, I've a notion I'd like some insurance."

"You're a great little kidder, Angela."

"No, seriously, I'm spending money like a match magnate. And my investments have gone wrong — "

"Yours and a couple of million other people's."

"I know," she said plaintively, "but that doesn't help me. Anyway I was never lucky. Buy high and sell low, that's me all over. I wish I didn't know so many good-looking brokers. I have no sales resistance. I really mean it, Jimmy. Suppose I do put something away now, where it will be safe?" She sighed, he could hear her over the humming wires. "Otherwise," said Angela, "I may find myself in such a position in my old age that I'll be out selling apples. By then I'll be too old to induce anyone to keep me. That's the worst of it. I don't need protection now and when I do I won't have any teeth — "

Jimmy hastily said he'd come, and slammed up the receiver. His boss was grinning at him, and Angela's voice was very clear.

Armed with model policies and information

on annuities, he went to see his wife's cousin. Angela was alone, in itself an event. She was brisk in tweeds, and businesslike, but her long eyes were amused. She gave him a drink, a cigarette and a chair and listened to his painstaking explanations.

"Must I really tell you my age?" she demanded sorrowfully. It was, after all, thirty-one. She also remarked that if he must send a doctor around it had better be a young one.

But she wasn't, it appeared, really interested in incomes. Lump sums had more glamour for her. Jimmy worked out a series of single-policy investments for her, finally. And that was all there was to it, unless you count her following him to the door and her soft-spoken good-by. "I *did* get you here, didn't I — under any pretext?"

He replied, irritated, "If it was a pretext we'll forget it."

That pleased her, she had gotten under his skin, he had at least admitted something. She said, soothingly:

"Of course it wasn't — entirely. Business and pleasure, a delightful combination. You may have saved me from a pauper's grave, I'm duly grateful." She added, "I'd be glad to see you again — without the papers, Jimmy."

But he didn't go again; and now she was in Palm Beach having, as her idiotic postals testified, an elegant time. "X marks the body," she wrote.

In a way it was a summing up of her whole life. *X marks the body.* And X was not, in this connection, a particularly unknown quantity.

In the early spring the main house was reopened and Sheila came back to it. She would remain there during the summer save for visits she might be prevailed upon to make, Bar Harbor, Newport, Southampton. She would not go abroad. Summer was the trippers' season and all the "little places," once so cheap and entertaining, had become commonplace and crowded. Perhaps in the autumn she might go over.

Jocelyn had "fitted" in. She had made friends. Nita Welles was one of them. No two people on earth could have been more unlike. Jimmy was faintly alarmed and said so. Sherry shook her head at him. "That's nonsense," she said. She laughed a little, her eyes tender and amused. "What a very conventional father you'll make some day," she prophesied.

"No, but really, Sherry, I think Nita'll be bad for her. She's not much older in years — three, isn't it? — but when it comes to experience — holy cat!" said Jimmy inadequately, "she's King Tut himself."

"She can't hurt Jocelyn. No one can," said Sherry, out of a vast trust and a world of unwisdom. "But Jocelyn may do her good."

Nita's reactions were mingled, and her mind beneath the wild red hair amazed. Damned if she could see what she did see in Jocelyn, she told herself. It was, she finally decided, because the youngster was so absurdly sweet — without whipped cream and gingerbread and Pollyannaisms — that she liked her. They got along well once Nita had stopped trying to shock the younger girl. Jocelyn was no Elsie Dinsmore. Moreover, she wasn't shockable. She stopped one of Nita's open confidences once, and firmly. She said, "I know all about that sort of thing. Where do you suppose I've been all these years? I have eyes," said Jocelyn, "and ears. But it bores me. It seems — "

"Very wicked?"

"No, just stupid," said Jocelyn.

Lorrimer Welles was pleased. He liked the little Lee girl, a nice child, with excellent manners; he wished Nita would emulate her. He wasn't even very much concerned with the fact that Jack, his unmarried son, a hard-riding young person of about twenty-six, supercilious, rather clever and an excellent business man, fell completely in love with Jocelyn — and with no encouragement. Jocelyn liked him, but as she said to Sherry frankly, when questioned, "No, nothing can come of it. After we've talked twenty minutes we've said all we have to say to each other, I suppose we could pass the time other ways." She laughed a little, mischief in her very clear gray eyes. "But that would pall, wouldn't it, after a time, and then we'd have to get back to conversation and what good would that be?"

Nevertheless her friendship with Nita and young Jack's assiduous courtship brought into her life a sparkle which it had lacked. She had for so many years been bound to a house and a troubled love and a desperate fear. Now, in a sense, she was free, the house vanished, the love a part of her inner life but no longer troubled and the fear realized and therefore conquered.

Angela came back and began a series of informal afternoon affairs, concerned principally with Holman Benson. He had come down to Florida with a party of men and had seen her. She had said, directly: "No, I won't put any money into your ventures, why should I? My gambling spirit exercises itself in other ways — but I can bring you into touch with people who have more money than brains."

She did so but money wasn't easy to come by these days. The theatrical season appeared, in the winter of '31, to be dead upon its feet. Then Benson met Sherry.

She came in after a day's shopping, and left the sweet spring dusk for Angela's crowded, smoky studio. Jocelyn was out in Rye, Jimmy off chasing some prospects to whom Mr. Welles had given him letters. Welles had been extraordinarily kind to Jimmy. He hadn't himself accepted any of Jimmy's eager, carefully thought-out plans, but he had sent Jimmy to his friends.

In the studio Benson saw her come in. She looked entrancing that day, in the sable-collared suit, her pert hat tilted, her cheeks a little flushed. "Who's that?" he asked Angela eagerly.

Angela explained. "I told you all about her — you met her husband, Jimmy Maxwell, one day last winter," she said.

"Oh." His interest flickered, then shot up again. "She's very good-looking," he said.

"*And* crazy about the theater. Quite in your line, Holman," Angela told him.

She went to meet Sherry, to draw her into a group, to present Benson to her. Presently Sherry found herself alone, in a corner, with the dark man whose eyes, surprisingly light in contrast with his swarthy skin, were so full of quenchless vitality and enthusiasm.

"Angela tells me you like the theater," he said conventionally.

Like, Sherry told him, was an inadequate word. She had, she added, seen *Good-by to Love,* a pity it had failed, it had no reason to fail.

"No, except a lack of funds. If I could have kept it on a little longer — " he deplored, shrugging, "but I couldn't. At this very moment I've a really remarkable play — by an unknown whom I've been staking for the better part of a year. I have the cast, that is, I know whom I want. But not, alas, the money," he added.

Would he tell her a little about the play? she wanted to know.

He would. But not here, he added, eyes clouding; noise and people and interruptions. Perhaps Angela and she would come to his place some time for tea? He would read it to them, if they liked. He had tremendous faith in it. He'd have young Richardson there. Really a tremendously gifted person, erratic, like so many of them, drank like a fish, had to be shut up in hotel rooms with a guard at the door in order to work — he didn't, said Benson thoughtfully, believe that the drinking mattered, in this case it was an

164

attempt to escape —

"Escape?"

"Oh, life, that sort of thing. He's married, has been since he was about nineteen. A dreadful woman in many ways. No, they don't live together, but he'd never been able to rid himself of her. Every so often she comes back and there's a reconciliation, emotion, all that sort of thing. Then a bust-up. It never fails and no one has been able to make him see sense. She had a hold on him that is really terrifying in all its implications," Benson told her.

He asked her presently if she had ever thought of the stage as a career.

"I suppose not," he went on without waiting for her reply, "although you seem to have so much for it — youth and beauty and one of the loveliest speaking voices I've ever heard. Grace, too, I watched you walk across the room; and interest in the stage as a living and vital part of life. But I met your very attractive husband," said Benson, smiling, "and Angela tells me you haven't been married long."

Sherry admitted it, flushing slightly. Benson regarded her with delight. She was new to him, refreshing, straightforward. He liked her. She said: "Of course, I've always been insane for the stage. My mother wouldn't hear of it, however. Then I married. I do belong to a group of new, very amateur players, out in my part of the world — and that has to suffice," she said.

"It shouldn't," he expostulated, staring at her, "that is, if you have talent. I don't know that, of course. Perhaps you'll let me come out some time when you're putting on a show, and let me judge?"

"I'd love it," she said, and added frankly, "and I'd be scared to death!"

She met Jimmy in town for dinner, as Jocelyn was going to be at the Welles'. She could talk of nothing but Benson and his plans and his contagious enthusiasm. Jimmy, with an unsuccessful day behind him and the knowledge that his record for the month had been far below par, listened without interest and with his mind elsewhere. He said merely: "I remembered him; looked like a slick customer. I'd steer clear of any of Angela's finds if I were you."

She said indignantly: "He isn't a find. Angela doesn't, really, know him very well. I'm going to give a little dinner before the next Thespian show, Jimmy, and ask him, if you don't mind."

He didn't mind and said so. He let her take all the reins of their entertaining in her hands. It had always been inconsiderable and very informal. And they were not of the generation who went into conventional mourning and stayed there. Even Jocelyn had not.

A week or so later Angela and Sherry heard the play read in Benson's attractive apartment over on the East Side. Young Richardson was there, a gaunt young man of thirty-odd, with blazing eyes and a city pallor, a weak, too well-modeled mouth and a stubborn chin. The play, declared Angela, was good and far too highbrow, but Sherry was intensely stirred by it. Her eyes and her shaken voice when the reading was over, and dusk had fallen and Benson amusingly busied himself with teacups as well as with a shaker, were tribute enough.

"It will take money," he said, "or we can't do it. It has to be properly put on."

Richardson agreed with him glumly. He believed in the play, he said, but in the face of so many obstacles he supposed that believing would be all the satisfaction he'd ever get out of it.

Sherry lifted a rather timid voice: there was a young woman, a minor part, a musician, she thought the character a little out of drawing. She turned to Angela, glowing, "If Mr. Richardson could meet Jocelyn?" she said. Angela nodded indifferently. She was rather entertained. Richardson did not interest her, he was not her "type." But while Benson did not, either, she was amused at his response to Sherry. Benson had a reputation for being very hard-boiled where women were concerned. There were times when he had had money and was seen a good deal on Broadway when he was literally surrounded by pretty girls, all angling for, at least, his professional, and most for his personal attention. He hadn't been moved. But here was Sherry, the rankest amateur, obviously making the grade.

The Thespian show went on. It was Barrie. Sherry had her dinner, and excused herself in the middle of it, making Jocelyn substitute hostess. Sheila was there, and Angela, Benson and Richardson had come out from town, and one of Sheila's satellites. It was a delightful dinner, well served, excellently cooked, in a pleasant atmosphere. Sheila had supplied extra help for kitchen and dining room from the main house.

Later they went on to the play. Richardson was frankly half asleep, waking only to ask Jocelyn in a pained whisper, "Why Barrie?" and to slumber again. He was in a somnolent mood. The dinner had been good, the liquor even better. Jocelyn Lee was the prettiest, the most soothing sort of girl he had met in years. She made him feel young and gay

168

and fatherly, all at once. He wished he had been able to persuade her to duck this idiotic evening and stay at home in that nice little house and play to him. He knew she played, he had managed to talk with her during dinner about the character in his drama, and she had offered some very sound suggestions.

Benson, however, was wide awake. He dismissed the rest of the company and concentrated on Sherry. Yes, she would do. Awkward, a little unsure, but charmingly intent, lovely to look at in her make-up, even with the inadequate lighting of the small stage. Yes. She could be trained. To hell, said he to himself, regarding Jimmy's face, a mixture of pride and embarrassment, with husbands!

But husbands could be set aside as of minor importance. He said to Angela driving back to town: "I think something could be made of that girl . . . If I could persuade her — "

Angela said, "It depends upon what you wish to persuade her — and what do you mean — made?"

"Don't be a fool," he said shortly. "I mean she has talent. There's even a part for her in Frank's play." He listened for expostulations, but Richardson was sound asleep in the corner. "The part of the sister. She could handle that, I think. But," went on Benson gloomily, "it doesn't look as if we'd ever get the money — "

"Sherry," said Angela lazily, "has money of her own."

He stared. He said, "Why didn't you tell me?" He added, "Of course, her mother, and all that — Funny woman, her mother, gives me the creeps — "

"If that's all she gives you — Yes, Sherry his her own income, and access to her capital," Angela informed him, enjoying herself tremendously, "and she thinks you're the new Messiah of the theater."

"Do you believe," he asked slowly, "that she would consider — ?"

"Faint heart," interrupted Angela, "never won fair angel. Try and see."

CHAPTER VIII

At the little restaurant which customers and columnists call merely "21," Holman Benson, Frank Richardson and Sherry Maxwell sat for a long time, upstairs, over coffee and benedictine. Benson had been, and at great length, what he called, smiling a little, "frank and earnest." And Richardson, staring moodily into space, had murmured, "Two such nice boys — one rarely meets them socially." But Benson ignored him. He had brought him along merely as atmosphere. This after-lunchon discussion was, his manner seemed to say, a matter which lay entirely between himself and Sherry. He put, he said, less banally but in effect, all his cards on the table; and managed somehow to invest the gesture with generosity. This play of Frank's was good. It shouldn't fail. He didn't, of course, mean to say it couldn't fail. Anything could fail, everything connected with the theater, and with, for that matter, life, was a gamble. But he believed in the play. In 1928, before the bubble burst, he could have had all the backing he needed and more besides. He wouldn't, however, have needed any in

171

1928. He had had money then — plenty of it. He hadn't now, which was what came of pinning your faith to matches instead of cigarette lighters, he explained, gayly enough, and to other things too, so far as that went. Last year he had operated on a shoestring, and if he had had the slightest margin over he would have been able to pull out with, if not a profit, then at least no loss. This new Richardson play would make the grade, provided the money for the production was forthcoming. If the play went on there was a part for Sherry in it, that of the sister-in-law. A small part, of course, but it had appeal and could be built up, he said. Richardson looked over at him glumly, with a twisted smile and an expression which changed to one of acute pain, as Benson's heavily shod toe connected with his shin. Sherry, her heart racing and her eyes enormous under the small unbrimmed hat, regarded Benson with something close to hero worship. She said, her voice husky:

"Do you really think . . . or are you just being kind? I mean, consider my absolute lack of experience. You saw me in the Thespian show. I know the part was too big for me to handle and the whole production a little haywire. But — I do wish you'd be honest with me and tell me exactly what you think — thought — "

Benson said, and quite sincerely:

"I thought you were very lovely. You need training, naturally, and, as you say, it wasn't your part. Not yet. But you'll learn. Everyone has to begin somewhere, you know."

He looked at her intently; he asked, "Mrs. Maxwell, would it be possible for you to find the money and to go into partnership with me — so that, together, we can put Frank's play over?"

She replied, after a minute, "I don't know . . . I'll have to talk to Jimmy first, of course. How much," she asked, stammering a little, "would it mean?"

"Twenty thousand," he answered readily, "with what I've scraped together to put into it. That's a lot of money these days — or any days — but I believe in the play," he told her. His eyes added . . . and in you.

She said slowly, "If I could think it over . . ."

"Of course," he said instantly, "but don't delude yourself. It isn't any *Abie's Irish Rose.*" Richardson looked up with a snort. His shin still smarted and he was in one of his moods of almost unfathomable depression. When he sat like this, in a pleasant place, watching the pretty women, the men, hearing the steps on the stairs, the clatter of china, subdued

173

but insistent, the clink of silver, the tinkle of ice; when he drank, slowly, in good company, not getting drunk enough to forget, but becoming so stimulated that every nerve drew taut, he thought of Elsie and wished that he, or she, were dead. To live with her was impossible, a constant routine of quarrels, recriminations, passionate reconciliations . . . to live without her was a deep misery. Where was she now, Paris, London . . . ?

She had brown hair and green eyes and a magnificent figure. She was shallow, unintelligent, selfish, grasping, a little common. He disliked her very much; and he was insane about her. It amounted to just that. Sometimes he thought she hated him. Yet there was something between them, something dark, something real, something essential. Something, possibly, evil. Yet he couldn't believe that, for it went deeper than good or evil, it was voiceless, it was mute, it had no name. It was like a tide in an underground river, flowing in secret, moved this way and that by some inexorable, fantastic, otherworldly moon.

They had never divorced, although each had threatened it on occasion. Elsie had her own money. She had had it before they married. One of the recurrent reasons for their quarrels, but only one of many, had been the source of that money. "What does it matter?" she asked him brutally. "I earned it, didn't I . . . ? before I ever met you?"

So here he was, listening to Benson try to put it over, listening to a pretty woman with shining eyes stammer her willingness, her excitement. Benson, he thought, was a decent sort. At least, he was honest in his belief in the play; at least the theater mattered tremendously to him. When he spoke of the theater he wasn't putting on an act. He was himself.

Wearily, Richardson supposed Benson attracted to Sherry Maxwell. He didn't blame him; she was good to look at, intelligent. Benson wasn't merely playing her for the miserable twenty thousand. Knowing him, Richardson could absolve him of that. As for himself, Sherry didn't exist for him. Few women did, except fleetingly, except as brief star-shot moments of forgetfulness. He thought of the girl he had met at the Maxwells' . . . the fair girl with the cool gray eyes and lovely hands. He had liked her, she rested him.

Benson was explaining further to Sherry. There would be a summer try-out of the play, in a little theater in the artists' colony up on the Cape. Then, if the money was available and the play held up, they would come to New York. He added that many of the plays now running had been tried out in that fashion. With, sometimes, a full professional cast, sometimes not. It wouldn't, however, be hard, he reminded her, to induce professionals to take the gamble and the small salary. It would have been impossible in the old days.

"When," Sherry wanted to know, "would the try-out take place?"

Benson calculated swiftly. It was now late in April. With any luck, a week's try-out on the Cape in, say, July. Some of the people he had in mind were settled there for the summer. That would mean rehearsals in the country, instead of rehearsals in New York. She would have to count on at least two weeks away from home. He looked at her, with his brows lifted slightly. "How will that strike your husband?" he asked her carelessly.

She did not evade it; said merely that she didn't know. She would talk it over with him. She added, "Perhaps, after we have talked, you and Mr. Richardson would come out to Rye?"

They left "21" something later than three o'clock. Sherry had come in by train. Now Benson put her into a taxi. She was going shopping, she told him. She leaned out of the cab, dark fur against her white throat, and asked if she might drop him and Richardson anywhere. They refused, they had an appointment, they would walk, they said. The cab drew out gingerly from the curb and shot away. Benson and Richardson stood looking after it. Benson sighed deeply.

"I think I've put it over," he said.

"Is that what it amounts to?" asked Richardson.

"I didn't mean it that way. I meant — hell, you know what I meant. She's really a lovely person," Benson said, his eyes warming, "and, honestly, I don't feel that I'm doing her in the eye or anything. Your play has guts, appeal, power. It's almost bound to succeed. And I think Sherry Maxwell has talent. If she has, it will be her opportunity as an actress, and it may make money for her into the bargain."

Richardson said slowly:

"You'll get her in a jam. Her backing will leak out, it's bound to. And there are too many experienced young actresses starving in agents' offices at this moment."

Benson shrugged.

"Come on, let's get going. That's as may be," he added, as they walked toward Fifth Avenue in the bright spring sunshine. Reaching there they stood waiting for the lights to change. "Depression," Benson exclaimed, lighting a cigarette, "it doesn't look much like it." He regarded the continuous stream of cars, a big black Rolls-Royce purred up the roadway, and then another. Richardson said, "You aren't looking in the right place for it."

He had been. He had been standing in breadlines, for material, he had spent days prowling along the Bowery, looking at the men who slept in gutters, who stood unmoving, only their eyes alive, in doorways. He had climbed rickety stairs in tenements, he had stood listening in front of soap boxes. He was going to do a great play some day, a play of the depression. That play had not yet been written, nor the book. Not the real things, the vital things. He would do it. Benson discouraged him. People weren't ready for it, they didn't want to be reminded. Good God, why pay money to see the things that went on about you all the time, and within yourself as well?

They argued this fiercely, night after night. The present play, in which Benson had such faith, was light, a little cynical, a parlor affair, with plenty of pleasant adultery and with a very modern ending . . . a play of passion in a penthouse. That's what people would pay to see, said Benson firmly. He wouldn't stake Richardson for a week to do anything else. But Richardson had his own ideas. If *Penthouse* went over, he'd take the proceeds and write his play and be damned to Holman Benson, much as he owed him, much as he liked him. He could write the play, he knew it. He knew a lot about hunger; hunger for food, and other hungers, physical, spiritual, mental. He'd call it that, he thought, *Hunger*. But hadn't Knut Hamsun been ahead of him with a book of that title?

"Well," said Benson, "we'll wait until we hear from her. Then, if things click, I'll hop a train for the Cape. I want Norma Mason for the lead, with David Burns. They're both down there for the summer. The rest of the cast can be scratch, except, of course, Mrs. Maxwell. We'll try it out, come back here with it, whip it into shape, get the rest of our cast together and — "

"If it isn't chickens you're counting, it's a dear little goose," said Richardson, walking along gloomily. He thought, It's a pity that all Elsie's acting talent is confined to a drawing room — or a bedroom. She would have been perfect in the part of Moira. But Norma Mason will have to do, at that she's pretty good. He couldn't, however, feel exhilarated at the off-chance of the play getting a production. Once a piece of work was finished, it was finished. He hated the polishing, the rewriting, the hysterical atmosphere of rehearsals. He always went on to the next thing, in his mind. His hands itched to put the depression drama down on paper . . .

Sherry, flying in and out of Saks Fifth Avenue, taking a taxi down to Best's on an errand for Jocelyn, and finally ending at the Waldorf where she was to meet her mother and drive home with her, as Jimmy was uncertain about the time he would finish at the office, was in a maze of excitement. She thought, Two weeks, perhaps more, at the Cape . . . and then perhaps a New York production. It was a dream, a marvelous, impossible dream. As for the money, she could, of course, procure it. A year's income. She would have to go into her principal, sell some bonds. But she was fired by Holman Benson's absolute belief in the play. She would make it back and more besides, she would have her own chance and the deep satisfaction of having done something worth while for that fabulous world of the theater which had held her, an outsider, enchanted, upon its difficult thresholds, since her childhood.

"Well," said her mother, over a teacup, "you look as if the world had just begun for you."

She thought she had never seen Sherry so animated, or so lovely since her marriage. "Don't tell me," she began abruptly, and clashed her cup in its saucer. Sherry would be just enough of a fool to look like that if she'd been to doctor and been told that layettes were in order.

"I'm not going to tell you anything," said Sherry gayly. She meant it. She had a horror of arguments with Sheila; she didn't want to tell her until the possibility was a settled fact. Sheila might disapprove, might try to get Jimmy on her side. Or, if she approved, perhaps that would put Jimmy off. Sherry had thought about it all that afternoon, darting in and out of shops, ordering, giving name and address, in a mechanical manner. Lord, she thought now, crumbling her toast, had it been blush rose or white that Jocelyn had wanted in the nightgowns? She had ordered the rose at any rate. No, she went on busily, in her mind, she'd wait to tell Sheila until after she had had her talk with Jimmy that is, if Jimmy concurred. But why wouldn't he? He wanted her happiness more than anything in the world; he had said so, and surely he meant it. He wanted her to spend her money as she saw fit, and he had said that, too, time and time again and she had no reason to doubt his sincerity. If he agreed with her and she went on with this adventure, it wouldn't matter about Sheila. After all, she told herself, things were between her and Jimmy now and no one else.

Her mother was gossiping, in short amused phrases.

"Nita," she said, "is running around with that good-looking riding master who has the new stables."

"No!" said Sherry, shocked.

"Yes. Lorrimer's wild and Lucy takes to her bed regularly with migraine and scented pads over her eyes. If I were you, I'd warn Jocelyn. It won't do her much good to be used as a blind. How is her affair with Jack coming on, by the way?"

"You *do* know a lot," said Sherry resentfully, "and it isn't an affair. He's crazy about her, of course." She stopped suddenly. That Jack Welles had asked Jocelyn to marry him she knew. But there was no use in letting Sheila know it.

"She could do a lot worse," commented Sheila carelessly. "After all, Lorrimer Welles' son is something of a catch. Pretty good for a youngster who comes out of the wilds of Jersey with absolutely no background."

"Background!" said Sherry hotly, "when she's Jimmy's niece, and the daughter of the finest people I've ever known! As for Jocelyn herself, I don't know anyone who can hold a candle to her in looks and disposition and character and intelligence."

"Of course," said her mother, "she's Jimmy's niece. But that doesn't — " She shrugged gently. "Have it your own way. But if Jack Welles wants to marry her, I'd advise her to oblige him, that's all."

She thought it was curious that Jocelyn Lee should be able, by all signs, to do so much better for herself than Sherry had done. It was ridiculous. Why Sherry with her appearance, her training, her connections and her money had chosen to throw herself away . . . Well, it was done and showed no signs of being undone, as yet.

The Nevins' estate wasn't as large as it had been, income taxes were appalling, and it took a lot of money to keep up the Quaker Hill establishment, to say nothing of clothes and all the rest. Sherry wouldn't inherit as much as Kenneth Nevins had intended her to, one day. Thank heaven, Kenneth had not seen fit to tie up her, Sheila's inheritance. It was not in trust for Nevins' daughter. Why should it be? After all Sheila had been Kenneth Nevins' wife and had been, according to her lights, a good wife. Sherry was a child when he died, almost a baby. If when *she* came to die . . . she ceased to think for a moment and the utter blankness of horror, the appalling incredulity which always seized her when she thought of her own departure from the world she so terribly loved, gripped her. It was impossible. It could not come to pass. She shook herself out of the chill darkness which crept like a fog from an uncharted sea, over the wastelands of her mind, and concluded her thoughts firmly — why need she leave Kenneth Nevins' money intact to Sherry? Sherry had her own income — and a husband.

They drove home together, each with her own thoughts. Once Sheila roused herself to announce that except for short visits she would not leave Quaker Hill during the summer. Visits had begun to bore her; you bought a lot of clothes, you sat up late, you drank too much; and the tipping was a considerable item. "Will Jimmy," she inquired, "take a vacation?"

Sherry supposed so, a little absently. When, she didn't know. But they did want to go back to Skytop again. Perhaps for their wedding anniversary. She supposed she was sentimental about it —

"Very," agreed her mother. She regarded Sherry in the dimness of the car and smiled. She said, "I find it wiser not to try to repeat an experience."

At home, finally, Sherry found that Jimmy had come out by train before her. He was playing Canfield with Jocelyn in the living room and there was the good aroma of dinner cooking. "Jimmy, you old idiot, you know Sheila and I were at the Waldorf, why didn't you stop in and come out with us?" she cried.

She took off the little bell-boy jacket of hunter's green, frogged in black braid, collared in Hudson seal, and dropped it over a chair. She stood up, straight and slender in the green skirt, the soft blouse of knit wool. She came over to watch the game which she had interrupted and said, "Red Jack on Black Queen."

"You would kibitz," complained Jimmy, laughing. He drew her down on the arm of his chair. She asked, after a moment, "Have you thought about Skytop, the first week in June?"

He had, he said instantly, as Jocelyn cried, "Don't think of me, I'll be all right here, alone. Or I can visit . . . in . . . Montclair . . ."

But Jimmy shook his head.

"We'll have to postpone it," he said regretfully. There was to be a special convention, at Atlantic City. He'd have to get on the bandwagon. There wasn't any way out, really.

Sherry's heart sank. She had looked forward to Skytop, blue mountains and rosy laurel . . . the walk to the water fall, the trail around the lake, just a year later, remembering, exulting — it's lovelier than ever, Jimmy — nothing dimmed, no glamour lost.

"You're not any more disappointed than I am," he told her, and kissed her.

Jocelyn watched them, smiling. Her mind went to the last letter from her father. He would be away six months longer, possibly more. But she was happy here. It made her happy to be in this little house; there was an atmosphere of gayety and gallantry in it to which she responded.

After dinner, when they had settled down for the evening, Jimmy asked casually, "Well, what happened in town? Did you see the boy friend?"

He had known she was to meet Holman Benson and Richardson. She had told him so. "I saw them," Sherry responded, laughing, "both of them. I believe in boy friends, tandem."

"Come clean, what happened?" he insisted, lighting his pipe.

All the way home she had rehearsed what she would say, had marshaled her arguments. It struck her then that, after all, she could not be so very sure of Jimmy's cooperation

186

or she would not have bothered. Now whatever arguments she had had in mind flew to the winds. It all tumbled out breathlessly . . . the money — the try-out — the chance of a part. She sat down on the footstool at his feet and laid her arms across his knees, Her face upturned to his was rosy with excitement, childlike with pleading, the hyacinthine eyes luminous . . .

"Jimmy, what do you think?" she asked.

Jocelyn, after one small gasp, had stolen quietly from the room. This was between them, she thought. She was determined to efface herself as much as possible at all times. She went up to her room and read her father's letter again. The telephone rang and she answered, as an extension stood by her bed. It was young Welles. Could he come over? He had been all day at the Blind Brook, and was sick of not seeing any women, he said.

Neither Sherry nor Jimmy noticed the ringing of the bell. They were intent one upon the other. He said slowly:

"It's your own money, Sherry. You do as you think best with it."

She asked, shocked by disappointment, "You don't approve the . . . ?"

"I wouldn't say that," he said carefully. "If you get a kick out of it, go ahead. It seems sort of risky in these — these times," he went on, fumbling, "but — sure, you go ahead and back it. There was, of course, *Abie's Irish Rose* — "

She discounted that, scowling a little as she did when she was serious and troubled. It lent her face a delicious expression it was as if a child pondered the problems of the world.

"I don't expect to make money," she told him flatly, "but I don't expect to lose it, either. It's a fine play, really. Holman Benson believes in it, he knows plays."

"He's never had a smash hit," offered Jimmy shrewdly.

"That wasn't his fault . . . it was — oh, depression and all that," she defended Benson eagerly, "and it isn't the money part, anyway, Jimmy, it's the chance I've wanted for so long."

Jimmy said evenly, "I suppose so." He looked at her with a little reluctant grin and touched the loose curls on her forehead gently. "Look here, couldn't you just back the play and stay in the audience?"

Her face fell. She said grievously, "Oh, darling, do you hate it so much — the idea that I might go on the stage?"

"Well, I'm not exactly setting them up to celebrate," he admitted, "but — after all,

Sherry, it would be pretty tough to be known as — "

"Mr. Maxwell?" she said, laughing. "But you *are* Mr. Maxwell and I'll stay Mrs. Maxwell."

He grinned again, more readily.

"That's right," he said, "I forgot that. But gosh, Sherry — " He bent and took her chin in his hand and lifted it and looked down into her eyes. "You're a thousand miles away," he complained.

Sherry got up, and sat down again, on his knee.

"There, is that better?"

"Much — "

She said, feeling like a child whose Christmas stocking is limp, lank emptiness:

"Jimmy, if you really care so much, I won't do it . . ."

"No," he said hastily, terrified, "no, you go ahead. If — if you're going to be happy that way, Sherry, why, that's the way it has to be. You — you try it, that's all, and I know you're square enough to quit if it doesn't bring you what you want. What *do* you want?" he asked curiously, soberly — "is it — to be famous and all that?"

"No. Yes. Oh, I don't know, Jimmy, that's part of it, of course. But mostly it's being a part of the theater, having something real

189

to do in connection with it. You don't know what that would mean to me," she said, low. "Ever since I was a kid — I've sat on the edge of my seat waiting for the curtain to rise. I known that it's lights and paint and that the people are playing parts. I've been back-stage too, a lot. But the illusion persists . . . I'd be so terribly happy . . ."

"I thought you were happy."

"I am." She put her arms about his neck, laid her warm, flushed cheek against his own, said practically, "You really should shave twice a day," and then went on, "Of course, I am terribly, beautifully happy. This is another kind of happiness. Don't you think I can have them both?" she asked him anxiously.

He said, "I hope so." His arms tightened about her. "You do just as you please, Sherry, and I'm all for you one hundred percent."

Jocelyn, coming down when Jack Welles was announced, surprised them, sitting there in the big armchair. Sherry got up smiling and without haste. She told Jocelyn joyously, "Jimmy says it's all right. How'd you like to have an actress for an aunt?" She was absurd, she was a little touching.

Young Welles came in, a nice, commonplace boy, correct and rather colorless. He

190

was taking Jocelyn for a ride, he explained, it was an elegant night. Would they care to come along? he asked, not too hopefully.

They declined with thanks. The door closed behind the youngsters. Sherry sat down again on the footstool.

"Let me talk, Jimmy," she said, "lots."

Much later that night, after Sherry slept, Jimmy Maxwell lay awake, thinking. He didn't like it. He faced that squarely. He didn't like the money side of it, he didn't like any part of it. But it was her money. He couldn't protest too much, he couldn't even bring forward his sound common-sense arguments against the expenditure. He was very sensitive where Sherry's money was concerned. She hadn't made him so, bless her. It wasn't that, it wasn't her fault. But there the money was, bonds, stocks, the income arriving regularly, solid, respectable, a nice little fortune. Sherry's. No amount of persuasion on her part could make him believe that it or any share in it was his. If he argued against her putting money into Holman Benson's venture, she would think — usual thing. It wouldn't, he told himself, be true.

They had been married a little short of a year. They were very happy. They had had nothing resembling even a minor quarrel.

Oh, irritations, little flare-ups, these things one expected, you couldn't get along without them, you more than "got along" with them. He couldn't jeopardize their relationship by a show of authority. He should be grateful that she had consulted him. After all, she was independent. Money made her so. Damn money anyway.

If he could persuade Lorrimer Welles to that two hundred and fifty thousand dollar policy, half insurance, half annuity, things would be better for him, too. Three percent wasn't such a bad commission. And his clubs were costing money, the house, no matter how simply they lived, cost money; the replacement of liquor cost money, everything did. And it bothered him because, after all, he wasn't supporting Sherry entirely. That was why he made her such charming, extravagant gifts every now and then.

He found himself cursing Angela. If it hadn't been for Angela, Sherry wouldn't have met Benson, wouldn't have acquired this bee in her bonnet.

He slept, finally, puzzled, definitely unhappy but determined to stick by his guns. Sherry was a sensible kid, after all. She had more sense than most of the women he knew put together. She'd see if the business was just a blind to get the money. She'd quit.

As for the money, he comforted himself, suppose she did lose it? Well, in a way that was all to his advantage. And perhaps she'd be cured. Unless, of course, she went over like a million dollars.

He was no critic, he knew very little about the theater, his appreciation of acting mechanics and technique was simply that of the average man in an orchestra seat. But it came to him dimly that Sherry had a long way to travel before she would be a Fontanne or a Cornell — his two great enthusiasms. Still, he was loyal and in love, and Sherry was very lovely to look upon . . . and he'd thought her swell in the Thespian show.

The next morning Sherry telephoned to Holman Benson. Holman turned from the instrument, his eyes blazing. Richardson, lounging in a big chair in Benson's apartment, grinned sourly.

"It's all right," reported Benson, fired with enthusiasm. "And we are to go out there to dinner tomorrow night."

Richardson came to life, a little. Perhaps, while they hashed over the details, he could persuade the gray-eyed girl to play to him?

On the way out, in the train the next night, Benson occupied himself with speculations. "I don't believe Maxwell is hanging out any flags," he said.

"Why should he?" Richardson inquired. "Few men like to have their wives' money, and also their wives' attention, taken from them at one fell swoop."

"I asked her outright," said Benson, ignoring him. "I said, 'Is your husband perfectly in agreement?' She was frank enough. She said, 'He understands of course, but I hope you will be able to infect him with a little of your own enthusiasm.' "

"That will be just dandy," prophesied Richardson gloomily.

But it wasn't so bad. The cocktails were good. The dinner was charming. The more he saw of Jocelyn Lee the better he liked her. He let Benson do the talking, watched him produce papers, figures, heard his cautious promises. "Mind you, I don't say that we will have a success. I've been in this business long enough to know that nothing's one hundred percent proof. But if we do — " He went on talking about grossing so-and-so much; about the cast he had chosen; about Sherry's really great opportunity. "I do believe in her, Maxwell; it seems to me that she'll have everything. After training, experience — "

He, Richardson, didn't bother to listen. Spoke when he was spoken to, that was all. But he persuaded Jocelyn to the piano after dinner and sat there, his chair drawn up close, brandy at his elbow, a cigarette smoldering between his fingers and a sort of hunger smoldering in his eyes. He'd never seen a girl as cool, as remote, as sturdily sweet without affectation or greensickness. Abruptly over the soft accompaniment he began to talk to her. The three grouped at the far end of the room were oblivious. He said:

"Go on playing. Let me talk. I don't know what there is about you, you're like something out of a dream. Look here, I'm going to write a play, a great play — it won't be pleasant, it won't wisecrack, it won't be love on fifty thousand a year and I-am-not-at-home-to-anyone-but-Mr. Van Hampton, Celeste. It will be life, hard and hurting, innocent people suffering and decent people bewildered and squalor and agony and courage. You can't understand that, can you — ? You haven't been touched by life."

Jocelyn lifted her gray glance briefly to the gaunt young face, the tormented eyes. She said, and went on playing, "I could try to understand."

She thought of Jack Welles as the low eager voice went on, saying things that puzzled and wounded her, twisted things, and she thought of this man who sat here talking,

feverishly, without reticence, sometimes in-
coherently. Jack was nice, she thought, a
nice boy. That was all. She had hurt him
badly, she supposed, telling him last evening
that it was of no use, it never would be of
any use. But he'd get over it. He was Lorrimer Welles' son. He would never know
hunger or thirst for food or drink. Or, save
in a minor degree, for anything else. This
boy — he wasn't much more, here beside
her, said something to her wordlessly. He
was ill, he was unhappy, he was out of tune
with life. She went on playing, and his eyes
were on her hands, beautiful, sensitive, long.
He said, "Look here, don't you feel it too,
we belong somehow . . . we can't just drop
out of each other's lives?"

"No," said Jocelyn, "I suppose not."

She lifted her hands from the keys a moment and regarded him. She was not in the
least attracted by him in a physical sense.
In that sense Jack Welles held more of an
attraction for her. But pity flowed from her
in a wordless stream and reached him. He
thought: If I had known her, long ago, before
Elsie. But she would have been a kid then.
Elsie's spoiled me for other women, except
the basest.

He thought further: If there were a remnant
of decency left in me, I'd let her alone, I'd

never see her again. She doesn't care anything about me, she's just sorry for me — schoolgirl stuff —

He knew, none better, that the dark power within him which could reach out across the miles and the hatred and the utter lack of understanding and bring Elsie back to him suddenly, strangely, could be used for other purposes. He could fling himself into the dream-brevity of a love affair, persuade himself and the woman. And then abruptly it was over and there was Elsie again, soft-footed havoc in his brain cells and terror in his heart, with her hard, sullen mouth and her green eyes and her long, brown hair . . .

Jocelyn was playing. He lay back in his chair. He said to himself: If Benson will stake me, I'll clear out somewhere, get a room in some little lost hotel, work on the new play . . .

Jocelyn was dreaming over the keys. She thought, It's so queer not to be needed any more. She wasn't really. She had been, at one time, by her mother; she had thought she had been, by her father. But there she had been wrong. And not to Jimmy or Sherry could she give anything. What was the matter with the strange, lean man, smoking furiously and in silence beside her? Was there anything in her that would console him, that might become important to him? She knew absolutely nothing about him. But she thought — if I can help?

CHAPTER IX

Now it was the first week in June. Sherry and Jocelyn were riding. They took back roads, winding, thick with trees. Summer was sweet on the dancing air, a scent of early roses, of salt and sun. Jocelyn sat the little chestnut mare from the Nevins' stables very well. Hatless, her hair was warm gold in the checkered light. She had learned to ride, and completely, although she would never achieve Sherry's magic with a horse, her light hand, her perfect confidence, grown to be an integral part of her, schooled in her since her very small girlhood.

They were walking their horses now, talking. Sherry asked:

"Aren't you seeing too much of Frank Richardson?"

Jocelyn turned slightly in her saddle. She said, as Cherubim danced delicately beneath her, restless: "I don't think so. You see, Sherry, he's really awfully unhappy."

"I know," said Sherry. She spoke carefully, feeling her way. Jimmy had a good deal to say about Jocelyn and Frank Richardson. He had appeared to blame her for the friendship.

Last night they had very nearly quarreled. He had insisted, doggedly, "It's your job to speak to her, Sherry."

"But I've no real right. After all, she's nineteen — "

"She was left in our care. Oh, I know what you'll say; you'll say she's my niece and the responsibility is mine — "

"I wouldn't. I had no intention of saying it!" she'd cried indignantly.

"Sorry. But the point is, there are things a man can't say without getting into a hell of a jam. You'll *have* to talk to her. She thinks you're the most marvelous person on earth. She'll take it from you; you'll know how to handle her — the best way."

Now she was trying. She felt exceedingly inadequate. Jocelyn's eyes were clear and astonished.

"Jocelyn, he's married."

"I know. He told me. He — he's in love with her, Sherry." She stopped. Impossible to tell even Sherry the things Richardson had told her, sitting there with him in strange little cafes, listening; things which had wounded, things which had amazed her, intolerably; things which seemed too sorrowful to be borne. So much muddling in this world, so much waste and wrong direction . . .

Sherry made a funny little sound in her

throat, part pity, part impatience. She said, "All the more reason . . ." She broke off, and leaning forward smoothed the satin neck of her horse. After a minute she went on, "I hope he doesn't tell you he's misunderstood!"

Jocelyn laughed, a silver tinkle of sound; her eyes laughed too, with a genuine hilarity.

"Of course not, silly. She probably understands him only too well. It's just . . . oh, I'm sorry for him, Sherry. He's so talented and so absurd. He's weak," Jocelyn commented after a minute, "and moody, and I don't suppose he has any character really."

"People will talk," said Sherry helplessly.

"Let them," Jocelyn told her serenely, "so long as I know things are all right . . . so long as you and Jimmy know it, what difference does it make?"

Sherry shook her head. She said, wondering if she was saying the right thing at the wrong time or the wrong thing at the right time: "Angela's been a little catty. So has Sheila."

"That doesn't bother me," said Jocelyn cheerfully. She looked at Sherry. Her words were a little shaken, perhaps because of Cherubim, perhaps not. "I don't count, really, except to you and Jimmy and Father, do I? I mean, I'm nothing in your mother's life, or Angela's. Nothing I can do would really upset or disturb them. I'm nobody, after all. So long as you and Jimmy understand, I see no reason why I can't go on being friends with Frank. I'm good for him, in a way," she said placidly, "and he's good for me — "

"How on earth can he be good for you?" asked Sherry, irritated. "He's gifted, I'll grant you that. But he's unbalanced, gloomy — and all the things you yourself admit he is."

"He's real, though," Jocelyn declared. "He's a part of life I don't know anything about. But I'm learning," she added after a moment.

Sherry looked at her watch. It was time to turn back, she decided. She said nothing more on the way home. Clarke took the horses at the stables and they went directly back to the little house, changed and then walked over to the main house for luncheon. Sheila was "having people," as she said, vaguely: Angela, who was staying with her for a few days; Nita, three or four others.

Sherry had dreaded it. Why do I go when I dislike it so? she asked herself every now and then. But she went, rather than have an argument, and was bored and exasperated. Walking over, she reflected that she had said very little to Jocelyn, that they were where they were before. She revolved phrases in her mind to placate Jimmy . . . If I talk too much she'll think we don't trust her, and we do. Can you imagine anyone you'd trust more fully? The last thing in the world I want to do is to estrange her from us. We're looking at it the conventional way, really; we don't doubt her common sense for a moment. It's just that Richardson is married and she's a youngster, but half the girls we meet are interesting themselves in married men far more seriously than Jocelyn, and we don't think anything about it.

Well, such phrases wouldn't do. They would go in one ear and out the other. Jimmy would say, she knew it as well as if she had already heard him, that ignoring certain social tabus was all very well for people he didn't give a damn about, but Jocelyn was his sister's daughter and he was responsible for her. And it would all amount to the same thing, Sherry's responsibility in bringing Jocelyn and Richardson together.

Luncheon was good, cocktails were frequent. Angela was very smart, and animated. Nita was sullen, under the red hair. Someone said, "I didn't really think you needed riding lessons, Nita," with a light, feline emphasis on the wrong word. There was, today, no discussion of Sherry's theatrical venture. No one here save Sheila had been told, by her; and of course Angela, by Benson himself. Sheila, to her astonishment, had shrugged and commented, "It's throwing money away of course — but if it amuses you — " and had let it go at that. And Angela had said merely, "You're a brave girl and Jimmy's a model husband."

Sheila's personal reaction was simple. Sherry had always wanted to go on the stage. Now she could go, and her mother was absolved of all responsibility. That Jimmy Maxwell wasn't exactly delighted at the prospect was obvious despite his gallant efforts to appear enchanted and in entire agreement with his wife. That was all right, too, thought Sheila. After all, a great many girls of impeccable social standing took their chances on the stage nowadays; and several young wives had done so also. If this venture left Sherry without a husband but with a career, that wasn't, after all, to be deplored. Not that Sheila believed, seriously, in the career.

Whatever Angela thought she kept to herself. She had seen Jimmy, however. She had dropped into his office, unannounced, to bring him a check for one of the single policies he had recommended. Her arrival had caused something of a stir, three ambitious life underwriters had been transfixed and wild-eyed, breathing hard with amazement and envy; and the eyebrows of the boss had done acrobatics all over his lined forehead. Jimmy had been startled but hospitable, and as Angela had come at just the right moment, what more natural than to take her up to La Rue's for luncheon?

Across the table she had regarded him. She'd said abruptly, "I think Sherry's a fool, Jimmy, and you know it. And you're a fool for encouraging her."

Her tone was entirely matter-of-fact, friendly; her eyes met his with directness.

He said, fidgeting: "I didn't encourage her. I don't like it very much." He added hastily: "Please don't quote me on that. Can't you understand my situation, Angela? I'm in no position to forbid anything. Sometimes I wish I were," he said gloomily. "Of course I know that's old stuff and doesn't come into modern marriage, but just the same, it had its good points."

Angela said: "Yes, I understand. You're a pretty good sport, James, my lad. Perhaps you're being wise, after all. Give her her head for a time."

She added, thoughtfully: "Holman Benson's all right. I think he's absolutely sincere. I'm certain it isn't entirely money with him."

He left her, feeling that he liked her better than he ever had. She did understand, and without too many words. She hadn't bothered to be exotic and provocative with him, hadn't intruded her own personality into the discussion at all. Perhaps he had done her an injustice. Being a little on the slinky side was Angela's way and she couldn't change it and she didn't mean anything, he supposed. The latest intelligence from young Post had somehow mitigated Angela's culpability in that quarter. Merry had become promptly entangled with some female or other in London, and his mother had departed to see if, with the help of God, a good lawyer — and a check book, she couldn't straighten out this unfortunate rebound. No, if Angela hadn't happened to Meredith Post, someone else would. Someone else had. He said as much to Angela, ready to admit himself in the wrong, before they left the luncheon table.

She nodded. "I thought you'd come to see it, after a while. The woman, by the way, is Elsie Richardson. I had a letter from some friends in London last week. I'm not, of course, telling Frank. He'll find out soon enough, he always does. It was just Merry's hard luck that part of his education was undertaken by two good-for-nothing so-and-so's — " she smiled, briefly — "One, myself, out of boredom and pity, and the other out of God knows what, but if I know Elsie at all, it wasn't pity and it wasn't boredom. That woman," said Angela frankly, "is a nymphomaniac."

Jimmy shuddered a little. He didn't like phrases which conjured up such wholly unpleasant pictures. He reflected, not for the decent reticence of a former generation. Only now people called it hypocrisy. Telling all seemed to be the slogan of the day; shout it from the housetops, they announced, and you'd get rid of your inhibitions. But did you get rid of them? Talking about things didn't, Jimmy thought, lessen the urge to do them.

As he put Angela in her car she asked him, "When's Sherry going up to the Cape?"

"Next month, I think."

"You going too, for the two weeks?"

"No," said Jimmy. "I offered to take my vacation then, although it really wouldn't be sensible, and I'd thought perhaps I'd take it in the autumn. But I decided against it. She'd be busy rehearsing and all that and I'd be as out of place as Walter Winchell at a Sunday-school picnic. So I'm staying home. Jocelyn's going with her. . . . She doesn't want to go alone; and there's some big pianist chap or other up there whom

Jocelyn's crazy to meet. Benson says he can work it for her."

"Meyerstein," said Angela. "Yes, he's there for the summer. He's a strange man but a great teacher." She said, after a moment, "Well, look me up while Sherry's away, perhaps I can find some mischief for you to get into — " She laughed, the car pulled away from the curb and she was gone.

Jimmy had decided to walk back to the office. He started now, thoughtful, not hurrying. Angela had been very reassuring. She'd said that Benson knew his stage groceries, that he was sincere, that it wasn't entirely the money —

He stopped suddenly, crossing, to the horror and profanity of a traffic cop. If it wasn't the money entirely . . . ? What had she meant? That had been, now that he considered it, an ambiguous sentence. He walked on again, successfully negotiating an avenue more fraught with danger, when the lights were against one, than a battlefield. The cop sighed deeply with relief and thought longingly of a very large glass of beer at Kelly's back entrance. Of course, reflected Jimmy, she'd meant merely that Benson believed in Sherry's talent.

He himself didn't know whether to believe in it or not. Either way, someone would get hurt. He didn't want Sherry to be hurt, ever, but if she failed, she would be. And if she failed, it would be all the better for him. But did he want that personal triumph at the sacrifice of Sherry's dreams and ambitions? Yet — if she succeeded . . . ?

American husbands were funny enough, according to the press and the foreign observers, without the added ignominy of Husband and So-and-so, he thought glumly.

However, there wasn't anything to do about it and cudgeling his brain until his head ached didn't make sense. Nothing to do but wait and see what happened.

Early in July Sherry and Jocelyn went up to the Cape. So long as they were going they might as well make a holiday of it, they decided. Jimmy, persuaded to take a few days away from work, did so, and drove them up in the roadster. Richardson went with them, as Benson had gone on ahead. Jimmy hadn't much cared for this arrangement, nor had Sherry, to be truthful. But it had come about so naturally that it couldn't be helped. Surprisingly he proved himself an entertaining companion. He wasn't, so far as Jimmy could judge, drinking; not what Jimmy called drinking; and he was gay and light-hearted, as if he had discovered somewhere the boy-out-of-school spirit. He and

Jocelyn laughed their way to the Cape, and had a very good time. Jimmy liked it too, he wished the trip might continue; he didn't like, as well, what was at the end of it. He would leave the roadster for the girls, he decided, and come back by train. Then he'd come up and drive them back when the time was over.

The glorious weather held, the roads were good, they poked along enjoying every minute of it. And finally, there on the curved tip of the Cape, the little town sacred to tradition, and O'Neill, with golden sand hot under a blue sky, a battleship at anchor, gift shops, hotels, shacks; and the streets filled with people, men and women with easels under their arms, men and women without easels, dark-eyed men and women who deeply in their blood retained the old Portuguese strain; children, trippers, writers, actors . . .

They had engaged rooms at the old red inn which stands directly on the beach, and which accommodates few people and those superlatively well. Jocelyn's room, on the first floor, opened directly on a path leading to the water, and Sherry's and Jimmy's was up a narrow winding stair, all chintz and mahogany, dimity-curtained windows, fragrance of salt and lavender. Richardson was stopping with Benson, in the house David

Burns had taken for the summer.

Jimmy stayed over night. They had arrived in the morning from their last stop-over and Benson had been waiting for them. There'd be a scratch supper at Burns', he said. Maxwell would be able to meet some of the gang. Benson was businesslike, alert, excited. Everything was going splendidly, Burns was enthusiastic over the play and so was Miss Mason. There had been a reading of it and some preliminary rehearsals, and they had got the rest of the scratch cast together. Sherry would like the people, he promised: young, zealous, filled with ideas and ideals.

The supper at Burns' rather attractive house was all right, Jimmy was forced to conclude. Burns himself, quiet, blond, pleasant, was all right too. Norma Mason, not as young as she had been when first she had made Barrie the carriage trade rage, following in the elfin footsteps of Maude Adams, was still a lovely woman, with great charm of speech and manner if, as Jimmy afterwards confided to Sherry, a little on the wistful side. She would play, and perfectly, the part of the wife who was so good that no man could be true.

Benson had succeeded in getting the girl he wanted for the other major woman's part, Dolores Demidova, half Spanish, half Russian, a very arresting personality, young, with one success and three failures on Broadway back of her. She was at the Cape visiting Norma Mason. The rest of the cast, the two unimportant men, the woman musician, were recruited from a theater group. Sherry, with the small role of the sister-in-law, was the only real outsider.

There was much smoky talk after supper. Richardson and Jocelyn slipped away — "You don't have to apologize," Richardson told her, "these people have never heard of the amenities." Later, after a walk on the beach, they went back to the inn, where in one of the small, enchantingly prim rooms she played to him on a very old piano, and he sat there and listened and watched her hands on the yellowing keys.

Back at the Burns' cottage they were not missed for some time. Everyone was talking about the play, most of them simultaneously. Norma Mason and Dolores Demidova were fencing warily, as is possible only between devoted personal friends and competitors. Dolores was so much younger than Miss Mason . . . but of course Norma's part was more sympathetic than Miss Demidova's. Didn't Holman think so? And shouldn't that last speech of Dolores be modified? After all, it left the audience in doubt as to whether

her motives had been entirely mercenary, and they had been, hadn't they? "Where's Frank?" asked Benson, unable to stem the soft, eager tide. But Frank wasn't available. Benson smiled at Sherry, raised an eyebrow and proceeded to be deft and clever, promising nothing, vaguely.

Jimmy enjoyed himself for a time. After a while he became bored. They seemed to him like greedy children in a bakeshop, each wanting the biggest eclair. He sat back and smoked and drank some execrable rye and watched Sherry. She was so eager, so excited, so — feeling her oats, a little embarrassed, but, yes, self-important too. Benson was charming to her, drew her into all the discussions. Miss Mason, Burns and possibly Demidova knew her connection with the piece. They were very pleasant to her at any rate, tried not to make her feel so strange.

It was late when they started back to the inn. Jocelyn was in bed, and Frank Richardson had gone long ago, he was walking alone on the beach, stopping to sit on a black bulkhead and look out over the anchored craft and the quiet bay under a rising, golden-red moon, asking himself a thousand questions. One was the key to them all. Had the ghost really been laid? Was what he felt for Jocelyn the thing which mattered, which

213

endured? Yet what he felt for Elsie had endured, to his misery. Yet Elsie was vanishing somehow, he couldn't as strongly feel the pull of the dark, the underground tide. He had heard the story connecting her with Meredith Post, whom he vaguely remembered meeting at Angela's. And it had not affected him — much. He hadn't cared — deeply. But Jocelyn was a silver singing in the night, a spring morning, she was all grace and a delight without fever and a peace without satiety. This she had become, the epitome of things he had never before known. Without the emotional attraction he told himself the whole business would have been too ethereal to be of any value. But the emotional attraction was there too, the trouble of young beauty in his blood and the simulation of chastity which, contrary to modern belief, still remains a very powerful magnet.

If he loved her — and he was telling himself that he did — did he love her enough to take the risk . . . the risk which would possibly exist as long as Elsie existed? He didn't think of the risk to Jocelyn.

Walking home through the warm lovely night, Sherry linked her arm in Jimmy's. It was grand, she said, exciting, she felt — she couldn't tell him how she felt, keyed up, keyed to perform the impossible, to justify everyone's trust in her. "Yours, mostly, Jimmy," she said a little shyly.

She looked in on Jocelyn before going upstairs. Jocelyn slept as deeply as a child, her face and her yellow hair buried in a great pillow. And she looked like a child, untouched by life. Sherry stood there, puzzled, worried a little. But she did not wake her, she went on upstairs to Jimmy; and forgot Jocelyn in the old, recurrent delight, which had lost nothing save strangeness and which had gained more than it had lost.

With Sherry lying close in his arms, as the moon climbed higher and flooded the polished floor with intangible gold, Jimmy reflected drowsily that there was something seductive about strange places, new places. Even the familiar face of the beloved took on new contours, different allure. He was very happy. He had forgotten his slight uneasiness in Burns' cottage, his feeling of being tolerated merely, his feeling that behind his back people were talking about him and that before his face they were thinking things they did not utter aloud.

But tomorrow was another day and Sherry kissed him briskly if tenderly and drove him to the train. The last he saw, she was waving to him, smiling, with Jocelyn beside her, and then she turned, with Benson's hand on her arm, and walked back to the car.

Sunlight was not moonlight, it was clearer, harder, more searching.

The two weeks which stretched ahead of him were intolerable, they held nothing but loneliness. After he had been home for a day or two he was moved by a sense of utter forlornness and so went forth, and in a pet shop on a side street bought himself a wire-haired pup with an engaging face and quivering whiskers. He named it Pinch Bottle, Pinch for short, and took it home with him. It would be Sherry's homecoming present. He remembered that she'd said, "Let's wait a while." But if she'd seen Pinch in the window, barking furiously, or sitting still in a litter of papers looking out so hopefully at the world, she could not have resisted him. Jimmy was a little uncertain about Katie and Mary. But they took to Pinch at once. Katie announced that she had a way with dogs, sure she'd have the pup trained by the time Mrs. Maxwell got back.

After all, the time would pass quickly, a week for rehearsals, a week of try-out in the small theater, the new one, a converted warehouse on a wharf. And then she'd be home again.

Sherry had not wanted him to come to the try-out. She would be nervous, anyway;

having him there would make her more so. It had been suggested that Sheila, Angela, Joe McKenzie, Jimmy and others go up and make a party of it for the closing night. But she had begged them not to; and Benson applauded her decision. Time enough for that when the play was put on in New York, he argued, so long as Sherry felt as she did.

So while Sherry started her first rehearsals, finding things very different than her Thespian experience had led her to believe, while Jocelyn sat, mouse-still, in the back of the warehouse with Richardson, and now and then escaped altogether with him, for the beach, with Benson tearing his abundant hair and asking frantically, "Where the ruddy hell is Frank *now?*" — Jimmy stayed home, with the office to occupy him daytimes and Pinch to welcome him back evenings.

Three days of it was plenty. Sheila took cool pity on him and made him come for dinner and bridge, which was almost as bad. Joe McKenzie dragged him out, in town, to an alleged stag. Dinner was stag, the rest wasn't. Jimmy stayed at the club all night and woke up with a head as light as a platinum blonde's. This bachelor stuff wasn't so good either.

He didn't, however, take Angela at her word until the fifth day, when he dropped in late in the afternoon. There were dozens of people there, and she greeted him as if she hadn't seen him in years. "You'll take me to dinner?" she asked. "You're a godsend. I was contemplating a tray and a bad novel after this gang of extras clears out." Jimmy said, all right, he'd take her, provided he could telephone home. "There's a husband for you!" someone said gayly.

But Jimmy grinned. "It isn't my wife," he explained, "she's away. It's a new pup."

How was Pinch? he demanded over the wire, while Mary's soft voice replied. Would she let him run and be sure to whistle him home again? He'd been a bit off his feed this morning. Mary assured him that the dog was in perfect health. Jimmy turned from the phone feeling encouraged. Someone yelled when he came back into the room, "Here is something new: man has to ask his dog's permission to take a woman out to dinner."

Dinner with Angela was pleasant. She listened to Jimmy's account of the Cape. After three drinks he grew rather funny at the expense of some of the star boarders. Angela listened, smiling. Jimmy began to fancy himself as a comic.

"Mean of Sherry," she said plaintively, "not to have let us make up that party for the closing night. It would have been fun. By the way," she added before he could answer, "I've tickets to a revue opening Monday night. Want to drag me to it? It's good, they say, excellent reviews from Philadelphia."

Angela was very decent, during the two weeks, which dragged themselves into three. Something went wrong at rehearsals, Burns had a touch of grippe which delayed things. Sherry wrote every day, little scraps, hasty, scrawled on a pad . . . It was infuriating, but she loved it, every minute of it. He must not be too lonely, she missed him terribly; she loved him, and loved him. She'd call up some night soon.

He had called her, several evenings, not reaching her; and had then taken to calling her early in the morning. Her voice was faint over the clear wires, and drowsy. It was consolation and exasperation to be able to hear her and not to see her, touch her. The night she called, finally, after a long and arduous dress rehearsal, he was in town with Angela. It was very late, after one, she had been sure of getting him. She heard instead Mary's bewildered voice and the bark of a dog. "What's that?" she wanted to know, and Mary told her . . . "The new dog, Mr. Maxwell's . . ." and then, remembering, "but it was to be a surprise!"

Sherry assured her she would not betray her, and hung up, wondering. Jimmy evidently wasn't staying home to mourn her absence. Silly of her to feel irritated and let down. It had been the dress rehearsal of course. They'd been at it since early morning. And why had Jimmy bought another dog without consulting her? Of course it was sweet of him, but still —

She fell into bed, her make-up half removed, dead for sleep, every muscle aching. She wouldn't have minded, she told herself crossly, if she could have talked to Jimmy and complained and been comforted. But that was childish.

Benson brought her the New York paper and set his finger on the column. It was the night after the opening of the show. He was inclined to be very sure of the play, it had shaped up well. It was too long, the opening had proven that, but such critics as had seen it had been kind, if cautious — Emory had come up from town as a special favor to see it. There was nothing to worry about and she had been splendid. Emory had asked about her.

She was still faintly ill with the nausea of last night's stage fright. The others had been kind, Mason, Burns, Demidova. They had helped her. Jocelyn had told her she was lovely. But the gray eyes had been anxious.

"What do you mean?" Sherry had demanded. Jocelyn had repeated it. Sherry said sharply: "I know I looked well — that doesn't matter. But — can I *act?*"

Jocelyn had replied, too quickly, "Of course, you were — splendid. Mr. Benson was delighted with you. Frank, too," she added. She lied. Richardson had said, "She can't act, darling, she's simply a quite beautiful stick walking around the stage, saying the things I wrote down for her to say."

He called Jocelyn darling, urged her to marry him. "I'll divorce Elsie . . . if you can put up with me, we'll be happy."

He had added, "At least I will. I don't know about you."

But she had shaken her fair head. She didn't love him. Yes, she did love him. But she wasn't in love with him. There was a difference.

Sherry wasn't, at the moment, concerned about Jocelyn, shutting herself more away from her day by day. That morning she was concerned with the New York paper Benson had brought her. He'd said lightly: "It was inevitable. You know Angela, she's known everywhere, she can't be seen places with anyone two times hand running without a lot of silly comment. I thought you'd rather see it than hear about it at third hand."

"People are wondering," wrote the columnist, "who has succeeded Meredith Post in Angela Ward's gay affections. She's been seen all over, in the most social speakies, always accompanied by the same young man. We hear he's a relative by marriage. Angela, who has plenty of what it takes, is the White Hope of the arty crowd which gathers at her penthouse to discuss — can it be art? — over the tinkling glasses . . ."

"That's Jimmy, of course," said Sherry. She moved her stiff lips and molded them into a smile. "It doesn't take a Philo Vance to see that — "

"No," agreed Benson negligently. "Now, Sherry, about your last act entrance . . ."

Angela, reading the same paper, smiled a little. Later in the day she called up Jimmy. He appeared, faithful to her summons, a little wide-eyed at her insistence, toward the end of the afternoon. "Have you seen this?" she demanded, and showed him the item.

He whistled as he read it. He said ruefully, "You're much too well known, Angela."

"It's the curse of beauty," she told him, laughing. Then she sobered. "Sheila's called up, and other people. Sherry won't like this, Jimmy."

"Oh, hell," said Jimmy with an ease he didn't feel, "she won't care. She knows all about columns and things. They have to have something to write about; no one takes 'em seriously."

"Sherry might. I'm so awfully sorry, Jimmy." She looked at him. "I — Lord knows I've never thought of myself as a *femme fatale,* but if this makes trouble between you and Sherry I'll never forgive myself. It doesn't do a bit of good, you know, to rush to the telephone and inform the scribe that you are my cousin's husband and everything is on the up-and-up. That only makes matters worse."

"Sherry won't see it," he said hopefully.

Angela laughed.

"You are an infant," she said; "of course, a thousand people will send it to her; and two thousand more will tell her about it, all adding their own embellishments. I'm just warning you. Of course, I'll explain — " she stopped. "That sounds as if we were very guilty, and you look it this minute." She put out a scarlet-tipped hand and patted his sleeve. "Forget it," she said. "It will blow over. Perhaps I've been silly to bother about it for a minute. The papers have left me alone for a long time . . . I was sick with worry when — Merry acted the fool.

But nothing broke." She lifted her dark head a little arrogantly. "After all, I'm not vulnerable, really. It's marvelous how a name protects you and a bank account. This" — she flicked at the item scornfully — "doesn't matter a good little damn. Unless it upsets Sherry."

"It won't," he promised stoutly.

He sent the item to Sherry himself, after a long consultation with Pinch, the dog's head on his knees, the moist black nose quivering, the hairy ears pricked up. "That's what we'll do, old man," decided Jimmy; "then she'll see how asinine it is."

So he sent it to her, and a gay letter over which he labored for hours. "Forewarned is forearmed," he said, "and you might as well know that I'm the Ethiopian in the woodpile. Not that it matters. Angela's sore as a crab, but I'm not worrying."

It was one of at least eight such items which reached her by mail. She thought furiously, Why can't people leave me alone? She was very angry at Jimmy. He might, she thought, have taken it for granted that she wouldn't mind, would understand. She'd call him up. No, she'd wait to hear from him.

But when she did hear it was that he couldn't come up and drive her back. He had to go to Chicago, big business, very important. The item departed from her thoughts. She hated driving back without him, she said, and she couldn't take Benson and Richardson. She and Jocelyn would have to come alone.

Jimmy saw that she couldn't take Benson and Richardson. That was perfectly patent. He was sorry, but it couldn't be helped. How had the show gone? She said so little.

She came, alone. There had been a little unspoken awkwardness in explaining to Benson. Benson had hastened to assure her that he understood perfectly. She supposed that he did; that he realized she had not yet reached the point where she would constitute herself Jocelyn's chaperon, driving the girl and two men down to New York from the Cape. So she came, with Jocelyn, tired, her nerves taut, but without accident. The play had shaped up, there would be rehearsals in September with the new members of the cast, and then the New York opening. The money had been arranged. She thought of the bonds she had sold at a loss, to the horror of Joe McKenzie who acted as her broker. Well, it couldn't be helped. The show would succeed, she told herself savagely, it *must* succeed.

Jocelyn was strange on that trip home,

quiet, subdued. Nothing Sherry could say could rouse her. The last night, in Boston, she sat on the edge of Sherry's bed and put her head down on her shoulder. She was shaking. Sherry held her close, frightened.

"What's the matter?" she asked.

But Jocelyn evaded her. "Nothing, just the jitters, I suppose." And then, later, she spoke to Sherry out of the darkness. Her voice came clear, the little distance away. "Things are awfully muddled," she said. "You know, Sherry, I don't suppose I really grew up till recently. I don't like it much." Then she was silent; and then she spoke again, "You and Jimmy," she said, "are pretty sound . . . something to hang on to, to believe in."

Things *were* muddled. Sherry reached home. Jimmy had not yet returned from Chicago. Jocelyn went to her room early that night; she was tired, she said, she had letters to write. Sheila came over. Sitting in the living room, the windows open to a breathlessly hot night, she crushed the red tip of her cigarette in a copper bowl. She said:

"This idea of yours was — not so hot. I suppose you realize that while you were away Jimmy embarked upon an affair with Angela?"

CHAPTER X

Sherry stared at her mother for a full minute. She made a curious, intensely angry sound in her throat. Pinch, the new wire-haired terrier, lying on a rug at her instantly beloved feet, looked up inquiringly and growled a little as if interpreting her mood.

"That's nonsense, of course; and you know."

Her tone was pure hostility, well iced.

"Very creditable of you, I'm sure," her mother responded smoothly. Then added, as if casually, "But I wouldn't be too sure."

Sherry looked down at the little dog. She had not, she reflected with the idiotic detachment which occurs in moments of crisis, given him quite the welcome he had really deserved. Jimmy would have been disappointed. But then Jimmy hadn't consulted her when he bought Pinch; and that, absurdly, had annoyed her.

As Sherry did not speak and it seemed that she never would, her mother went on coolly.

"It's decent of you to rush to Jimmy's defense. But I must say you take it calmly

227

— after all, you've been married only a year. One can reasonably expect fidelity for twelve months."

"Naturally," said Sherry, matching her tone, "I take it calmly. Because it isn't true."

She had a wild and entirely ludicrous desire to scream. She felt something for her mother that was part dislike and part sheer pain. Of course it wasn't true. If it were, would Sheila have told her, in just that way? She was afraid that she would. That was what hurt.

The dog stretched, put his black nose on the toe of her slipper. She wiggled her foot a little, just to show him she knew, was aware of him. His silly tail thumped, he grinned broadly. No, Jimmy hadn't consulted her, buying Pinch. She wondered — thinking that he might consult her on more important things — on, for instance, being unfaithful to her — if her mind was affected.

"I hope it isn't true," said Sheila after a moment. "There's been plenty of talk. Oh, before you went away. And there's always the fact that Angela was interested in him for a long time — before he was your husband, in fact."

"If," said Sherry angrily, "you want to believe all the gossip columns broadcast!"

"'There's an old saying," her mother told

her, "relative to smoke and fire. I'd remember it, if I were you. I have no intention of advising you how to handle the situation. Much good it would do me, if I had. You always listened to what I had to say on any given subject and then did as you thought best. It's an excellent thing," she concluded carelessly, "that you have found another interest, I suppose."

"I? What on earth do you mean?" Sherry's eyes were blazing. Her mother met them with amusement.

"This stage business. What else should I mean? How, by the way, did things go?"

"Well enough," Sherry told her dully.

"That's good." Sheila rose. "I'll go back to the house now. I haven't had a decent night's sleep in weeks." She looked it. Sherry went with her to the door. Her mother paused there, the screen let in a gust of warm, enervating wind. Sheila said irritably, "I loathe summer." She turned and touched Sherry's shoulder lightly. "I know you despise me for saying what I did. But after all," she explained in some astonishment, "I *am* your mother. You have never seemed to feel that I have your welfare closely at heart. But I have . . . I'll talk to Angela, if you like," she added with unusual hesitancy.

"I don't like," Sherry said sharply. She

was unwillingly stirred at her mother's concern, a concern she recognized as genuine enough, as far as it went. She added, more gently: "I'm sorry. Tired, I guess. It was a long trip. But there's nothing to be gained, that I can see. Besides, it isn't true. Angela would — laugh. You know," insistently, "that it isn't true, it couldn't be." She wanted to say, We love each other, Jimmy and I, more than anything in the world. That meant everything. But it wouldn't, she reflected, mean much to Sheila. She would be faintly embarrassed by such a statement.

"Well, good night," said Sheila after a moment.

Sherry watched her walk away down the little path and turn into the road to the main house. After a moment she went back into the little house and closed and locked the doors. She turned into the living room and Pinch met her, vocal and excited. "Drat you," she said absently, with some tenderness. She unlocked the door again and let him out, and waited on the steps in the breathless night until he showed symptoms of rejoining her. Then for the second time she locked the doors.

She saw Pinch safely into the basket Jimmy had bought for him, on guard in the little hall. Then she turned and went slowly up the stairs. Jocelyn's light still burned. She looked in on her, and found her, letter to England stamped and sealed, on the desk, and herself, lying partly dressed across her bed, the bedside lamp burning.

"Did Mrs. Nevins go?" asked Jocelyn, stirring. "I meant to come down and say good-by."

"That's all right."

Sheila sat down on the edge of the bed a moment. Jocelyn looked tired, all in. She asked her, "Are you all right?"

"It's the heat," Jocelyn explained. "I've never stood it very well."

It wasn't perhaps all the summer season, close and exhausting. Sherry, too preoccupied with herself to notice, kissed the younger girl and went into her own room. Jocelyn rose after a moment and took a step toward the door. Should she talk to Sherry? If she could talk things out perhaps they would become clearer. But Sherry seemed shut away from her, somehow.

Jocelyn went back to her desk. She picked up a sheet of paper stamped *Little House, Quaker Hill* and started to write. "Dear Frank," she wrote in her round, childish hand. . . . She must tell him that it was no use, that she could not consider marrying him over, as it were, Elsie's live body. She

231

was afraid of Elsie. She couldn't, she wrote, make him happy. She was sure of that. No, she thought, and the pen rested, waiting . . . no, she wasn't sure.

On her own bed, in the darkness, in a nightgown that was the sheerest of chiffon, Sherry lay and questioned herself. Did she believe that Jimmy and Angela — ? No, she didn't believe it, she told herself truthfully; it was fantastic, too absurd, too dreadful to contemplate. Turning her head restlessly on the pillows fast losing the coolness and smoothness of their fine linen, she felt, however, that she couldn't forgive Jimmy for having placed her in a position where she was forced to question — no matter how reassuring the reply.

Jimmy did not return for three more days. During those days Sherry had several feminine callers, and one masculine. The feminine callers were good friends. They told her so. They said, in effect, If I weren't a friend of yours, Sherry, I wouldn't bother. And I wouldn't have said a word, either, if it hadn't broken in the column . . . but I saw Jimmy and Angela last winter — lunching together . . . they seemed entirely absorbed.

Or one had seen them together in Angela's car; or another had observed them at Angela's place, during a cocktail party. It all amounted to the same thing.

The masculine caller was Joe McKenzie, dropping in after something or other at the Hunt Club. He was unusually agitated. As a rule he carried his forty years of eligible and imperturbable bachelorhood with great equanimity. He was perhaps Jimmy Maxwell's closest friend. He said so now. He said diffidently:

"I suppose you've heard the gossip — and seen that neat little item? I — it's a damned shame, Sherry. There's nothing to it, of course. I know Jimmy. As for Angela, she likes everyone to believe that she's having an affair with everyone she's seen with twice. That's her game, she eats it up. Nine-tenths of the time it isn't true. This is the nine-tenths, all right. But — God, how I hate people!"

Then as Sherry mustered a smile and met his pleasant, anxious eyes frankly, he smiled, too, and mopped his broad brow.

"Hot, isn't it?" he asked simply. "I knew you weren't worried or anything. But I heard a bunch of the gals putting their dear little heads together at the Tennis Club — and so I thought, I'll go see Sherry and tell her — it's a lot of hooey, and she's not to pay any attention to it. You know, I think you're pretty swell, you and Jim," he concluded simply.

Sherry thanked him, mutely, with her eyes. She said gayly:

"That goes for us too — the way we feel about you. But I'm not bothered, Joe, at all, why should I be? Anything for a gag, nowadays. These things start — they're like snowballs, rolling downhill. Sometimes you get hit by them, and there's a chunk of ice, all nicely wrapped up. But, I know — and you know — and that's all right, isn't it?"

McKenzie said it was all right. Relieved, he asked the usual questions about the play. When would it open — what were its chances — how did she like embarking upon a career? He'd give her the party of her life after the New York first night, he promised; and later, after a highball and a cigarette, lounged out of the little house and into his car, feeling pretty well satisfied with himself. He had issued a warning and Sherry had understood and that was that. They were two good kids, they mustn't break up because a lot of unhappy people would just as soon they'd join the gang at the wailing wall. Not if he, Joe, could help. When Jim came home he'd put a flea in his ear.

Jimmy came home the following day. He telephoned Sherry before leaving Chicago.

How was she, how was Pinch? It was hotter than the seven brass hinges where he was and the lake breeze was a blast from a steel mill. He'd be damned glad to get home, he said.

She met him at the train he took directly after reporting to the office. He was out of the car and down the platform before the wheels stopped turning. There she was, looking cool, looking lovely. Lord, how he had missed her! If it hadn't been for that Chicago business —

He had her in his arms, kissing her, regardless of onlookers. There were few people getting off; those who did looked amused and that was all. Jimmy raced back for his bags, raced to the roadster, in which Sherry had by now installed herself, climbed in and grinned at her.

"All set?" he asked.

She was all set. He wanted to know a million things at once. All about the Cape, and the show, the things she hadn't told him by letter or over the wire. Was she really going on with it? How was Jocelyn? Did Sherry think that she was seriously interested in Frank Richardson? Out there in Chicago he had wondered about it, been worried. Perhaps Jocelyn shouldn't have gone to the Cape, after all. Did Sherry like Pinch?

Fine! She couldn't help it, could she? He was, said Jimmy, awfully like old McTab. She hadn't been sore at his springing the pup on her like that, had she? Had she seen Angela since she returned? he asked.

She looked at him, a shade intently. But his eyes were without guile. Something sang in her heart. She couldn't believe that he would look at her like that if — if —

She thought, I won't say anything, I won't speak of it at all — it's better that way.

It was a resolution. She meant to keep it.

But she didn't. That night in their bedroom as they were undressing, he said casually, wandering into her dressing room, sitting down and bending to untie a shoe lace: "It was worse than lonely with you away. Angela took pity on me, dragged me around." He looked up, grinning, his face bronzed with wind and sun, "I suppose that's no news to you, after the column," he added lightly.

Best way to say it, he thought, carry it off with a high hand. A joke, that's all. A bad one but a joke. He added, "Angela was pretty sore about it."

He'd written her that; the repetition irritated her. She forgot resolutions. She said sharply.

"I should think she would be; and you too. It's all over that you two are having an affair. About six people have told me so — oh, not all in so many words, but I have had plenty of callers who came out of what they called friendship and considered cocktails, or tea, the funeral baked meats. They condoled with me, and liked it. I didn't."

Jimmy was aghast. Twice he had sputtered into her sentence only to fall silent. Then he said, laughing, "Well, of all the damned fool . . ." He stopped laughing and his jaw set slightly. He said, "That's a nice little accusation to come home to — "

Being innocent, he both looked and sounded guilty; being innocent, he was at once upon the defensive; being on the defensive, he took the offensive.

Sherry said tartly, "I haven't accused you of anything, Jimmy."

"I suppose not." He ripped at the offending lace, broke it, swore, took off the shoe and dropped it. It fell with a sharp thud on the polished floor. He said, "I didn't exactly like your tone."

"What was the matter with it?" There was a sudden rising hysteria in her throat. She tried to control her voice but it soared up the scale. "You were in an awful hurry to deny — the accusation."

"Then it *was* one?"

"I didn't say that."

Shoeless, coatless, in shirtsleeves and trousers he came over to the dressing table where she sat and looked down at her. "I — you can't believe this, Sherry," he said, and his voice was sullen with his wound.

The sullenness reached her; not the hurt. She said, "of course I *didn't* believe it."

The emphasis was obvious. He asked, "That means that you do now?"

She swung around on the bench. She said shrilly: "It doesn't mean anything. I don't know why you're quarreling with me. I just told you what people were saying. It — it was stupid of you, Jimmy, yes, *stupid,* to put yourself in a position where they could say anything. I didn't believe it. I don't now, I suppose. But your attitude is awfully strange."

"Attitude? What attitude? It's all a damned lie," he said angrily, "and as unfair to me as it is to Angela."

That was unfortunate. She said softly, turning back to the mirror, her cheeks flushed, her eyes overbright and her lips slightly unsteady: "It's chivalrous of you to think of Angela. But she can take care of herself. She always has."

Jimmy turned from the dresser. Everything he said was the wrong thing. He jerked at his braces, aggrieved. This was a swell homecoming, he thought, perfectly dandy. Everything was going just fine.

There was a silence. Jimmy turned and went into the bedroom.

Later, standing at the open windows in his pyjamas, he said, without turning, "I'm sorry, Sherry — but — Lord, it was a jolt to come home and find you thinking — "

She came close and stood beside him. She said, fighting the easy tears, "I didn't think anything, Jimmy, ever, not really."

"Well, then," he wondered aloud, in great amazement, "what was the matter with us anyway?" He took her in his arms and kissed her. Suddenly she was crying, desperately, hopelessly, clinging to him, shaking.

"Hey, go easy," he said, troubled. He held her close and tried to quiet her. "Don't, Sherry — don't. Please, darling. It's all right, everything's all right."

He was deeply disturbed. He had seen Sherry cry before, but not often and never like this. During their engagement there had been moments when taut nerves had snapped, when they had quarreled and kissed, and she had wept. During the first months of their marriage there had been other little scenes of emotion. But nothing of this sort; nothing that hadn't ended in kisses and laughter.

Here were kisses, but no laughter. Much later, thinking about it, unhappy, wondering, he found reason for dread in the fact that they hadn't laughed about it, he and Sherry. Surely it rated laughter? There was a laugh in it somewhere.

After a long time, she quieted. Jimmy was frightened, the time was so long; because he was frightened he was conscious of a curious impatient anger with her, beneath the protective tenderness which tried to console her.

"I suppose I'm awfully foolish," she said when she could talk, "but somehow— No, Jimmy, I didn't believe it . . . I don't . . . I don't . . . but somehow I was so frightened."

They were both frightened. Two frightened people, taking comfort from touch and sight and murmured sound.

Across the hall Jocelyn lay mouse-still in bed. Her door was open. Her room did not face the prevailing breeze and was very warm. Through her open door from behind the closed door that was Sherry's bedroom she heard sounds . . . voices raised in anger, tense silences, the violent sobbing.

Three frightened people . . .

"It was just," Sherry explained, "just thinking if I ever lost you — I knew I hadn't, but it was the first time I realized that I might."

"It isn't humanly possible," he declared stoutly.

But that night, tired, sleepless, she thought of loss; loss by death. She had never thought of that. They were very young, their lives were ahead of them. Because one loss, not by death but by life, had threatened, her thoughts turned to darkness and silence and the unanswering voice. Cold crept over her, in the hot night, under the single sheet, she was shaking with chill, creeping from feet to head. Yet her slim body dripped, suddenly, with sweat, and she moaned aloud softly, anxiously. Jimmy did not stir in his bed; he slept deeply. She wanted him to stir, to wake. She couldn't think beyond the blank wall which shut out her mind from consciousness. It wasn't possible, it could never be. She slipped out of bed and went to him, and called him, urgently, touching his hand, laying her wet cheek on his shoulder . . . "Jimmy — *Jimmy* — "

He muttered something, turned, flung out a hand, striking her across the cheek "Hie, what's up?" he demanded, wide awake.

"You hit me," she complained, between laughter and tears. "I — I can't sleep," she said, "I'm lonely, Jimmy."

That was it. Lonely. Terribly lonely. Love

dug a little grave for this perpetual aloneness but not deep enough, never deep enough. Loneliness was the human portion, you never quite forgot it. You took out insurance against it. You denied it. You drank deep with all your senses of the wine that would cloud your awareness of it. But it remained. It was a burden and it was a premonition.

"Well," said Jimmy, "there's room enough for two."

She lay beside him, straightly, in the narrow bed. Too straightly she lay; and too narrow the couch she lay upon. But she could touch him, wake him to instant response, hear his breathing.

He slept again, murmuring something. Sherry lay awake, deriving such comfort as was possible. She thought, I'm going a little crazy, I suppose. She thought tenderly, He's dear. The thermometer stood at eighty-eight outside their windows and they lay there together, oppressed and uncomfortable. But he hadn't laughed at her or complained.

No, she could not endure his loss. She told herself she believed in him, fully, completely. Then why did she torture herself with fleeting visions of Angela, long-eyed, mocking, her glance careless yet cautious under the dark wings of hair? Thoughts of the women Jimmy might have known, had known before he married her, had never troubled her. He had tried to tell her about them. She had stopped him, a slim hand across his stammering lips. "I'd rather not know, Jimmy." That was true, she had not wanted to know. It was all before he'd met her, nothing very dreadful, nothing at all important. Now she began to wonder, more than a little. Now she began to sicken with detestation of the strange women who might have lain as she now lay.

If Angela . . . But Angela did not exist. Jimmy had told her so.

Dawn came, scarlet and gold across a sky deepening into blue. Birds sang with a sudden piercing sweetness in the trees at Quaker Hill. A little breeze, cool and blessed as water, sprang up and ruffled the curtains. Sherry crept back to her own bed and fell suddenly and profoundly asleep.

CHAPTER XI

Waking was like rising slowly, struggling a little, to the surface of a strange and moveless sea, so deeply had she been immersed in sleep. It was an awakening to strangeness, for although the little breeze, fainter now, still persisted, fluttering the curtains, although a streak of sunlight lay golden on the floor, there was something wrong with the morning. Sherry turned a little, still with the undercurrent of that sea of sleep in her ears, and looked at the double-faced clock which stood on the bedside table. It was very late; and Jimmy's bed was empty.

She swung her slender feet to the floor and rose, and walked to the door. She staggered a little, from drowsiness and exhaustion. But she felt light, as if she floated, swaying. She opened the door; and listened. The house was very still.

Jimmy had gone, rising softly, dressing carefully, in order not to wake her. Standing at her door, in her sheer nightgown, she became very wide awake, she remembered. There was an ache, somewhere, like a bruise. It was not the hurt of a wound which had healed, for of course she had not received that wound. It was merely a sore place in her consciousness, the scar of a blow one had not suffered but which one had feared. A psychic bruise, an almost invisible tear in some fragile fabric which would never again, perhaps, recapture its smooth completeness.

Jocelyn's feet were light on the stairs. Sherry called. Jocelyn came faster, reached the stairway head. She said, disappointed: "Oh, you woke. Jimmy said you must sleep till noon. I'll tell them downstairs to fix your tray. I'll bring it up, Sherry."

Sherry smiled. "No, I'll come down. In ten minutes."

She went back to her bedroom and into the bathroom. There she stripped and stood under the shower, tepid at first, then running cooler, then liquid ice as her hands directed. The water ran in swift downpouring streams over her rosy body. She gasped, and moved her bright head, shaking water from it. Presently she stepped out and blotted the water from her cool skin with a huge towel and rubbed vigorously at her hair until it curled damply all about her face. Then, still girt in the towel, she went into the room and found a pair of one-piece linen pyjamas, thrust her feet into mules and went down to the dining room. The scent of coffee greeted her, and a great glass of orange juice waited at her place. Jocelyn was there, her gray eyes faintly shadowed and pallor under her tan. She sat down at the table while Sherry ate. "Too hot for eggs," said Sherry to the little maid, "just some toast please, and perhaps some marmalade."

"Jimmy get off all right?" she wanted to know.

"He almost missed the train," Jocelyn told her; "he had to run to make it."

"I didn't hear him, not a sound. He must have been awfully quiet or I must have been almost dead," Sherry said. "It's the first time it ever happened."

"Yes. He said not to wake you."

There was a little silence. Jocelyn thought, What happened last night? I heard you crying, Sherry, what was it, is it something I can share? But she knew it was not. She thought, We're so terribly shut away from each other, all of us. You think you're not, and then suddenly there's a barrier, a glass wall; you can see through it dimly, but you can't get by, reaching out is just pushing against an unyielding smoothness, your hands slip, you have no grasp.

Nevertheless she made an effort. She said abruptly:

"Frank wants me to marry him. He'll divorce his wife."

Sherry laid the piece of toast down on her plate, carefully. She said after a minute, "But — you *can't*, Jocelyn." Then, as the other girl said nothing, she added urgently, "You don't love him. Or — do you?"

"Yes, I think I do. I'm not in love with him, if that's what you mean. But he's lost, somehow. Nothing to hold to, drifting. If I could help . . . ? I think I could. I don't believe he's in love with me either," she added reflectively. "I think he'll always love her. But she's so awfully bad for him, Sherry. If I could — "

Sherry said violently:

"Don't. Don't even consider it. It's fantastic — it's entirely mad. If you loved each other— You don't, though, you've said so. Even loving each other it's such a terrible risk." She leaned across the table, earnestly. "How old are you now, Jocelyn — nineteen? You've no right even to think of it. In another year, two years, five, there'll be someone, someone you'll want terribly. Time enough to take the risk then. You can't — "

She broke off, helpless. Jocelyn was listening to her, but something in Jocelyn was shut against her. Jocelyn said slowly, tracing circles on the cloth with the tip of her finger:

247

"But — if even when you are terribly in love it's a risk, isn't it better to take the risk with someone — I mean, it wouldn't matter so much if things went wrong if you weren't, yourself, so desperately involved."

Sherry sat staring at her. Jocelyn rose. She said, "I'm playing golf with Nita, and then swimming — " Her tone was even, matter-of-fact.

Sherry rose too. She said, still with the freighted feeling as if her hands were tied and her feet leaden and her tongue without any magic of persuasion, "Jocelyn, please — before you make up your mind — won't you talk to Jimmy and to me, and won't you wait until your father gets back?"

Moving beside her out of the room, bright with sunshine on the gay striped linen and the peasant pottery and the flowers branching from a center bowl, Jocelyn said: "I don't know, Sherry. I expect I have to think it out for myself, don't you?"

Sherry went back to her room to dress. She had a charity relief meeting in the town to attend. Perhaps afterwards, if she got away in time, she could swim at Calves Island with Nita and Jocelyn. But she didn't want to, very much. She wanted, she thought, dressing listlessly, more than anything in the world to go somewhere where it was quiet, and cool, and where she could be alone and think, untangle the thoughts which seemed knotted in her brain. She must think about Jocelyn, what she should do about her, how best to advise her. But Jocelyn was a knot that somehow she couldn't untie. She kept thinking back to last night, to Jimmy and herself. There was, of course, no sense in that, it was over and done with. But there, too, there was a knot which eluded her efforts.

As she was leaving the house Holman Benson called her. He said, after the preliminaries: "Everything's set. I'd like to see you, though, and talk things over. I hesitate to ask you to come into town — "

Suddenly she was brisk again, all the brain surfaces smooth. She would, she told him, be glad to come in. Tomorrow, perhaps. As she replaced the receiver she thought that perhaps she could speak to him about Frank Richardson and Jocelyn. After all, he knew Richardson very well, he would understand her worry and alarm, he would be able to advise her. Better, perhaps, until she had seen him, not to worry Jimmy.

Jimmy came home, late, fagged out, but grinning. He had completed, he said, the working out of the policy for Lorrimer Welles; it couldn't fail; anyone with half an

249

eye and common sense must see it. He'd
tackle him shortly. He understood he had
gone to Maine for a couple of weeks, or
more. But when he came back . . .

Nothing further was said that night. There
was an impulse in each of them to reopen
the subject for the sake of reassurance. But
Sherry thought, If I say anything he'll think
I'm not convinced; Jimmy thought, If I speak
of it, she'll believe I've a motive, protesting
too much. There was an awkward "Did you
sleep late? I knew you must be tired . . ."
on his part, and no more. Jocelyn had some
young people in after dinner, Sheila came
over, the evening became bright with talk
and chatter, radio music, bridge. And nothing
was said.

On the following day Sherry went into
town by train with Jimmy. She did some
shopping, looked up an old friend who was
enduring a depression summer in an apartment overlooking the park, and met Holman
Benson for luncheon on the St. Regis roof.
He looked well, eager, tanned, enthusiastic.
They sat overlooking the city, listening to
the music, talking. Everything was going
along smoothly, he assured her, the new Manhattan Theater booked, rehearsals would be
called the first week in September, not far
off now. She said, trembling a little: "You

have no idea how it frightens me. I get a rather gone feeling when I think of it."

That, he assured her, was nonsense.

Frank, he said later, was working on a new play. Benson didn't approve of it, he thought there was nothing of value in it, but he couldn't, of course, do anything about it. Once rehearsals started Frank would have to be on the job, and there would be polishing and rewriting to do and, Benson thought, cutting. Here was Sherry's opportunity. She was worried, she said directly, about Frank and Jocelyn.

Benson shrugged his shoulders.

"I've talked myself blue in the face to him," he admitted, "but — you know how it is. Every so often it happens to him; a girl, someone who can make him believe that Elsie doesn't even exist. In this case, I'm sorry, I feel as if in a way it were my fault. Jocelyn's a sweet person. She isn't seriously in love with him, is she?" he asked.

Sherry shook her head. "She says not," she answered.

"Then," said Benson, relieved, "it will be all right, I'm sure of that. The play will engross him, it will have to. After its production he'll go back to work on the new one. When he works he's like nothing human. No one matters to him. He'll be inaccessible.

The little romance will be forgotten, an interlude. I know this, because I know him. But I was frankly anxious about Jocelyn. So long as you assure me that she isn't — "

"I can't do that," Sherry interrupted. "I'm only telling you what she said. You — you don't know her, of course. She's different, awfully, from most youngsters. Pity, I think, moves her more deeply than anything else; and she's sorry for him."

"That's too bad," commented Benson. He frowned, black brows drawn. "You see, he doesn't rate it, really. This business with Elsie, it's a madness, an obsession. But he makes no real effort to free himself, I don't believe he wants to, in a sense. I sometimes think he has a vision of himself as the Spartan boy with the fox gnawing at his vitals, or as the gentleman in the poem who was faithful in his fashion. He's — and I feel no disloyalty in saying it, I've said it to him often enough — he's entirely unreliable, blown by every wind, a straw. He's gifted, I know that and you know it, but he has no emotional stability. I should feel sorry if Jocelyn believed herself in love with him."

"He wants her to marry him — wants to get a divorce," said Sherry.

Benson stared at her, utterly aghast. He said, "But that's incredible!" He said further,

252

"If it's true, it's more serious than I believed, on his part."

"I know," said Sherry. "I shouldn't, I suppose, discuss it with you. But you're his friend. And I do feel responsible for Jocelyn. Her father left her in our care. But I hate to talk her over with Jimmy — he'd go right up in the air, and go at her the wrong way. He's already spoken to me about it, he doesn't like the association — he's worried."

"I'll have a talk with Frank." Benson's jaw was set. He thought, The damned young fool, more complications, when I need every ounce of gray matter; he's got to see the show through properly.

"If you would," said Sherry, smiling faintly.

He was shocked, not for the first time, into a personal realization of her charm and her honesty. "Of course, even if I weren't interested, I'd do what I can, for you. You're pretty fine. I keep thinking, If I let her down with the business I'll — well, I won't shoot myself," he promised, smiling, "I'm too much of a coward, but I'll wish I had the nerve to do it. After all, I got you into this venture and if it doesn't succeed — "

"It will," she said strongly, "it must."

"If you say so — " He smiled at her across the table. "But I do feel pretty responsible, you know."

His eyes were dark with something warmer than mere friendliness. Sherry was uneasily conscious of it. It affected her, a little. It embarrassed her, and although it awoke absolutely no response, it was exciting and not unpleasant. Any woman knows how she felt. Males, as such, were trees walking, to Sherry Maxwell. She was too utterly in love with one man to feel the slightest pull of attraction toward any other. But she was also too utterly feminine not to hear that little cat, Vanity, stir and purr sleepily under the caressing hand of Benson's admiration.

He said abruptly, "Just my luck to have you come along — married."

It was less embarrassing to have things put in words. You could ward off words with words of your own. She said gayly, "That's a line of course, a nice one."

"I've no doubt you've heard it often enough." He looked at her, without smiling. "Still, it remains true." His gravity broke. He laughed. "Naturally I've had narrow escapes, every bachelor has them. But that was because the exactly right combination never came along — before."

She was silent. He said, "You don't want to know the combination?"

"I could make a dreadful pun, something,"

she replied, "about safes." Her eyes, lambent and amused, met his own. "Of course I want to know. I have my share of curiosity."

"Beauty then, and youth; intelligence, ardor, sensitiveness, and understanding of the theater, a real love for it — "

"Such a combination," she said, "shouldn't be hard to find — "

"Perhaps not. But so far as I'm concerned, you've a monopoly on it."

She looked at the little watch on her wrist. She had, she told him, an appointment. And she'd be late.

Benson beckoned the waiter, and paid his check. He followed her a moment later from the room. Going down in the elevator he said: "I'll call you — about Frank. No, perhaps it had better wait till I see you. Which won't be, I hope, very far in the future."

They hadn't, he reminded her, talked about clothes at all. He had his own ideas, so had Frank. The costuming of the play mattered, modern clothes notwithstanding. At the Cape try-out, of course, it had been merely a matter of suitability.

She said, "I know, I'd thought about that." She laughed, looking up at him, "We clashed dreadfully — Miss Mason and I in the last act. The colors screamed at each other."

Out on the street she let the taxis go by

one by one while she discussed the matter of her frocks with him. There was only one change — a tailored suit for her brief appearance in the first act, an evening gown for the third; she was not in the second act at all. She would, she said, have some designs drawn, to show him, in ample time.

Finally she hailed a taxi and directed the driver to go to the Chrysler Building. Benson walked on to his own apartment. Richardson was living there with him. He wondered, as he walked, if he would be in, and how best to approach the subject of Jocelyn. Walking fast, ignoring the blazing sunlight which beat down upon him and his fellow pedestrians and softened the asphalt, he thought, I can't afford to have any emotional complications. Whether he was issuing a warning to himself as well as to Richardson he did not know.

Frank was in. He was lying on the couch in the living room, supine, an ash tray standing beside him was filled with cigarettes, half-smoked. A letter lay on the floor beside him, crumpled, crushed into a ball. Benson let himself in with his key and walked into the room.

"Not working — ?"

"No," said Richardson dully.

Benson sat down in a chair near the couch. He said, after a moment, "Look here, what's all this about you and the Lee kid?"

"What about us?" Richardson asked, not moving. But a muscle in his cheek twitched.

"I mean— Look here, Frank, you can't throw monkey wrenches. A lot's involved. This play, for instance, it means the making of you as a dramatist, it means as much to me. I've staked a lot on it — "

"Twenty thousand of someone else's money," said Richardson.

"That, too," Benson agreed evenly; "and if you get yourself in a jam with this girl there's going to be hell to pay, all around."

"I'm going to marry her," Richardson said after a moment, "if you consider that a jam — "

"Don't be a damned fool," said Benson angrily, "you can't marry anyone — you're married — "

"I won't be, long." He gestured toward the letter, there on the floor. "I've had a delightful communication from my wife. She wants a divorce. She wants it badly. She's found someone who wants to marry her. She's quite girlish about it all. What's the use, she wants to know, of going on like this? When we can both find happiness. She's willing to do it all in order. She's coming back, she'll return in the fall and go out to Reno. She hopes I won't contest it. She'll

257

always be fond of me, she says."

Benson was an imaginative man. The slow venom and raw pain mingled in Richardson's voice affected his nerves, set them quivering.

"Frank — look here — I know you're pretty well shot over this, but — "

"Not at all," denied Richardson easily. "Our letters crossed. I wrote Elsie, when we got back from the Cape. I said I was in love, wanted to marry, to settle down — and would she consider a divorce. In a measure she beat me to it, which will always be a satisfaction to her." He swung his legs to the floor and sat up suddenly. "So that's that. Everything's lovely."

He was disheveled. The muscle still twitched in his cheek. It was like a pulse, it was painful to watch. Benson turned his eyes away.

"You and Elsie have gone through this before. It's never come to anything . . ."

"No," agreed Richardson, "but this time it will." His gaunt young face was naked with rage and shock.

"You didn't mean it — about Jocelyn — You couldn't. You don't care for her — "

"I do," said Richardson stolidly. He looked up and a brief unpleasant smile marred the weak, handsome lines of his mouth. "We'll be extremely happy," he announced with a curious formality.

Benson gestured helplessly.

"You don't. You'll despise her, in a week. And what she'll feel — I can't contemplate it. . . . You couldn't be happy with her, or she with you. She's a child, really, ignorant — " He broke off. He thought, Without guile, without sensuality. She couldn't be happy, she'll be wretched and tormented. He can't be happy either. That woman's made him immune to happiness, his work will go to pieces, he could write, hating Elsie Richardson, loving her, waiting for one of their mad reconciliations and afterwards, drained, exhausted, work was like a drug to him. But this will ruin him. Aloud he said, as Richardson waited, still smiling, for the conclusion of his sentence, "Has Jocelyn said she'd marry you?"

"No, but she will."

Richardson rose and went over to a table and flipped open the leather box of cigarettes which stood there. His mouth tasted like leather, his throat and eyes were sore with smoke, the scent of tobacco made him faintly ill. Nevertheless he lit the cigarette and drew a great breath of the smoke into his lungs. Expelling it, he said, "And it's none of your business, Holman."

Benson replied, irritated:

"I'll make it my business. The girl isn't in love with you, Frank, there's that much to be thankful for, as I see it."

"Who told you she wasn't?"

"Sherry Maxwell," replied Benson briefly.

Richardson said nothing. He went through the room silently and into the small bedroom which Benson had allotted him. Benson sat where he was, hearing the sound of paper being crumpled and torn, the slight noise of a cover being ripped from a typewriter, and the clatter of keys, then silence. He did not go in. After a while he went out of the apartment. He had an appointment to see Norma Mason.

Alone, Richardson sat slumped over the static keys. When he had asked Jocelyn to marry him, when he had said easily, "Elsie will give me a divorce," it had all seemed very simple, very normal. Now with Elsie's letter still lying where he had thrown it, there was chaos in his mind. Another man, she had written. Other men there had been, in profusion, he thought. But somehow this was different. . . .

There was one thing to do: force Jocelyn to marry him, throw himself on her cool mercy, be upheld by her pity, absorb her into the self which suffered, as a man dying of thirst flings himself down beside a spring of clear water. It was not water he desired, however, nor was his craving for its colorless healing.

He rose from the typewriter and presently left the apartment. He would take the first train he thought, to Rye. If she was not at home, he would wait for her.

CHAPTER XII

Sherry's taxi drew up at the Chrysler Building. The driver leaned casually from his perch and opened the door with a ham-like hand. She descended, paid and tipped him, and he awarded her a graceless grin, compounded of an astonished gratitude and masculine appreciation. He knew a good-looking dame when he saw one, was his instant reaction. He suggested, with the chronic hoarseness of Manhattan cab drivers, "If you ain't going to be very long, lady, I could turn off the clock and wait."

Sherry smiled at him. "No, thanks, I don't know how long I'll be — " and the driver nodded. "Okay," said he briefly, and pulled reluctantly away noting, as he did so, the long, dark lines of a parked car. Sweet job, mused the taxi driver aloud as his vehicle rattled on. He spoke without envy, being past that.

Sherry turned, to enter the amazing door of the building. A voice spoke, amused and lazy. "It's Sherry."

The long dark car waited. Angela leaned back against its upholstery, the door was open, and Jimmy, hatless, had his foot on the step.

Sherry was conscious of a little shock, blank dismay. The picture was very clear. Angela waiting. Jimmy. Sherry stiffened, figuratively, her straight little backbone and walked over to the car. "Mr. Maxwell, I believe?" she said to Jimmy, with formality.

Jimmy laughed. He said, "You almost missed us — "

"So I see. I thought if you weren't busy — we could do a movie and go home to-gether?" She looked at Angela. Angela smiled at her, and spoke.

"I went to see Jimmy on business. I've got a prospect for him, he'll be at my place presently, I had just persuaded Jimmy to come back with me now. Get in, Sherry, and we'll all go."

Sherry hesitated, a fraction of a second. Then she got in and Jimmy followed her. He sat between them, legs stretched lux-uriously. "It isn't every day that two beautiful women seek me in my lonely lair."

But he wasn't wholly at ease; Angela knew it; Sherry knew it. Angela said presently, as they rode up Park Avenue:

"I've been wanting to see you, Sherry. While the big insurance men foregather, we can have a nice old-fashioned heart-to-heart

— and an old-fashioned without the heart — if you care to. Why not stay to dinner with me, I'm alone. We can have something out on the terrace where it's cool. Do — "

Sherry said, a little starchily, "I don't know — Jocelyn's alone — "

"Phone her," suggested Angela. She looked at Jimmy. "Persuade your wife, won't you?"

"I have no influence over her," said Jimmy glumly. "You try."

Sherry said briefly, "We'll stay, Angela, it will be nice — " She addressed Jimmy casually, "Thought you were being very busy?"

"I was — all morning. Thought I'd hop an early train out, this afternoon," he said, "and then Angela came. I told her you were in town."

"I had lunch with Holman Benson, at the St. Regis," explained Sherry, to no one in particular. Angela laughed.

"Jimmy is a very complacent husband."

"And I," said Sherry angrily, "am a very complacent wife."

Jimmy shrank to a miniature of himself between the two of them. He felt like a fool, as a man always feels in those circumstances. Angela's very red lips were pursed to a whistle. She said, "I doubt that, darling."

There was a silence. They reached the

apartment and were taken up in the lift. Angela rang her bell. She asked the preternaturally solemn manservant who appeared, "Has Mr. Nelson come yet?" He had not. Angela looked at her watch. "I thought," she murmured, "he would be here before three-thirty." Sherry had two simultaneous thoughts, one being that Jimmy had thought so, too, and the other that Angela had never thought so.

Mr. Nelson did not arrive until half-past four. Prior to his pompous appearance on the scene Angela, Sherry and Jimmy sat out on the terrace. Cold, long drinks were served them there, and Angela talked a great deal about nothing very much and asked innumerable questions about the play, when would rehearsals start, had the cast been entirely assembled, what did she, Sherry, think of it, really, and how was Joe McKenzie's party coming along? She understood he had asked half Manhattan and all Rye and Greenwich and was taking most of the orchestra for the opening night.

Once Sherry left them alone, shortly after their arrival, to telephone Jocelyn that they would dine in town but would not be late reaching home. When she returned to the terrace Angela looked amused and Jimmy looked annoyed. Angela said, almost at once,

"Jimmy tells me you were upset by that asinine clipping — "

Jimmy said shortly, "I told you nothing of the kind."

Sherry had an impulse to throw something at him, an impulse she controlled. She couldn't, it seemed, be absent for five minutes without a discussion ensuing. Jimmy, she thought bitterly, should have better sense and more loyalty than to discuss her with Angela. She said coolly, "I wasn't upset, I was entertained."

"Atta girl," applauded Angela softly; and regarded her cousin with something approximating admiration. She said briskly: "It was awfully stupid. I think a good counter-irritant would be if we appeared, the three of us, in public together occasionally." Then: "I'm sorry it happened, Sherry. But nothing nowadays pays but the worst possible construction — "

"It's all right," said Sherry. She essayed a smile and found to her astonishment that she did very well. "When I said I was entertained it wasn't perhaps all the truth. I was also — a little annoyed. For your sake as well as Jimmy's."

That was even better. Angela suppressed a genuine "Bravo." She thought, after all, there's not much kick in combating a washrag. Sherry's no washrag.

Before Mr. Nelson arrived Angela explained him for Sherry's benefit. Shrewd man, very *nouveau*, married, of course, but not working hard at it, rather impressed, Angela told them casually, with her particular *milieu*. She had met him at Southampton this summer. Had an excellent business, of which he was the brains. She had cultivated him lately, for Jimmy's sake — and had told him about Jimmy. There was a chance that Jimmy could underwrite some business insurance there, said Angela, finally; no harm done trying.

Mr. Nelson was announced, portly, florid, with something of a manner, split infinitives and a certain aura of real power. He joined the terrace group and accepted a tall glass and the conversation became a little stodgy and very general. It was a considerable relief that, after an hour or so, he turned to Jimmy and said, "Miss Ward tells me you're the smartest life underwriter in New York."

"Oh, not quite," said Jimmy modestly, "but at that I'm fairly bright."

That amused Mr. Nelson. He laughed, he smote Jimmy on the back. He said, "Drop in at my office and talk turkey with me, some time." He added that he spent most of his days kicking insurance agents out of his office, so this *was* an occasion.

"Eventually, why not now?" asked Angela. "I've some frocks to show Sherry and a lot of gossip to tell her. Can't you two entertain each other while we secrete ourselves and converse on those frivolous and trivial subjects which interest women and infuriate men?"

Mr. Nelson nudged Jimmy vastly. Jimmy received the strange elbow in his ribs with tolerance. Mr. Nelson remarked that when the girls got together they didn't want the stronger sex around, did they? His wife now —

Angela was patient about the unknown Mrs. Nelson. She even looked at a photograph of the three Nelson children, produced from a wallet, and exhibiting them as a trio of low-grade morons, which was a real injustice. She made the usual remarks. The kiddies, said Mr. Nelson, were what held a home together. He inquired of Sherry whether she had any kiddies. Sherry replied in the negative. Mr. Nelson looked sorry for her; his wife, he said, was a wonderful mother, she thought the world and all of the kiddies. At the same time his rather protruding blue eyes were appreciative of Sherry's figure.

Angela, an affectionate arm through hers,

led Sherry from the terrace, into the studio, and down the stairs. Once in her bedroom she cast herself upon the chaise longue and indulged in profane laughter.

"Isn't he swell? You know he is, Sherry. And impossible. He thinks I'm the cat's. I've had lunch with him twice and in his eyes it has reached the proportion of an affair — just short of the inevitable conclusion. That's why he talked about the wife and kiddies. Spurs of conscience, to say nothing of guile, in exhibiting himself before you and Jimmy as a family man; He's grand. Someone wrote him. He isn't real, you know."

Sherry, in a deep chair, opened a box of cigarettes standing on a small table beside her and lit one reflectively.

"I don't think he's so funny. He seemed sort of pathetic to me — a little boy, boasting. Why do you bother with him if you feel as you do?"

"Oh," said Angela lightly, "he'll be a great addition to some of my parties. He'll give them all a kick — and get one himself — "

"That's pretty cruel," said Sherry.

"I don't think so. He won't know it," said Angela, with scorn. "And, besides, I thought he'd be useful to Jimmy."

He was being useful at that very moment.

269

Jimmy was doing some explaining. "If you should die," he was saying, "and your business should go into the hands of your wife — what then? Even clever women err in business. I would advise a policy which would turn over your stock to your business associates and pay your wife an income. — Look here," producing papers, "suppose we run over these together?"

In the bedroom Sherry was saying, regarding the tip of her cigarette, "You're awfully solicitous of Jimmy."

"I thought so!" said Angela suddenly.

"Thought what, Angela?"

"That that was your attitude. Look here, Sherry, don't be a little ass. I'm awfully fond of you — you're not only family, you're a friend. I'm fond of Jimmy too. If I dragged him around with me while you were away it was just because I like you both and he was lonely and at a loose end. If you are going to give credence to all the gossip you hear, I'm warning you, you'll give yourself a rotten time, with very little reason."

Sherry said, after a moment:

"I suppose you're right. But it isn't very pleasant, Angela, to hear things — from close quarters."

"You mean Sheila," said Angela shrewdly. "Don't you know her by now? Sheila isn't capable of admitting an innocent male and female relationship — except her own. That's the way her mind works. And she didn't like your marrying Jimmy. Can't you see that? It's the way she's always been with me. I don't know how often she's told me unpleasant things about myself — and added, 'Not that I think so, but So-and-so said So-and-so and I think you should be warned.' Oh, I know she's your mother, and my aunt, but I see no good reason why we shouldn't look at relatives with a comparatively clear eye. After all, they're just people, aren't they? Sheila's a trouble maker, she's always been one. She can't, however," arrogantly, "make trouble for me." As Sherry, flushing faintly, said nothing, she added, "By the way, did you hear that Merry Post wants to marry Elsie Richardson and she — like Barkis — is willing?"

"He must be years younger," said Sherry, startled.

"Considerably. I heard it in a roundabout way. I don't think Frank will ever permit her to divorce him though," said Angela, "unless," she added, looking keenly at her cousin, "he's really serious about Jocelyn."

Jocelyn mustn't enter this, or any, discussion with Angela. "Oh, I don't think so," replied Sherry vaguely.

Angela was not an idiot. Thinking her own thoughts, she went back to her previous topic.

"I'm glad of this opportunity to talk to you alone. I think Jimmy's been pretty dismayed by all the talk, poor dear," she added, with tender amusement. "Of course it's been augmented because I did see a good deal of him before you were married, and people always exaggerate those pre-marital friendships into something legendary. But I don't care what they say, or think, so long as you aren't harboring any cockeyed thoughts. I'll be frank with you — " Angela was always dangerous when "frank." "If you weren't married — I didn't, you know, half appreciate him when I knew him first — but you are, and he's family, and it's all been very innocent and pleasant and it would trouble me deeply if I thought you believed otherwise."

Sherry asked slowly, "Are you trying to tell me you're in love with Jimmy?"

Angela sat bolt upright. There was no change in her dark eyes, in her delicate coloring. Her eyes widened a little. That was carrying the attack into the enemy's camp with a vengeance. She wouldn't have believed it of Sherry. She had always liked the younger woman, partly out of habit, partly out of a good-natured tolerance. Now she respected her, suddenly . . . but as one respects a worthy adversary.

"No, darling, I'm not in love with Jimmy. I doubt," said Angela, for once with entire truth, "if I've ever been in love with anybody. I merely meant that if you hadn't married him I might have — been interested. I'm a worthless son-of-a-gun," said Angela, red lips grave, "and I have to have a lot of excitement to keep me going. But I don't get far. Excitement wears off. I do think your James is terribly attractive in a nice and — forgive me — quite unsophisticated way — "

Sherry couldn't forgive her. The picture of Jimmy as a rather sweet and naïve sap annoyed her. One doesn't want to think of one's husband as a danger to women, God's gift to the female, the cinema Man-of-the-World — yet — at the same time . . .

Angela was continuing evenly. "But you needn't worry. He's in love with you." She added, with less veracity, "And even if I could, I wouldn't go hunting in another woman's back yard — "

Sherry said, "You must think me unsophisticated too. We all pretend we're above being influenced by gossip, but we're not. And when it comes at you from all sides, it's pretty damned disconcerting."

"Well," said Angela, "don't let it disconcert

you. You and Jimmy and I will do some turns together. And that will stop the talk. Sister act," she said, smiling. She rose. "I, wasn't lying when I told you about clothes," she said. I've some new summer things, you may like them. To whom are you going for your stage frocks, Sherry? Bergdorf Goodman . . . or Saks Fifth Avenue? I think they'd do awfully well for you. Or how about Hawes? She has a flair— You saw the frocks she did for the dark girl — what's her name? — in that Molnar show last year . . ."

She walked into a vast closet and came out, her arms heaped with bright materials. There was no further talk of Jimmy.

After a time they joined the men. Nelson was beaming rubicundly. He was convinced. He and Jimmy had an appointment to meet next day. He tore himself away with reluctance and another drink. When he had gone the three of them looked at one another. Jimmy cast himself face down on the big divan in the studio and beat his fists feebly against its luscious pillows . . . "for the wife's sake . . . and the kiddies," he moaned, in anguish. Angela and Sherry laughed hysterically. "How about dinner?" asked Jimmy, sitting up. "My party. Let's go out, Angela, or have you ordered something that won't keep? I want to go where there's music and lights and large mugs of beer and a breeze."

Angela knew the very place, in the Sixties on the East Side. An Italian garden, synthetic and charming. The beer was good, the food was excellent, there was music, dancing. Jimmy divided his attentions with a scrupulous fairness. Once, when he was dancing with Angela, tall nondescript head bent close to her dark sleekness, Sherry, watching, thought, angry with herself, I should be reassured, of course she's right. But I'm not reassured. What's the matter with me anyway?

The garden filled up quickly. It was a rendezvous for Angela's crowd . . . Angela waved here, called there. People joined them, sat at their table. Sherry found herself with plenty of dancing and drinking partners. Shortly after ten, while they lingered, reluctant to leave, Holman Benson stood in the doorway. He came over, smiling, and spoke to them. He said to Angela severely, "This girl should be home nights getting a lot of sleep." But he took Sherry's hand and drew her out on the floor. "I think Frank's gone haywire. He's left the flat. My man came in while he was still there. He thinks Frank told him he was going out to Rye."

Sherry said, distressed, "Oh, I hope not.

I think, if that's the case, we'd better go home."

Benson agreed with her. She hesitated before she spoke to Jimmy. No, why upset him? Besides Richardson might not have gone out to see Jocelyn. She thought, I'm neglecting her, I haven't meant to, I meant to be so careful. She thought again, But you can't chaperon a girl every minute, she'd resent it terribly.

She went back to the table and spoke to Jimmy. "I'm tired," she said, "let's go, shall we?"

Angela was agreeable; and certainly Jimmy was yawning. They left immediately, and Angela's car took them to the station. At Rye they picked up a taxi. Sherry was conscious of terror as they approached the house, but it was dark, save for the hall light. Jimmy opened the door. Pinch greeted them with sounds of welcome, fury or pleasure.

"That will wake Jocelyn," said Jimmy, quieting the dog, "as well as any neighbor within six miles. Probably carried to the Westchester-Biltmore," he added.

They tiptoed up the stairs. Jocelyn's door was closed. Sherry wavered before it. But Jimmy whispered, "Come on, she must be asleep."

In their room he put his arm about her.

"You looked like a million dollars," he said, and he added, "You know, Sherry, I'm jealous of Benson."

It was evenly said and amiably, and his eyes laughed a little. She looked at him however, aghast. "You're not, really?" she asked, in horror.

"Perhaps not really. But he *does* have proprietary airs. After all, you're partners. I feel pretty left out of it — "

"Jimmy, it isn't too late. I can get out. Not the money, but the part."

It was a hard offer to make, but not as hard as it might have been. All her trust and confidence had come back in a great surging wave, lifting her heart. She thought, I should make it up to him, for thinking things — or thinking that I ought to be thinking things! and for going all emotional and hysterical on him. If this is what he wants . . .

He said, low: "You're a marvel. No, of course not. You go ahead with it, you'll be a success and I'll get a kick out of it, I'll be so proud," he said, and tried to believe it. They kissed, as solemnly as children. "When," asked Jimmy, "are rehearsals?"

The first week in September, she told him.

"Angela," said Jimmy, "wants to go to

Montreal for the eclipse. A party of us. What about it?"

Angela again, arranging their lives! But there was no reason to refuse. Sherry said, "It might be fun — "

Jocelyn in the morning had nothing to say, save that Frank Richardson had come out unexpectedly and that she had given him dinner . . . Sherry didn't mind? She'd asked Nita over for a third, and Mrs. Nevins had come in later. He'd left early. She hadn't known he was coming, he'd arrived after Sherry phoned her.

Sherry could say nothing; Jocelyn's frankness tied her hands. But Jocelyn did not add that he had flung himself out of the house, enraged, unhappy, without the promise of solace he had come to procure.

She had not agreed to marry him. She couldn't, she said. She had thought it over. She did not believe that she could make him happy. He had stormed and pleaded, clutched at her hands, clutched at her cool, small body, working himself up into a condition of frustration and misery in which he believed she was the only thing in the world that could save him from himself. Then Nita had come over, pert and self-sufficient, and later Sheila, amused and a little disapproving. And so he had gone.

The following week Sherry, Jimmy, Jocelyn, Sheila and half a dozen others drove up, in several cars, to Montreal, and took rooms at the Mount Royal. There they dined and wined and danced and on the following day drove up the mountain in a procession of slow open carriages, passing the amazing pilgrimage of people on the way, and regarded the eclipse from the top of the big toboggan. It was something of a flop, complained Angela discontentedly, making faces at the clouds which provided their own eclipse, and she thought they might have stayed to play contract at the hotel.

But there were glimpses of pale strange segments floating in the strange air, appearing through the clouds. There was sudden darkness, eerie, still, the birds hushed, even the trees controlling the trembling of their leaves. Sherry stood close to Jimmy, her hand in his. This night-in-day frightened her, this sense of all things waiting, mute and breathless, for a miracle and a wonder.

Then, back to the hotel, the heavens' show over, to more brief amusements. And the uneventful trip home.

On arrival Sherry was plunged into conferences with dressmakers, with Benson and with the first rehearsals. She appeared at home at all sorts of odd hours, sometimes she did not come at all but stayed at Angela's, Angela having put the apartment at her disposal. She was fagged and nervous, excited and stimulated. Things went badly at first. Frank Richardson was never to be found when needed. Norma Mason was bitter about her part. Dolores Demidova smiled silkily, she couldn't have improved upon her own. The echoing stage, the dusty house, empty save for the small group, depressed Sherry, she felt like a stick walking. Whenever Richardson was located he was sulky, unwilling to work. He had torn up the first draft of his depression play. It was lousy. He was lousy. He couldn't work except under the right conditions. And the conditions were all wrong. Daily he expected Elsie in New York on her way to Reno. But she hadn't arrived. What he didn't know was that Mrs. Post and a cordon of lawyers were frantically trying to persuade Mrs. Richardson to take the cash and let the credit of a really startling marriage go; and that Elsie was lingering in London in an endeavor to strengthen her influence with her "fiancé," afraid to leave him to the argumentative mercies of his mother and her legal advisers.

Left to himself, while Sherry occupied herself with rehearsals, Jimmy found himself more and more in Angela's train. It was all

280

very plausible. "Let's go to a show and come back to the studio. Sherry will be in, I think, and you can take her home." Or, "Sherry's spending the night with me. You stay, too, Jimmy, there's room for you both, we can amuse ourselves until she comes back to the flat." Or, "How about lunch . . . if you aren't too busy . . . Or — "I've someone here you should meet, it may mean business."

Looking back later, he didn't quite know how it all came about. Then, he was grateful to Angela, she had been awfully decent. She was especially so about the Lorrimer Welles' fiasco.

That happened this way. Mr. Welles went to Maine, returned, went West and was finally available. The policies were argument proof. Two hundred fifty thousand, a lump payment. For that you drew a guaranteed annuity beginning at the end of the first year — and dividends. At your death the payments ceased and your life insurance in the full amount of the two hundred fifty thousand became payable to your family. The income and inheritance tax advantages were worked out, the annuity income and the probable dividend scale. It couldn't really miss. It was drawn in two separate contracts, based on Mr. Welles' age, which was fifty-one and one-quarter years.

It was unfortunate that Mr. Welles believed that no one could be a good business man, a reliable one, and a playboy as well. Mr. Welles, on the trip west, had encountered one Daniel Nelson. Mr. Welles had made himself agreeable to Mr. Nelson, whose account was not to be sneered at by any banker. They had had a pleasant evening together in St. Louis and Mr. Nelson, who drank, although Mr. Welles did not, became confidential.

Angela had had her fill of Mr. Nelson. He had signed on the dotted line for Jimmy, he had amused some of her crew, and that was all that was necessary. When Mr. Nelson became importunate, having taken a good deal for granted and thinking himself a gay dog, but willing to make up for it to his wife and kiddies by a diamond bracelet and a pony, he had received his congé accompanied by considerable hearty laughter. "But, my good fool!" said Angela, exclamatory.

He was verging on fifty; he had become romantic, and romance had received a death blow. He was also something of a snob. Angela was a flower any man might wear, not too openly, in his lapel. A rare orchid, perhaps, a gardenia. But Angela had had enough.

Mr. Nelson put two and two together and made eighty-one. He spoke of Jimmy Maxwell, upon learning where Mr. Welles lived when at home. He spoke of Jimmy Maxwell and Jimmy's wife's cousin at length when he learned, further, that Mr. Welles knew the young Maxwells. Mr. Welles returned home frowning. He made a comment or two, asked questions. Nita could answer these. "Everyone," she said, "knows that Angela Ward has been in love with Jimmy for years and that they're having an affair. Too damned bad."

Mr. Welles, a suppressed man, was unable to believe that any man who would stoop to an affair with his wife's cousin could be a good business man. He rather imagined that the incident of Mr. Nelson had been engineered by Angela, for Jimmy's percentage's sake. In which he was perfectly right. He was an upholder of the sacred hearth. The fact that he couldn't keep Nita warming her hands at these innocent fires made him more than ever a defender of the Home. He despised Jimmy in proportion to his former liking for him. And when Jimmy came to him, bearing policies in triumph, he said, abruptly, that he had changed his mind. No, not now. No, not in six months. No, not ever, said Mr. Welles. "And will you forgive me, Maxwell, I have an appointment."

Jimmy left the office, an extremely unhappy young man. He had counted on this, on his commissions, to free him from debt. He was out of kilter for the rest of the day. He went back to Rye and shot a terrible game of golf with Joe McKenzie. He said to Joe gloomily, at the nineteenth hole where he was trying to make a quart in one, out of sheer disappointment:

"I took it on the chin today. The Lorrimer Welles prospect. Nothing doing."

McKenzie was in Jimmy's confidence. He knew, none better, how hard Jimmy had worked on the policies. Welles was a tough nut to crack. He murmured sympathy and refrained from asking questions. But he thought, Lorrimer Welles doesn't look like a good risk.

That was how it started. McKenzie spoke his thought to someone else; and somehow the thought went a little further, at third hand. "Maxwell underwrote a big policy for Welles the banker — and it fell through. Seems he was a rotten risk."

And this is how it went on. Lorrimer Welles, in his private office, shaken with a righteous anger, haggard after a scene with Nita, whose riding-master had cropped up again, in the new guise of a blackmailer, sat looking older than he was but younger than he felt. And into the office came a friend of his wife's for some advice. He was barkingly courteous and the advice was perfunctory. He was thinking, If I pay the scoundrel, he'll never stop bleeding me . . . on the other hand, there's the scandal . . .

So his wife's friend went home and reported to her husband that "dear Lorrimer" looked very ill indeed. And her husband said, "My God!" remembering something someone had told him, someone who had heard it from someone who had met Joe McKenzie at Blind Brook.

Lorrimer Welles' bank was a private affair, large, stately, solid. It was an entirely solvent bank. Yet banks tremble when the one brain back of them is threatened. There was suddenly a withdrawing of accounts; not a run in the ordinary sense, of lines of weeping, shivering, cursing, frightened people. But on the day before Sherry Maxwell made her first appearance on the Manhattan stage, the bank of which Lorrimer Welles was president closed its doors "temporarily," unable to withstand the continual drain upon its resources. And behind those closed doors were Jimmy Maxwell's small thrift and current checking accounts. It was unbelievable, and no one was more ignorant than Jimmy that the breach in those seemingly impregnable walls had occurred primarily at the nineteenth hole.

CHAPTER XIII

Frank Richardson's play opened on a Thursday, an unseasonably warm night in late September. On Wednesday afternoon the early editions of the newspapers had their headlines, and Jimmy Maxwell, crumpling a sheet in his hand, rhymed breadlines and headlines without much difficulty. He telephoned to Rye, completely forgetting that his wife was not there, that she was stopping at Angela's, and that she would not be home that night. So he called Angela instead.

"Have you seen the papers?" he asked her.

"No. — What's wrong, Jimmy?" she asked him quickly.

He told her. There was a second of silence on the other end of the wire and then her voice came to him again, warm, bracing and vital.

"It must be temporary," she said, "some canard stated in these times of panics and canards."

"That's as may be," she replied gloomily. "Lord knows I hope so. — I suppose Sherry hasn't seen the papers. I — completely forgot about her being at the theater and called home, and then when I remembered I thought — if we can keep it from her."

"She won't look at a paper," Angela told him, "until Friday morning. Jimmy, buzz around here, will you? Phoning's pretty unsatisfactory."

He remarked that he might as well, but without much enthusiasm. Angela hung up and sat thinking for a minute, then she went to give her orders. Scotch and soda in the studio, and she was not at home to anybody. She looked in on Sherry's bedroom before she went upstairs again and noticed that the wild confusion of the early morning had been repaired by the maid. She smiled slightly and went back to the studio. The telephone rang. It was Sheila.

Sheila was exclamatory. She had seen the papers. She couldn't understand it. Everyone had believed Lorrimer Welles' bank in the strongest possible position. She thanked her gods that, friendship notwithstanding, she banked elsewhere, as did Sherry. But Jimmy had transferred his account to the Welles bank after he had met Lorrimer Welles. He thought it good policy. Of course, she added, she was much disappointed in Jimmy. Angela suggested that Jimmy had had nothing to do with the bank's closing, which, although she did not know it, was not strictly true. Sheila, irritated, brushed that aside. Sheila concluded, discontentedly, "It would have to happen just when Sherry is so nervous and on edge, with the opening tomorrow night."

"She won't hear about it until after the opening," said Angela. "She hasn't a thought for anything else. She's like nothing human. I saw her this morning before she went to the theater. They've been calling extra rehearsals and heaven knows what. She sat with a breakfast tray in front of her, at an ungodly hour and shook like a leaf."

Sheila said after a minute:

"The Welles house is in an uproar. I hear Lorrimer is turning over almost everything he has to save the bank. His wife, of course, has had an immediate nervous breakdown. I don't know anything about Nita. Not that she matters. Is Sherry staying with you? How long?"

"Till after the opening. I understand that Jocelyn is in Montclair with some friends until tomorrow," said Angela.

"Oh, Jocelyn!" Mrs. Nevins dismissed her with an inflection. She said further:

"If the play fails — and with this bank business and all — I don't know what they'll do, Angela. I won't — I can't support them

— both." She added, "If it were a question of Sherry now — "

A little later Angela hung up. She was thinking in the brief time which elapsed before Jimmy came that Sheila would not be noticeably unhappy if Sherry came back to her — without the impediment of a husband.

Jimmy came in. He looked white and wretched. His tie was under one ear. Angela straightened it for him. She poured him a stiff drink, shot soda into it from a siphon and put it in his hand. "Hey, feller," said Angela kindly, "pull yourself together."

His grin was feeble enough. He said after a minute:

"I'm not worried about the ultimate outcome. The bank will reopen all right. Only just now — " He searched his pockets and forced his grin to broaden, "I've about twenty bucks between myself and a flop-house."

"We'll fix that," said Angela briskly. "Take a couple of long breaths and relax."

"You're all right," he told her gratefully. He looked up at her frowning. "But I don't want to borrow money from you, you know that. It's damned silly, isn't it? No cash, can't draw a check. Sherry's safe, thank heaven, and I suppose she won't mind assuming things for a little while. But — "

Angela said firmly, "When you leave here,

my lad, you'll leave with a check. You can deposit it tomorrow morning. Not in the late-lamented Welles organization. It will be enough to go on until you and Sherry get straightened out and some more commissions roll in."

Jimmy shook his head.

"Nope. Thanks a lot just the same. I'll go to Joe McKenzie."

"Don't be a damned fool," said Angela irritated. "Go to Joe if you want to but let me help out. It's just a tide-over. As you say, Sherry's all right, but you'd rather not go to her for cigarette money. Is that it? I thought it was. Let your sainted mother-in-law, my benevolent aunt, wait for her rent. Then you and Sherry can work out a budget together until the bank opens and until more business comes your way. I'll never miss it; you can pay me back as soon as something comes in."

She walked over to a desk and took a check book from a small drawer. She thought, writing the figures, that this might prove to be the best thousand dollars she had ever spent. It was, she knew, a safe gesture. But it was a gesture which she also knew would fasten Jimmy Maxwell to her with bands of steel. He was that rare human being, one with a sense of gratitude.

She put the check in an envelope and came over and put it in his breast pocket. She patted him briskly.

"That's that; and not another word out of you or I'll scream and hop out of the window; and it's a long way down. Don't feel forced to say anything to Sherry about it — or Sheila. Let it be between friends, that's all."

Jimmy pulled out the envelope and looked at the check. He said, flushing, "Gosh, Angela, you're a regular person."

"So are you," she said, smiling. She poured herself a small drink and splashed a little soda in it.

He said, after a moment: "I suppose I should be glad I fell down on the Lorrimer Welles policies. If I had underwritten them I would have stuck my commission in his blasted bank and there would have been that much more to regret."

"That's one way of looking at it," Angela agreed, laughing. She sat curled up in a corner of the dining divan, sleek black hair in wings about her face, her red mouth grave.

"Sherry's counting a lot on this opening tomorrow night."

"Poor Kid," said Jimmy, "she's edgy as hell. Jumps if you speak to her. I've got to get hold of Joe and some of the gang and tell 'em for heaven's sake not to say anything about this bust-up until the opening's over. She has enough on her mind as it is. For the last two weeks she's been looking through me and not seeing me at all. It's a funny feeling," he added, swirling the whisky around in his glass. "I suppose I was spoiled or something, but now that I don't rate anything I feel like something left out overnight."

"Well, it's natural enough, isn't it?" asked Angela after a moment. "It's her first opportunity and her big chance. Sherry always had a single-track mind," she went on thoughtfully, "one thing at a time, and everything else excluded. Just now it's the show. She always," added Angela negligently, "wanted a career, you know."

Jimmy looked up quickly.

"Does that mean, if she gets it, that she will go on being single-track about it?" he asked soberly.

Angela laughed a little.

"I wouldn't worry. Once she gets into her stride she'll adjust herself to a career and a husband, if that's what's bothering you — " She halted on an inquiring note.

Jimmy asked, "Well, wouldn't it be likely to?" and Angela nodded her black head.

"But don't let it," she recommended comfortingly. "Of course, I suppose it would —

you. Not a lot of other men. Some of them, especially this era's breed, would get a terrific kick out of a wife in the limelight — " Her voice trailed off and Jimmy had a sudden, very unpleasant vision of a wife in the limelight.

He said gloomily, "Publicity and all that eyewash, I suppose."

"It has to be," answered Angela after a moment.

Jimmy sat considering it. There had been publicity already. Young Society Matron Chooses Career. Benson had a good publicity man. There had been pictures of Sherry and Little House, pictures of Sherry and Pinch, pictures of the main house, the estate. The debut was being played up considerably in the press.

There had even been one picture of Jimmy, looking at one and the same time crushed and fatuous, and taken, as he said, over his dead body, in the midst of violent and profane expostulations on his part. He mentioned it glumly.

"I saw it," said Angela. She added consolingly, "Have another drink?"

It had been fairly late when he arrived. It grew later. Jimmy shifted in his comfortable chair. Twilight fell, and no lights had as yet been turned on. In the dusk Angela's white face was a pale blur, dark at the reddened lips. Jimmy asked, ending a long silence:

"What about Sherry? Will she be home — soon?"

"I don't think so," Angela told him. "I imagine they'll have sandwiches sent in and rehearse late tonight. We'll have some dinner here if you like, or shall we go out?"

"I still have twenty bucks of my own," he reminded her; "but, no, I'd rather stay if you don't mind."

"I don't."

She rose and came over to him and pulled him to his feet. "I'll order something," she said, "and change my dress — and leave you to the papers — "

"No, thanks — !"

"Well, magazines and a pipe then." She stood facing him, her hands still caught loosely in his own.

"Don't look so tragic," she ordered gayly, "everything's going to come out all right. We have to be merry and bright for Sherry's big night, tomorrow, remember. After Joe's dinner we'll have the whole gang back here, with the cast and all. It's going to be fun, Jimmy."

"I hope so," he said without much conviction.

Angela leaned forward suddenly and laid

her lips lightly on his own.

"That's for courage," she said, and left him. He stood quite still and was exasperated at his own instant response to her caress. After a moment he switched on two or three lamps and tramped about the room with his hands in his pockets. Presently he stood still by the mantel to light his pipe. He thought, She didn't mean anything by it, Angela kisses everybody, it's all of a piece with the way she calls everyone darling and all that rot — and *I* didn't mean anything by it —

He was worried, he was forlorn, he was unhappy. Sherry had become a nervous, irritable stranger in the last few weeks. She kissed him carelessly, she spoke to him, often, sharply. She asked his forgiveness, abjectly — "I'm so nervous, Jimmy — you must think I'm gaga," and then ten minutes later it would happen again. He missed her: the smile which was for him only, the eyes luminous with love, the spoiling, the pretty lovers' byplay. But Sherry was too tired for a lover nowadays and too engrossed for a husband . . .

He shrugged his broad shoulders. After tomorrow night it would be all right. After tomorrow night he would tell her about the bank failure and they would get down to brass tacks. Every cent she spent on items which were his concern he would return to her, with interest. Angela's loan was short-term. Must be. Just as soon as some money came in he would pay it back.

He thought with bitterness of the thrift account: it hadn't seemed very big but it loomed enormous now; and of the substantial sum in the checking account. Vanished. He supposed, he hoped that the Welles organization would one day pay one hundred cents on the dollar, but in the meantime he would have to hustle and start all over again.

Twenty thousand dollars out of Sherry's principal would make a difference in her income. And if she lost it, for good —

Angela came back, in periwinkle blue, graceful, appealing, a very demure frock. There were cocktails and desultory talk and later a simple but quite perfect dinner, the two of them alone. She would, she said, put up Jocelyn tomorrow night, the child wouldn't want to go back to Montclair after the party. "But what about you, Jimmy? Would you mind a shake-down on the divan? No sense in trekking back to Rye in the wee sma' hours."

It was arranged. Later some people came in, Angela permitting them to do so. After all it was wisest, she thought. And when they left it was nearly one o'clock.

Jimmy left with them, to drive out to Rye and the deserted little house. He took Pinch's head on his knee gratefully. There remained someone, he thought, to welcome him home.

Sherry came in at Angela's shortly after he left. She looked absolutely fagged out and her teeth chattered with a species of nervous chill. It had gone as badly as possible, she told Angela, undressing rapidly, to fall helplessly into bed, huddled under a down quilt.

Angela sat on the edge of the bed. "It always does," she consoled her. "You get some sleep. Sleep all day tomorrow if you can, till it's time to go to the theater." She added casually: "Jimmy's been here, he had dinner with me. Albert Saks and his wife came in later, and some others, we played bridge a while."

"Jimmy?" said Sherry. She was so tired that words didn't make sense. She roused herself finally to a real effort. She said, "Poor darling, I've been neglecting him shamefully."

"You can make it up to him," said Angela. "I told him he could stay here tomorrow night; and Jocelyn too. I'll phone her in the morning. You gave me her number, didn't you?"

There was no answer. Angela looked down.

Sherry was sound asleep, the sleep of utter exhaustion. Angela opened the windows, turned out the lights and went from the room.

Jimmy came in about noon the next day. Angela met him, smiling. "She's awake," she said, "but I've made her promise to keep quiet. She's just having breakfast. Benson has phoned twice. I wouldn't let him talk to her. Sheila called too but I wouldn't let her talk to her either."

"That's the ticket," applauded Jimmy and went into the single room which had been Sherry's temporary shelter for a good many nights recently. She was sitting up in bed, a lace jacket about her shoulders, sun on her wine-brown hair. She pushed the tray aside and smiled at him, radiant with welcome. Jimmy sat down on the bed and took her in his arms.

"Oh, be careful," she cried — "if you spill — "

"I won't." He held her very close. "Gee, Sherry, I've missed you."

She said with compunction, "I'm a rotten wife — but after tonight — " Then she began to shake again. She said, low, her face against his breast, her words blurred, "Jimmy, do you suppose I'll be any good? If you knew how frightened I am . . ."

"You'll be swell," he told her. She drew away from him and took a long breath. "What are you going to do after the party?" she demanded.

"Angela says I can sleep here, in the studio," he told her. "Jocelyn will have the other room . . ."

Angela came in, standing at the doorway. She was dressed for the street. She said briskly: "Flowers have started to come, here to the house, already. And Holman has called twice."

"He has!" Sherry's eyes widened. She reached for the telephone extension by the bed and gave a number. Holding the instrument across her breast she looked at Angela with frightened eyes. She asked, "What in the world do you suppose he wants?"

Before Angela could answer the voice at the other end of the wire spoke and Sherry said, "It's Sherry. I just woke up. Is anything wrong?"

Benson's voice was bracing over the wire, full of vitality and reassurance. Nothing was wrong. Had she slept? Everything would be all right. She was not to worry. Angela and Jimmy watched her replying, her face fleetly dimpled with smiling, her eyes shining, her lips curved. She bloomed before their gaze — Jimmy's blankly astonished, Angela's quietly amused — and flowered into life, and a murmur of soft mirth. Presently she replaced the receiver and turned to the two who watched.

"I was terrified," she confessed, "but he says everything's fine, and that final rehearsals are always as ghastly as yesterday's."

She shivered, remembering: remembering the stage manager's hairtearing despair, Norma Mason's hysterics, Dolores' display of foot-stamping temperament, the low, incessant O-my-God! of David Burns; remembering, too, Holman Benson's white, concentrated face and Frank Richardson's barking laugh, wholly without merriment, compounded of disgust and cynicism.

"Well," said Jimmy inadequately. He went to the bed, leaned over and kissed her, brushing his lips across her cheek, awkward under Angela's smiling observation. Sherry locked her arms around his neck. "I won't see you again," she said, "until — until after it's over."

He patted her on her slender back, with his big hand. "Hey, cut out the nerves. You'll knock 'em in the aisles."

At the moment he believed it and sincerely, for her sake, wished it for her. Sheila's chauffeur, he said turning to go, would bring his dress clothes to town; he hoped to heaven

300

Mary wouldn't forget essentials — such as trousers.

Sherry in a gale of wild laughter said, "Can't you see the headlines — Brilliant Young Life Underwriter Attends His Actress Wife's Opening Performance Minus Pants!"

Angela laughed with her.

Jimmy said, "Angela says I may dress here — you won't be needing the room till pretty late. Well, cheerio," and went to the door.

Angela made a movement to follow him but checked herself and remained where she was. Jimmy, in the entrance hall, regarded the long boxes of flowers which had not yet been opened and swore softly to himself. She must, of course, have flowers from him. Orchids, gardenias. If she didn't, she'd feel hurt, and justly. But, he thought, out of Angela's check, safely deposited that morning in the bank from which he had transferred his funds not so long ago! He flushed, recalling the manager's lifted brow. "So you've come back to us, Mr. Maxwell?"

Well, it couldn't be helped. Sherry should have her flowers and Angela would be repaid. He'd get out and hustle. He went back to the office now, determined to sell a hundred thousand dollars' worth of insurance before time to dress for McKenzie's dinner.

He didn't sell a hundred thousand, but he had a good day nevertheless. He returned to Angela's feeling rather set up. There wasn't a great deal of time. This was one occasion when a dinner party would begin on the dot and the theatergoers would be in their seats at the curtain's rising. Angela was not to be seen when he arrived, she was dressing, and he heard through the closed door separating the room Sherry used and Angela's own, a soft quick flurry of conversation and one or two mild oaths.

His evening clothes were laid out for him. He bathed, shaved and dressed, whistling tunelessly. The flowers had been dispatched to the theater; Sherry would have them before the curtain rose. He heard the doorbell ring and Jocelyn's voice in the hall, heard Angela go out to meet her, and went out himself, in shirtsleeves and braces, his hair ruffled and a streak of strictly masculine powder on one smooth-shaven cheek.

"Snap into it, my girl," he ordered Jocelyn cheerfully.

Jocelyn, looking, he thought fleetingly, extraordinarily tired, nodded and blew him a kiss. Led by Angela, who wore a coral silk wrap caught about her sensational lingerie, Jocelyn went into the other small guest room and the door closed behind her. Angela was saying, "When you want Marie's help, let me know."

The door to Angela's bedroom stood open. The room was in a pleasant and fragrant confusion. Marie, aproned, capped, moved about quickly, demurely, straightening up, setting bottles and jars back in their places. Jimmy still lounged against his doorway and now Angela stood a few feet away facing him. Her hair was sleek and dark as a blackbird's shining wing, her long narrow eyes were very blue under their brushing of a violet, metallic eye-shadow. She was delicately tinted and extremely good to look upon. She asked, laughing, "Jimmy, you aren't by any chance looking at my legs, are you?"

He was, although he hadn't realized it. Pretty legs, a gossamer silk sheen over them, high-heeled slippers. The coral wrap was very scant.

He said, grinning, "Well, now that you call my attention to them — "

She laughed. "Get back into your lair," she said, "it's a little confusing to have a great tramping male around the house, in this intimate fashion."

And *that's* a lie, thought Jimmy, returning to get himself properly dressed and to batter down his thick mouse-colored hair. But he thought it genially enough. There was a knock at the door. And on a tray a lone cocktail glass, but a large one. Jimmy took it and thanked the man-servant. He set it down on his dresser. Angela was a swell hostess, he decided, sampling the drink. It was, he discovered, an exceptionally good side-car . . . and just enough of it to set him up for the evening.

They were ready in time, Angela in a straight, severe frock of gold lamé with a high neck line and the lowest back this side of Polynesia. There were emeralds in her ears and one big emerald on her slender left hand. Jocelyn, very sweet in pale blue, looked washed out beside her, despite her authentic prettiness and the touch of rouge on her cheeks.

"Two elegant gals," Jimmy flattered them gayly, an arm around each. "Let's go."

Angela's wrap was lamé and sable, Jocelyn's velvet and lapin. They went to the apartment McKenzie maintained in town, for their cock-tails. Everyone was there, Sheila exceptionally regal in black velvet and pearls, and a dozen others. They were a little late for dinner, in the St. Regis Sea Glades, but not too late for the theater, arriving in their allotted seats just as the house darkened and the stage glowed out rosy-golden, in the twitter and soft sounds of programs turning, subdued coughing and rustling which always attends the curtain's rise.

"I wish," thought Jimmy, between Angela and Jocelyn, "I wish I hadn't come."

The play was a blur to him, it made no sense whatever. He was impervious to Norma Mason's wistful charm, to the Dolores girl's dark, hard handsomeness, to David Burns' really excellent acting and appearance. He saw no one but Sherry. She had never looked lovelier in her life. But he was forced to admit that the stage dwarfed her. The small stages of the amateur performances with their curtains which stuck, and their tolerant audience and their inadequate lighting, had been a different matter. There, she had dominated. But she couldn't dominate here. She was smaller, somehow, less vital, less assured. Her frock was lovely, her make-up professional, her low voice losing its tinge of nervousness as the play went on, had charm. But —

In the lobby, smoking, they stood in knots and talked. They heard others talking. "Where are you going?" asked one critic of another. "Back to my stud session," was the response. "I hate nightmares." "What do you mean, nightmares?" asked the first critic's current girl friend. "Well," responded the second, "I can't keep awake, and when I sleep, I dream. That's that. Good-by, and God help you."

Jimmy was red with rage. "Never mind," said Angela soothingly, "they always talk like that."

Jocelyn demanded, her mouth drooping, "Wasn't she lovely? She *is* good, isn't she, Angela?"

"Of course," said Angela.

"Who," asked a columnist with a slim, lithe figure and a shock of sleek silver hair, "who's the pretty amateur?" A dozen people told him. Someone said benevolently, "She's adequate, of course." And someone else stated, with less beneficence: "It can't be done. Or rather, only once in a blue moon. The road isn't royal or Social Register. It's up from the bottom, stock, variety, God knows what. There is of course Hope Williams. But she's a natural. In both senses. I watched her walk across the stage, that first show and the audience rose to her, like a fish to a special. But this girl — " He shrugged and lit a cigarette.

Jimmy said, "Let's get back to our seats."

Joe McKenzie clapped him on the back. "Why so nervous, old-timer?" he asked. "She isn't in this act, you know. Want to go back-stage?"

"I wouldn't," advised Angela swiftly. "She's awfully nervous, probably."

"No," said Jimmy. "I won't. Angela's right."

In the dressing room Sherry sat with her head in her hands, not moving. The stage fright, the sickness had passed, but she still shivered. There had been applause on her first exit. How much of it came from the McKenzie party she didn't know. Benson knocked and came in. She sat there in a belted robe and scarcely turned her head to greet him.

"I was unspeakably bad," she said tonelessly.

"You weren't," he denied. "Why, you're shaking." He went over to her, and put his arms around her. "Be quiet just a moment," he said, "try to relax. Everything is going very well. I've heard some excellent comments."

He was strong, he understood, he was a decent person, really. She leaned her head against his breast and closed her eyes. The room was full of the intangible odor of the theater, perfume, powder, grease paint, dust, perhaps, and the faint, sweet scent of forbidden tobacco. Sherry for an instant leaned on this masculine strength with a complete impersonality. Benson stood there, just behind her, one arm about her shoulder, looking in the mirror, with its hard, brilliant lights, at the abased head, the closed eyes, with their mascaraed lashes, the painted, young face. He thought, I'm in love with her. I've been in love with her for a long time. Even, he said to himself, after tonight.

There was a light knock; neither heard it; neither moved. The door opened and some of Joe McKenzie's party filled the room. Not Jimmy, not Angela, not Joe, but Jocelyn and Sheila and several other women.

Benson stepped back quietly. Sherry's eyes opened, they were for a split second quite blank of intelligence. She had never been so tired in her life. Then awareness came back to them. There was talk, exclamations, flattery, fluttering, and introductions. Every woman in the room had seen what she had seen and thought her own thoughts. Later, there would be a time for speaking, whispering, sidelong glances and shocked laughter which is so pleasurable to the person who laughs and the person who listens.

Sheila's eyes were bright with astonishment; Jocelyn's dark with pain. Presently Benson said, "If you want to be in your seats when the curtain goes up — ?"

They moved in a delicate flurry of lovely colors and materials toward the door. Jocelyn said, low, to Sherry, "Do you want me to stay with you — during this act?"

But Sherry shook her head. "No, run along. I'm all right. I was — tired, I guess, couldn't even move to change."

"There's plenty of time," said Benson, smiling.

Jocelyn followed the others to the door. Benson thought, If she says anything . . . they saw, of course they saw — they'll put their own construction on it. But Sherry said nothing except, "I wonder why Jimmy didn't come around — and Angela?"

"Perhaps," Benson suggested smoothly, "they realized you were nervous and would prefer not. I must say the others showed little consideration."

No, she said nothing. Because she felt nothing, realized nothing. The moment she had leaned there tired and speechless had rested her. It had been a gesture almost childlike in its naturalness. And Benson had not moved away in the haste and awkwardness usually contingent upon such a situation, and which would have aroused her to embarrassment.

After a moment or two he left her. The dresser came in. Sherry flashed into life and action. She said aloud, "I've forgotten my third-act lines." Her sides in their blue paper cover lay on the dressing table, crumpled, worn. She snatched them up.

The dresser out of her long experience said, "No, Miss Nevins" — they wouldn't call her Mrs. — ever — "you haven't forgotten them. Try to rest a little. Relax — "

Jocelyn slipped into her seat after the house was dark and the curtain up. "Did you see her?" whispered Jimmy. "If I had known you were going — but I was out smoking. How is she? What did she say?" Someone shushed him violently and he subsided into a penitent murmur. The bit which the pianist role had was in full swing, a tall girl with slender hands was at the piano. Benson had procured someone who could really play. Norma Mason made her second-act entrance. The audience stopped its rustling and settled down again. Jocelyn shook her head at Jimmy and laid her finger upon her lips.

She was faintly sick. The opening of the door, the instant, brief electric silence, Sherry abandoned to a curious moveless peace, her wine-dark head against Holman Benson's breast . . .

Returning, in the passage behind the boxes, someone had caught at Jocelyn's arm and swung her around. It was Richardson, in a serge suit, his tie rumpled, his hair wild, his face the color of ashes.

"Why won't you see me, why aren't you

home when I call? You must, Jocelyn, you must. I tell you I've been in hell — "

She had escaped finally. And now she was back in her seat, her heartbeats blurring her sight. It hadn't meant anything, she told herself, her mind going back to Sherry, it couldn't. If it did, her world would fall to pieces. Absurd, childish to build a great part of your world on the integrity of three people: your father, Jimmy, Sherry. But so she had done; so she was fashioned.

The curtain fell on the second act. Now it rose on the third act and there was applause for Sherry's entrance. Swiftly the play ran to its close.

That it was a good play there could be little manner of doubt. Or that it had been. But it had been ironed out, cut, rewritten, polished until it had achieved a brittle brilliance, a striving for cleverness, an economy of phrase which sacrificed blood and bone and the texture of living flesh. It was an amusing play; one you enjoyed, and forgot.

Jimmy and Angela, Jocelyn and Sheila were back-stage. Sherry, radiant, taut, now that it was over, received them with indiscriminate embraces. She was filled with an idiotic love for everyone; even for Angela.

"Was it so bad?" she was asking breathlessly. "Was I so bad?"

They reassured her. Jimmy kept looking at her in a sort of mute misery. She didn't belong here; she was strange to him; the room was strange, the atmosphere. Norma Mason was crying in her dressing room. She always cried after openings. People hurried by the partly open door or stopped to peer in, to exclaim, to prophesy. Holman Benson looked in on them, smiling.

After what seemed like an eternity, they were back at Angela's, all of McKenzie's party, the cast, Benson, Richardson. The flowers which had come to the theater for Sherry went too. The studio was dimly lighted, the bar set up, there was someone in McKenzie's party who played good jazz. There was dancing, laughter, and Sherry sat on the divan, Jimmy's orchids pinned to her frock. They were lovely, she told him, and so extravagant. Angela, hearing, smiled a little to herself. She did not even glance toward her cousin's husband.

Everyone smoked too much, talked too much, drank too much.

"It isn't a hit," said Norma Mason, drinking champagne.

Benson shook his dark head at her. "You've always been a gloom," he said. "I heard otherwise. Wait and see."

Clear to the corner where Sherry sat, a

voice rose from one of the McKenzie party, a man's. "I hear that Lorrimer doesn't care whether his bank failed or not — at least it has served to rid him of Nita's riding-master."

Nita wasn't there. Sherry for the first time missed her. She shot a startled look at Jimmy, standing back of her. He swore, not too gently. She asked, frightened, paling, "Jimmy, is this true?"

"Yes. Not to the degree you think. We'll talk about it afterward," he said.

A woman came up to claim her, to tell her how lovely she had been, how perfect in the part. "I envy you," she said, looking across the room at Holman Benson, "he's the best-looking man I've seen in years."

Jimmy heard and frowned, very slightly, and Jocelyn, sitting at Sherry's feet, put her fair head against Sherry's silken knees. She was terribly tired. Richardson had claimed her, instantly, in the studio; had literally backed her into a corner. Had sworn that he couldn't live without her, that he needed her. The play was a flop, the new play would be a failure. Her fault, she had obsessed him to the point where he couldn't think, much less write. Elsie was, he thought, on her way at last. In another three months or so the divorce would be a fact. Jocelyn must give him her promise to marry him. She said faintly, "I don't love you, Frank. What I feel for you — yes, I do feel something — isn't love."

"What is?" he asked her.

Suddenly she was confident. The little scene in the dressing room faded as if it had never been. She made a small gesture with her sensitive hand. "Sherry," she said, "and Jimmy — "

"My poor child," said Frank Richardson, "that marriage will be washed up within a year. Maxwell's insane over Angela Ward — and everyone knows that Holman's — "

"Oh, stop!" said Jocelyn, and put her hands to her ears. "I won't listen," she said and then, strangely, "I *can't*."

He had left her without farewell or apology a little later. And about one o'clock the others began to go, the people who were motoring back to Westchester, the cast.

Later, Jimmy sat on Sherry's bed and watched her at the dressing table. She asked, putting down her hairbrush, "It means, doesn't it, that all you have is wiped out?"

Here was the opportunity to tell her of Angela's generosity. He didn't. He thought, She'd hate it. She'd think — things. She'd insist upon paying her back. He replied instantly.

"Not quite. I — I had something in another

bank. Look here, let's not talk about it any more tonight, you must be dead tired. And tomorrow's another day. The bank will re-open, I'm not worried about that. And I made some money today."

"I'll transfer enough to your account," she began. But he shook his head.

"No, you won't. It won't be necessary. If I get in a jam this month, bills, and the rest, all right, you can shoulder it if you want to. But I'll pay you back, Sherry, as soon as things get straightened out."

She said, irritated: "Don't take that tone. Aren't we — married? I mean, of course, I don't want you to pay me back. I have some bills this month, my clothes, and all that. But I can meet them. If I run short, I'll sell something. Then there's my salary. And if the show's a hit and has a long run I'll get my money back."

Angela knocked and entered. "Do let her go to bed, Jimmy," she begged, "Jocelyn went ages ago." Jimmy looked up. "It's about the Lorrimer Welles business. She overheard someone tonight — " he said.

"That's too bad," Angela commented. "We tried to keep it from you for a few days, Sherry, we thought it best." Sherry turned, exasperated. *We* tried, *we* thought. Her old antagonism toward her cousin came nodding back. Because of it, her good night to Jimmy was casual, almost formal. "I won't sleep late," she said. "I must see the papers."

Jimmy and Angela left the room. The studio, Angela told him, was in a mess. But the worst had been disposed of, it had been aired, the couch made into a bed, his things brought up there. "I hope," she said, "you'll be comfortable." She stood there beside the divan, looking at him. "Don't worry so. Sherry's nervous, of course, and hearing about the bank bothered her. Naturally." She put her hand with the emerald shining on it in the dim light on the pillow and pulled it here and there to her satisfaction. "One blanket be enough?" she wanted to know.

She left him presently, looking back, at the doorway. The lamplight was rosy on the lamé gown, the earrings caught fire. She smiled, very faintly. She said, "It's nice to think of you — here."

Jimmy sat down on the divan and took off his shoes. He thought inconsequentially, They're too damned tight. He dropped one, dangled the other from a lax hand. Something had gone awfully wrong with the evening. It had been exciting, feverish, people, color, applause, all that. But something was wrong. Between Sherry and himself. He didn't know what. He didn't wish to inquire, at the moment.

CHAPTER XIV

Angela, Jocelyn and Jimmy breakfasted early. Sherry had insisted that she would return to Rye in the morning. "I can't get into the way of usurping your place, Angela," she said, "I'll learn to commute without much difficulty." So many stage people did, she explained, from Long Island, from Westchester. Besides, she felt as if she hadn't seen Little House in years. She needed clothes, she needed everything. Angela mustn't be bothered with her any more. She'd take a train out before noon.

"Well, sleep till train time," Angela had advised her. But they were still at the table, papers spread out all around them, when Sherry appeared, her eyes anxious, a robe belted about her slender waist over silk pyjamas.

"Brutes, not to wake me!" she said. "What — what do they say — ?"

Angela poured coffee. It was she who replied. "They aren't bad, Sherry," she told her cousin.

"That means, not *good*." Sherry's face was miserable. Jimmy had an immediate shocked

317

conviction that she would cry. She didn't. She rallied beautifully. She put her hand out. "Well, let's see the worst," she said lightly.

The worst was tepid. Critics disagreed, as they generally do except upon outstanding examples, very bad, very good. The play showed "promise," the play was "spotty," it was "fairly entertaining," it was "light." The acting was good. Norma Mason, almost a legend now despite the fact that she was not yet forty, received her usual careful praise; Burns was well treated; Dolores, however, was the hit. Angela was mentioned in just two papers — in one as "the pretty society amateur," in the other as "A" Miss Nevins. "Miss Nevins was neither bad nor good in a minor role."

Sherry laid down the sheets, carefully. She said, "Well, it might have been worse."

There was nothing they could say to mitigate it. It wasn't bad enough to arouse their dramatic fury and consolation, it wasn't good enough to select, in consolation, here a word and here a phrase. They sat and looked at her and murmured inanities. Jocelyn's eyes were bright with nervous tears. Angela said: "Perhaps it isn't quite the part for you, Sherry. Too smart-aleck. The next part will be different, more yourself. Don't be discouraged so early in the game."

"I'm not." She set her lips, her little chin was stubborn, her eyes defiant. She drank some coffee, reached for a piece of toast. She said, "If only the notices — as a whole — had been better. I'm not thinking about myself."

The telephone rang. It was for Sherry. The butler came and plugged in an extension wire. Sherry took it at the table. It was Benson. Of course, Benson, thought Jimmy, lighting a cigarette. He heard the snatches of conversation.

"You've seen the notices . . . ?" Nonsense, I got what I deserved. But, the play itself — ? What do you think — ? and Frank? Yes, I'm going back home this morning. Sheila, my mother, is leaving for Hot Springs today — Hot Springs — and she'll let me have her car and chauffeur while she's away."

That was news to Jimmy. When she had replaced the receiver he asked when Sheila decided to go away.

"Oh," Sherry told him indifferently, "some time ago, didn't you know? It will be easier, my having a car to get about in. I don't like the train, I'd hate to use the roadster, and after all, Jimmy, I can't interfere with you to the extent of having you drive me in and out every day."

That was thoughtful of her, he said. At

his tone she looked up quickly, frowning, and Jocelyn shrank a little. Angela rang for more coffee, and created a diversion with some gossip she had just heard. The papers lay on the floor. Sherry rose, after a moment.

"I'll dress," she said, "and go home. What the house looks like I can't imagine!"

It looked all right, Jimmy told her. He, too, rose. He said, "I'll get to the office. Jocelyn, you going out with Sherry?" Jocelyn said she was in a rather subdued tone. "Will you be home to dinner?" he asked Sherry courteously, "or have you other plans?"

Of course, she'd be home, she told him, astonished. Dinner at six. He didn't mind? That would give her time to eat, drive in, and be at the theater on time. The late curtain risings were really a blessing, after all.

Jimmy went on to the office. It occurred to him walking to the Chrysler Building for air and exercise through a gray autumnal murk, that the running of their household must now be adjusted to Sherry's career. He recalled the papers. Career? But he wasn't as sure as he had been that she'd quit, finding she had, if not failed, then at least not succeeded. He'd been certain before. But if this was in her blood, wouldn't she go on, year after year, finding sometimes little parts in the hope that one of them would prove the beginning for her? Not that she would be able to sink twenty thousand dollars in every new show, he thought; and would she get a part without that gilded string to it? He halted himself suddenly disliking his thoughts and the way in which they were leading him.

In Benson's apartment he and Frank Richardson sat in a similar whirl of newspapers. Benson swore, with a restrained savagery. "When they damn you with faint praise — " he murmured.

Richardson, gone very haggard but very youthful, somehow, in his fatigue, looked at him sardonically. "I still maintain that if you'd let me leave it alone it would have had something to offer. As it is it's gone stale, all the freshness ironed out."

Benson jumped to his feet . . . if they called rehearsals, if they returned to the first version? Richardson shook his head. "That won't do any good, and you know it."

Presently Benson said: "I think with ballyhooing it's good for a couple of months. At least the notices aren't such as to make it fold in a week or two."

Richardson said: "All right, if you say so. But there won't be any profit. What price throwing good money after bad?" He added negligently that Sherry Nevins was probably in tears over her notices — or lack of them. "Not that the part matters, but it's all of a piece with the whole thing. An amateur production despite the utmost efforts."

He was impossible, Benson told him shortly. Richardson shrugged. He thought, Elsie will be here now, any day. I've got to see Jocelyn, got to make her promise. In his frantic and fantastic terror he clung to the thought of her, the proverbial straw. She must, she should save him from drowning once more in those dark waters which were so fathomless, which had such strange unhappy tides. With the thought of Jocelyn, the promise of her cool hands and eyes in which there was the wisdom of innocence, the promise of her chaste and slender body, he could be fortified against Elsie's claims. He thought, But — if when we meet she decides against the divorce? She mustn't decide against it. She must go through with it, marry, leave this earth so far as he was concerned, with no chance of return. He thought, I should have killed her and myself long ago, we would have both been better off dead — even in the grave we would have been aware of each other, I suppose, hating, loving. He thought, Once I get her out of my nerve fibers perhaps I will be able to write her out of my system, a great play, sinister, exotic. It began to take formless shape in his mind. He was afraid of it, and elated. Some day, perhaps that corroding love — was it love? — might come to a sterile fruition.

Love. He thought of Jocelyn. She knew nothing about love, she never would. What she would have from him would pass for it, it would content her, she was very young, very ignorant. As for himself, he did not desire it again; did not want what he had had, nor that from which he could not be released.

Sherry returned home. Life in the next few weeks adjusted itself to her meal hours, her late sleeping, a horseback ride, a game of golf, a light luncheon, rest, people, and then time to dine and go into town again. They were playing to houses which, if not packed, were adequately filled. They were making expenses by a narrow margin, managing, and that was all. No profit.

"If," said Benson, "if we can keep it on long enough— And there's always the motion picture sale."

But his figure was too high; the first tentative offers were made, and refused. No others came. Benson refused to be discouraged. If the play had a three or four months' run — surely then they were bound to make their profit and the motion picture sale also.

Jimmy was looking for business; getting it, too, in some instances. The Lorrimer Welles bank had not settled its affairs, but his bank account grew. He was able to pay Angela something, not much, but something on account. She laughed at him. "Keep it," she said, "I'm no Shylock." He told her that he knew it, but he'd feel better, paying.

Sheila was at Hot Springs. Jimmy, when the play had run four weeks, went to Hot Springs also on the trail of an elusive prospect. He was there three days, golfing with his prey, wondering if he had been wise to risk the expense. He was justified, it appeared. He told Sheila so, in triumph, lunching with her the day he left for home. Sheila, looking very fit, and ten pounds lighter, with no less than three idle and personable youths in tow, had a word of warning for him.

"I'm not thinking of the expense and I'm glad you did what you came for," she said, "but was it sensible to leave Sherry?"

Jimmy laughed, without gayety.

"She won't miss me. I see very little of her," he said truthfully. "She has a regular routine now. I suppose she must have. New photographs, interviews when Benson can wangle them, exercise, sleep, the theater, meeting what she calls the 'right' people.

Just now she is all pepped up over some unknown playwright from the West. She met him at Benson's. Frank Richardson's vanished into the blue. Left Benson's flat and gone off somewhere, I don't know on what. I'm glad, for Jocelyn's sake. I think he was beginning to worry her."

"Never mind Jocelyn; Sherry's your real concern. She's seeing," said Sheila bluntly, "a lot too much of Holman Benson. You'd better know it. Everyone is gossiping about it. You, of course, would be the last to hear."

"That's damned nonsense," said Jimmy bleakly.

"No, my dear, it is not. Sherry is a very attractive girl, and Holman Benson is an attractive man. They are thrown together, day after day, intimately. He makes a point of being at the theater. He is seen with her a lot. On matinée day she dines with him. I know that they are business partners as well as producer and actress — but," she went on reflectively, "after all there are limits. I know that in this particular profession people may appear extremely intimate without being so — sometimes. I was shocked, however, to walk into the dressing room that first night and find Sherry and her producer in what virtually amounted to an embrace. I wasn't the only one who saw it," she said hastily as Jimmy's too-ready color flooded up to his eyes, his direct gaze dark and murderous. "Jocelyn was there, ask her, and half a dozen others. I know, and you know, it doesn't mean anything. Theatrical people are always embracing — with a knife in the hand concealed behind the back. But — people will talk and all the women who saw *have* talked, with the exception of Jocelyn and myself. I think if you would be a little more attentive it would repay you even more than chasing good prospects to Hot Springs, wouldn't it?"

He said heavily, "I can't believe you."

"You needn't. But it is true. After all, why should I lie about it? Sherry may be your wife, but she's my daughter. She was my daughter for twenty-two years before she was your wife, remember."

He left, his mind a chaos of speculations and unbelief. When he arrived in New York he stopped at the office to report and then went straight out to Rye. Purchase Street was lovely in autumnal colorings, still holding in that mild weather. It had been just about now, the middle of October, when he had planned a vacation. But vacations without Sherry would be no fun; and Sherry wasn't available. He approached the house in the taxi, exceedingly sorry for himself, worked up to a combination of rage and misery.

But Sherry wasn't there. It was matinée day. He might have remembered it, but he hadn't. He found Jocelyn alone, at the piano. She whirled on the bench to greet him.

"Why didn't you wire?" she cried. "Sherry's been waiting to hear."

He had forgotten, he realized, to wire. He had the taxi man drop his bag in the hall, paid him and went back to Jocelyn. He asked abruptly, without any warning, "Jocelyn, is Holman Benson in love with Sherry?"

By her slight stammer and the heightening of her color he knew that she believed so. But she said loyally, not looking at him with the eyes which mirrored her instant disturbance, "No, of course not." But then, as he remained silent, standing, looking down at her, as if waiting, she went on hastily, with anger, "You've no right to ask me that anyway. Or — or to discuss Sherry with me. I care a lot for you both — too much to — " She broke off, and turned on the bench again and crashed her slender hands discordantly among the keys. Discord slipped into melody. She said, not regarding him, over minor chords and little runs like silver bells, "I've been thinking — perhaps I'd better go to Montclair. To the Gowans'. They want me, they're lonely since Edith married.

And I had a letter from Father today. His return is still delayed, he's going into Germany, now that the English branch has been established."

"That's nonsense," said Jimmy. "Your place is here, with us. We want you — "

"I wanted to come," she told him. She lifted her hands from the keys. She swung around and faced him, her hands clasped in her lap. "I was happy here. You never made me feel as if I — interfered. Plenty of people have told me that — I did. A third person — " Her voice trailed off, she was thinking of Sheila, her careful feline utterances, of Nita's more frankly outspoken disapproval, and others.

Jimmy said strongly, "If you're going to listen to what people say!"

"You can't help it, can you? And no matter how much you try it makes an impression."

"Forget it," he said brusquely, embarrassed at the emotion in her voice. "You belong here." But she was not to be diverted. He said, before she could reply: "I'm sorry you took what I said about Sherry as you did. I wasn't discussing her with you in the sense you mean. But — "

"You've been listening to people, too," she ventured shrewdly. Without considering where it would lead, remembering his trip, she added — "Mrs. Nevins?"

"Then it was true!" he shouted at her so loudly, so suddenly, that she winced.

"What — ?"

"What Sheila said — about the night of the opening — and going into the dressing room and seeing Benson and Sherry — "

Too late she saw where her conjecture had led her. She answered stubbornly, "I don't know what you're talking about."

"Yes, you do. You went back that night, with Sheila and the rest. When you came back to your seat you were bothered about something."

"Not about Sherry, something else."

"What did you see?" he demanded, ignoring that, not believing it.

She flung back her fair head and met his eyes directly.

"Nothing," she answered.

She was not a liar. But if she could lie for Sherry, for Jimmy —

Jimmy turned, took a cigarette from a box, tapped it against the cover. The small muffled sound was louder than trumpets, so thickly did the blood beat in her ears. "You're protecting her. I don't believe you." He said, further, as if speaking to himself: "I've hated it all along, distrusted it. I might have known — She's always been crazy about the stage.

I thought if I put up an argument I'd lose her, in a way. After all, the money came into it. I couldn't very well kick about that, could I? So I didn't. And what's happened? Benson falls in love with her, he has everything I lack, interest in the things she's keen about — good looks — glamour, I suppose you'd call it — "

"Sherry loves *you*," said Jocelyn.

"I know." His voice softened for a moment. "I don't doubt it. But — "

"If you know it, what else matters?" asked Jocelyn. She waited for his answer as if it were vitally important to her.

"Nothing, essentially. No, that's not true. Things do matter even when you don't doubt . . . you're made that way, I guess — worrying."

Jocelyn rose from the piano bench. "Have you had lunch — ?"

"No, I came right out. I forgot it was — matinée day."

"Sherry went into town by an early train," Jocelyn told him. She walked toward the door. "I'll order something," she said, "for us both."

"No, never mind." He looked at his watch. "I'm not hungry. I'll take the roadster and drive back. As a matter of fact I shouldn't have come home. There's plenty for me to do in town. I'll drop around to the theater before the matinée's over, perhaps Sherry will have dinner with me."

He walked over to Jocelyn, touched her shoulder awkwardly. "Don't be sore at me, youngster. Things have gone haywire somehow. They'll be all right again."

The door slammed behind him. Jocelyn stood as he had left her. Her face was still and without distortion. But the bright tears ran silently down her cheeks. "Things have gone haywire." They had. She thought, Anyone's crazy to think life goes along beautifully, with just the inevitable big things, birth, death — crazy to believe in people.

This is no era for idealists. Perhaps any era makes their curious irradiated road difficult. She had grown up in a world which ceaselessly sought to adjust itself. She belonged to that generation which is post-postwar; reactionary, swinging back, looking for the older standards, sick and bewildered by the antics of its elders. She had been sheltered but she was not ignorant. And she had to have something upon which to center her belief. Jimmy and Sherry were more than beloved human beings, they were symbols, they had a significance to her beyond their mortality. She had tried to tell Frank Richardson. He had said: "Don't feel that way.

You'll get hurt. After all, they're just another young married couple, like thousands of others. Aren't they?"

Perhaps he was right. But she refused to believe it. Average, yes, attractive and average, if a little better off in material things than the run of young married couples. Average in that way, she admitted. Nor had they any special gifts; Sherry was an amateur actress turned professional, possessing an Equity card and a salaried job. Jimmy was a good life insurance salesman. They had average brains and average humor and more than average education. She knew all that. But the love between them, the integrity, that was something else again, an anchor in a drifting, unhappy world.

Sherry had failed her. Not wholly by the scene in the dressing room, one could mitigate that, explain it, excuse it. And yet, could one? Jocelyn thought, I couldn't tell Jimmy, I lied, I couldn't be sure that — that he'd believe as I do that it was innocent, that it didn't mean anything. And Jimmy failed her, asking her — *Is Benson in love with Sherry?* not carelessly, not with laughter, but with estranged and frightened eyes, dark with suspicion.

She had thought to be a part of the pattern of their lives, not interfering, not of course indispensable. But a part. She couldn't be. No one, she thought, needed her. She hadn't expected these two to need her, she knew, she had thought she knew, that they were sufficient unto themselves. But still she had thought to be a thread running through the closely woven fabric. She wasn't, that had been childish. No one needed her except, perhaps, Frank Richardson.

If it were true what he had said, that romantic love didn't endure, didn't, perhaps, exist, that people who started out with what passed for it were soon disillusioned, then perhaps what he offered were best after all, a person who belonged, in a sense, to you, a common purpose, a heart which needed you.

CHAPTER XV

"I promised Holman I'd have dinner with him, but he won't mind," said Sherry, laughing, "he'll let me off." Traces of grease paint made her eyes bright and dark, deepened them to violet. Her hair was pinned back with a towel. Jimmy lounged against the wall and watched. She suggested, "Perhaps the three of us — ?"

"No, thanks, I'm not in the humor. You keep your date," said Jimmy.

He'd been there ten minutes. She had been glad to see him, he told himself that over and over. He had reported the successful outcome of his trip, and mentioned seeing her mother. She said now, wiping her face, powdering it, tracing her pretty mouth with a reddened fingertip, "Of course I shan't. Your first night back! — I'll explain."

Benson tapped, came in at her clear call. She said swiftly, "You won't mind, Holman, Jimmy's just back, he has a hundred things to tell me . . . may I break our engagement?"

Benson was understanding, even gracious. Jimmy resented it. Too gracious, he thought, almost benevolent. Sherry slipped the silken wrap from her shoulders and reached for her street frock. It was unconscious, she was unaware of the two men in the room. After all, Jimmy tried to remind himself, she was more dressed in her straight slip than in an evening gown. But the casual intimacy of it affronted him.

He did not mean to quarrel with her. They went to a near-by speakeasy for dinner. He told himself afterwards that nothing was further from his mind than a quarrel. But Benson's name came up frequently, and before he knew it he had spoken out, abruptly, angrily; and she had listened with wide eyes, not entirely incredulous. After all, she was adult, she knew her way about, and supposed bitterly that it would have been too good to be true if Jimmy had accepted her association with Holman Benson for what it was.

But what was it exactly? The evening Jimmy left for Virginia she had gone out on a rather mild party with Benson, and he had taken her back to Angela's, where she would spend what was left of the night. And there he had talked to her, in the studio, while Angela had gone downstairs for something. There he had told her first of all that it was a matter of weeks before the show would close; that there was no profit; that he deeply regretted having let her in for this. That had been a body blow — she had perhaps known it all along, but had evaded it. And then he had said " — all the worse because I'm so terribly in love with you. Is there a chance for me, Sherry?"

Astonished, yet not entirely astonished, she had said the stupid thing — "But I'm married!"

He had rung all the old changes; married, yes, to a boy who neither understood nor appreciated her. It all came down to one thing. "Divorce Maxwell, marry me — I'm not licked yet. We'll do things together, big things. In the theater. We'll have a colorful life, a real life, one which matters — "

Angela heard; Angela listened frankly, outside the open door. She heard Sherry say: "I'm sorry. I do like you so much. But you see I'm in love with Jimmy."

Remembering this, sure of her own integrity yet not quite guiltless, Sherry stared across the table at Jimmy, in the low-ceilinged room filled with the odors of food and drink, with chattering people, and carried the war into his own camp. Angela? What about Angela? He saw quite as much of Angela as she of Benson. No, she hadn't forgotten. Had he thought she had? She'd been a good sport about it, she hadn't believed things against him. But of course, if he was going to believe things about her, just because she was thrown with a man in the pursuit of her career . . .

Jimmy made a bad mistake. He said "career?" and laughed. He said, because he was angry and because he was frightened: "You can't act for sour apples. Nothing but your money and Benson's influence put you on a Broadway stage. And you know it. When this is over, and there's no more money forthcoming, we'll see about the influence. You'll be washed up, Sherry, and you know that too."

"If that's the way you feel — !"

"That's the way I feel, all right — "

She pushed her plate aside. "I have to get back," she said, after a moment. Jimmy paid the bill, and they left. They drove in silence to the theater. Arriving, he said awkwardly, "I'll call for you after the show."

"You needn't bother," said Sherry, "I've Sheila's car."

He watched her go in at the stage door, slender back erect. He thought, I've made a damned fool of myself. Because he had, he was hot with anger against her. Ordinarily a fairly peaceful and certainly a merciful person, he longed for a nose to punch, preferably Holman Benson's, and for an alley cat to kick. He drove toward Fifth Avenue and presently found himself on Park and at Angela's.

Angela was home, there were people with her. She greeted him with no astonishment. She got rid of her guests presently, and so deftly that even Jimmy didn't realize it.

"Well, how was the trip and what happened? Did you see Sheila?"

He told her, not caring.

"What's wrong?" she asked him, sitting down beside him. Then she frowned. "Oh — " she said, *"that!* Don't pay any attention to it. Boys will be columnists. At that," she added, smiling, "it's a little of our own back, isn't it?"

He didn't know what she was talking about. "Didn't Sherry tell you, haven't you seen her?" she asked.

Sherry, he said, had told him nothing.

"Oh," said Angela lightly, "my error, in that case, forget it."

But he insisted. So she brought him the paper, laid her finger on the item. "Someone," said Angela, shrugging, "would call it to your attention tomorrow."

The columnist with whom she had talked briefly a day or so previously had been faithful, both to her and to his craft. The item was brief. It was merely in a sprightly manner that even if Sherry Nevins couldn't act she was an angel just the same. "We understand," it read further, "that she has sunk twenty grand in the current Benson show, which is being kept on its feet by will power, money and publicity. Angels rush in where financiers fear to tread. This one is pretty as something off a Christmas tree, trust Benson for that."

It said nothing, and it said a lot. Jimmy flung the paper on the floor. He said plenty, and none of it was fit for even a gossip column to print. Angela agreed with him. "It's too bad; but it was bound to happen."

"He's in love with her," said Jimmy after a moment. He waited for the denial. None came. He asked angrily, "Isn't he?"

"Perhaps," Angela replied, "but so long as she's in love with you, what does it matter?"

"It matters a lot," said Jimmy.

"You mustn't," Angela warned him, "get all hot and bothered. His intentions are perfectly honorable."

Then she told him, not omitting the last thing she had overheard. "You see?" she said.

But the fact that Sherry had told Holman Benson that she was in love with her husband didn't impress him. Angela hadn't expected that it would. But she had covered herself, cleverly. She looked at him anxiously.

"Jimmy, don't," she said, "it doesn't mean a thing . . . after the show closes, things will be as they were before. Holman has had his congé, he won't turn up again."

"Things aren't ever as they were before," said Jimmy. He sat staring in front of him.

Angela put her hand on his knee. "I'm sorry," she said, "I wish I hadn't told you but — she doesn't give a snap of her fingers for him really, Jimmy. There's nothing to worry about. I wish to God there were."

He stared at her, then said, "You wish — what on earth do you mean?" he asked angrily.

Angela rose and walked away.

"Oh, nothing." She stopped beside a table and picked up a cigarette. She lighted it with steady hands. She said, over her shoulder: "Just that I've been in love with you, Jimmy, for a long time. By all the canons of fiction Holman and I should get together and console each other. Only we won't. Run along now, will you, it's getting late."

He experienced all the embarrassment and resentment, gratitude and anger of any man in the like situation. He rose, after a moment, and went over to her. He asked tentatively, "Of course you're kidding?" He asked it rather hopefully. But Angela shook her dark head.

"No, I'm not, Jimmy. But don't let it

upset you. I'm not the type to put my head in the oven just because one man doesn't know I exist. I'll get over it, I always do. After all, there are hundreds of men."

Her eyes mocked him, he was irritated, completely masculine, angry with Sherry, with life, with himself, with Angela. The speakeasy liquor had been potent, quarreling with Sherry a dry business. He circled Angela's slender wrist with his hard fingers, pulled her to him and kissed her without tenderness and with rebellion. He did not love her and if in that instant he desired her it was without cooperation of judgment or volition.

After a moment she spoke, as coolly as possible.

"You'd better go," she said.

He went, without another word. Later, standing beside his car, breathing the crisp air, he wondered just how much of a fool he had been.

Driving home, with an inspired recklessness, his thoughts moved in a pattern, touching salient points, Sherry, Benson, Angela, himself. He was, he acknowledged, bitterly ashamed; yet, in a way, elated. He had asserted his manhood — or had it been asserted for him? — he and Sherry were quits.

But eventually there was an element of penitence to trouble him. He thought, letting himself in quietly, waiting for Sherry in their room, When she comes, we'll have it out. I'll apologize for tonight. If she tells me of her own accord what Angela told me, then I'll know, I'll be sure.

But Sherry did not come home that night. At half past three he called Angela. "No," replied Angela, wide awake, "no, she hasn't been here." He left her questions, her intimate murmur unanswered, hanging up the receiver. What was he to think, dared he think at all? Jocelyn, lying wakeful, heard him walking about, heard the scratching of innumerable matches.

At breakfast in reply to her questions, he said briefly that Sherry must have changed her mind after he left her at the theater and gone to Angela's. But the walls of Little House were not sound proof. Jocelyn had heard him call Angela's familiar number.

At the office he looked blankly at his appointment pad. Between appointments he telephoned Rye: twice, three times, four. No, Jocelyn told him, Sherry hadn't been there. Then there could no longer be any pretense that he believed her with Angela. But he was past caring.

He was at the theater waiting when she

drove up in Sheila's car. For once he did not speak to the driver, had no eyes for anything but Sherry. He took her arm, roughly. He said, still not caring, "Where in hell have you been?"

There were people about the alley. She said: "Please, let's not make a scene on the street. The theater's a more appropriate place." She walked past him to the entrance, speaking to the doorman, smiling. In her dressing room he shut the door behind him and asked again, "Well, are you going to answer me?"

"I went to a hotel," she said.

"That's *very* likely!"

"The Warwick. You can check on it if you like," she said, taking off her wraps. "Did you expect me to come home? If you did you were crazy. And I'm not coming home for a while. I'll send the car out with a note to Jocelyn, ask her to pack some things for me. I'm tired, the trip's hard. And I don't intend to be upset. Even if I can't act for sour apples," said Sherry evenly, "I don't want to be any worse than I am, if I can help it."

That was that. He left before the curtain call. Other people came in, Benson among them, impervious, friendly. Jimmy loathed the sight of him. He bolted, he had to bolt.

He went to a booth and called up the Warwick. He despised himself. They told him, yes, Miss Nevins was registered —

Returning to Jocelyn's waiting, miserable eyes was difficult. He explained awkwardly. Sherry was tired, she would stay in town for a while, she was sending Jocelyn a note, when the car came back —

He thought, I always believed things happened differently, a big smash, not this matter-of-fact business out of the blue. Nothing dramatic about it. There was a quarrel which ended nowhere and your wife walked out on you. Just like that.

He stayed away from Angela's, driving out doggedly nights, to Rye, and sitting in uncomfortable silences with Jocelyn. When she touched the piano his nerves snapped and he shouted at her. Sometimes they played two-handed bridge. Once or twice people came in and there were explanations and polite murmurs and entirely incredulous smiles. One night he got magnificently drunk with Joe McKenzie. But even drunk he held his tongue.

Angela called the office. He would not answer. One late afternoon she walked in; he was alone save for a couple of clerks. She shut the door to his office behind her.

"Look here, what's up? I've talked to Joc-

344

elyn. She told me Sherry's staying in town. Was it — anything I said — ? I'm dreadfully sorry, Jimmy."

He asked, fussing with a blotter which wasn't quite straight on his desk, "Are you, Angela?"

"No. Yes — in a way, I am. Tell me, Jimmy."

"I don't know what it's all about," he answered truthfully. "Let's clear out and go somewhere and eat. I have to talk to someone."

They dined; they returned to the studio.

"I'll make an early train. I didn't drive in, something wrong with the feed pipe. The bus is laid up. You're good to tolerate me, Angela, even Pinch avoids me, I'm lousy company."

"Tell me," she urged again, gently.

He told her. "She's at the Warwick," he concluded. "She won't see me. I've phoned a couple of times. When the show closes, she says — "

Angela was silent.

"It's an impossible situation. I'm shot. If you knew how I dreaded going home," he said with violence.

"You needn't," Angela told him evenly. "Don't think for a moment I don't know what I'm saying — or doing. I know you

have nothing to give me but a sort of dis-
gusted pity, the kind of pity with a smirk
behind it which a man gives a woman who's
insane about him and for whom he cares
exactly nothing. But I'll take that — and
like it. We're both pretty miserable. Stay
here, tonight."

CHAPTER XVI

Sherry had returned to Little House. The play had closed. Sherry had come home without elation, without triumph. She was incredibly tired.

Benson had said to her: "If you knew how I feel — I can't humble myself sufficiently. There's still a chance of a motion picture sale, you may be able to get back something — Lord knows we kept it going on our nerve, a paper house, publicity — but I'd like to hear you say that you forgive me."

She smiled, gallantly enough.

"Of course. But then there is nothing to forgive, really, is there? I mean, it was a gamble, I went into it with my eyes open, you held out no promises."

He straightened his shoulders.

"I'm not beaten yet. Some day I'll produce a play that will shake this old town to its foundations." He stopped a moment. "Richardson's found a producer for this depression affair of his. I told him I had no belief in it, and — " he smiled wryly, "no money to back it. He'll rewrite it, of course;

meantime he's got his advance. I saw him briefly a night or so ago. He's entirely uninterested in what's happening to this one, he's gone on to the next. In a way, his is a lucky temperament. He's living somewhere, Perry Street, I think. What about him and little Jocelyn?"

Sherry had been astonished at her own reply. "I don't know," she said truthfully, "I haven't seen Jocelyn, really — for so long."

Jocelyn had gone finally to the Gowans' in Montclair. Worse than the awkward silent evenings with Jimmy had been the evenings when he did not come home at all. There had been a good many of them.

"What are you going to do?" Benson asked Sherry.

"I'm not sure. My mother wants me to join her in Hot Springs and then go on to Palm Beach with her. I'm awfully tired, Holman, really."

"You mustn't," he warned, "give up."

"I think I have. After all — " she shrugged her shoulders — "it was nice while it lasted, but I think," she went on, trying to laugh, "you may announce my permanent retirement from the stage."

"No," he said, "of course not. You're worn out, that's all. Go away, have a good rest, and you'll see how you'll feel, in the spring. By then I'll have dug up something — "

Leaving her, he held her hand a long minute.

"I'm not going to reopen that tabu subject. But if you change your mind . . . I'm always somewhere, waiting, loving you — "

But she did not want him, nor his waiting nor his love. She went back to Little House and wandered about its charming rooms looking at it with clear and tired eyes. Why had she quarreled with Jimmy? Because of Angela — ? No, not because of Angela. Because of Holman Benson? No, not that, either. Because, perhaps, he had told her she couldn't act. That was the root of it, she decided. She'd been a pretty poor sport. She couldn't take it. She knew now, and definitely, her limitations. She had lived long enough in the world of the theater to get a perspective of herself. But she had been tired and troubled and Jimmy's brusque statement had flicked her on the raw, and intolerably. He hadn't been, she mused forgivingly, very tactful.

She had returned the morning after the closing performance. She had not been in the house ten minutes before she went to the telephone and called her husband's office. She said, merely, when the connection was established, "I'm home, Jimmy."

349

There was a brief silence. Something beat in it, something she sensed and which disturbed her. He said "Oh — " blankly; and then, "I'll be out tonight."

He had been staying at the Yale Club recently, not bothering to return to the empty house. Sherry's voice came back to him, disappointed as a child's.

"I thought perhaps — you could take the afternoon off? Or shall I meet you in town?"

"I've appointments," he said, "I'll be out as early as I can."

He replaced the receiver and sat down at his desk, his legs straight out before him, his hands in his pockets and stared into space. His secretary came in and he barked at her and she went out again, astonished. She harbored a silent devotion for Jimmy Maxwell which did not prevent her from being engaged to no less than two nice boys in Jersey City and she was pained at his unusual display of bad temper.

"It must be the missus," she confided to her girl friend in the rest room, rerouging her lips, "it's always one of three things with men: money, the wife or last night's poker game."

Sherry is back in Little House, thought Jimmy.

He remembered in every detail the last

time he had seen Angela, three nights ago. He had said, "I can't go on with it, Angela, I feel — rotten."

"It's a pity," said Angela, "that you were born with a conscience. I wasn't."

"I must have been crazy," he said bluntly.

"That's not especially flattering." She came and sat close beside him and put her hand on his own. "Do you hate me — terribly?"

"No," answered Jimmy, considering it. "I don't hate you, at all. I like you, Angela, I like you a lot." He was astonished to find it was perfectly true. He did like her. He did not approve of her, approval had never been included in his attitude toward her, at any time. But he liked her. "The only person I hate is myself."

"Americans," stated Angela, "have a lot to learn. Good husbands" — she looked at him sidelong and saw him flinch — "and bad lovers. Bad lovers because they can't forget they're good husbands."

"Stow it," he said irritably. He turned and looked at her, at the brittle, tended beauty of her face and body. "I'm letting you down, of course."

"No," denied Angela, "you're not. If I had had any sense I'd have known. You can't make a sow's ear out of a silk purse, I suppose." She gave him her most unusual smile, not the faint slow one which had disturbed a good many men but an impish little grin which transformed her face. She asked, "Look here, Jimmy, why did you stay — that first time?"

He questioned slowly, "Shall I tell you the truth or the other thing?"

"The truth. I know, I think, but I'd like to have it confirmed."

He regarded her with some admiration. "You're a good sport, Angela."

"No, only when it suits me to be. I can double-cross with the best of 'em," she said gayly. But her eyes were not gay. She thought, Is it possible that I'm going around the rest of my life remembering a failure?

"Let's have it," she suggested after a moment.

"I stayed," he said slowly, "because I've always thought Joseph a sap. I stayed because you're a damned attractive woman and because I was lonely, and because I had quarreled with Sherry and because I believed she no longer cared for me very much. I stayed because I wanted to, and because — "

"That's plenty," said Angela, a little pale. "I wish it had been otherwise. I wish you could see as I do that there's so little love in this world that even the emotion we call love, but think of by another name, is worth while, for the forgetfulness it brings, if only for a moment."

He shook his head. "I can't see that."

"No." She regarded him thoughtfully. "The absurd thing is that you aren't a prig. You're just a decent bewildered average sort of man trying to figure out what it's all about. You haven't progressed from your Puritan ancestors. Black is black and white is white. There are two kinds of women. Good and bad. You fall in love with the good ones and marry them. You have your moments with the bad ones and regret them. That's all."

"You talk like a book," he said, irritated. He had expected scenes, tears, braced himself for them, had experienced the inevitable there-there-little-girl reaction prematurely. But here sat Angela, smoking a cigarette and discoursing of his ancestors.

Angela said reflectively:

"I am rather like a book. One you read and which amuses you and which you forget — or lend to your friends," she remarked a trifle bitterly.

But she wasn't a book; she was flesh and blood. He knew, he remembered, he stirred restlessly. He didn't love her, he would never love her, but he would not forget her. . . .

"Sherry," said Angela, "should be grateful to me. You've learned something, in what

I may call an intensive course."

"Leave Sherry out of it!" ordered Jimmy.

Angela laughed.

"Of course, the perfect, and the expected remark. You do run true to form, Jimmy," she said. She leaned back against the cushions. She waited until his quick betraying flush had subsided and he had said, with some humility, "I'm sorry, Angela, that was lousy of me."

"I've always," she went on, ignoring that, "done pretty much as I pleased and made my excuses later. I won't make any now. I've wanted you for a long time. I got a lucky break, that's all. I knew how you felt — or how you didn't feel. I thought it would last longer, but it hasn't. Perhaps it's as well. It may amuse you to know that this is the first time I've been in a position other than that of kicker-out."

She added, irrelevantly, that she thought Schnozzle Durante was marvelous.

Jimmy was not concerned with Mr. Durante.

"Look here, what are we going to do?"

"Do?" she inquired in amazement. "Why, nothing at all. I thought that was what you came to tell me."

"You know what I mean. Please, Angela, be serious."

"I can't permit myself to be serious," she retorted. "Do — ? What is there to do? You'll go back to Sherry, make up your little differences, be twice as considerate of her as you were — before — in order to placate your remorse and to make up to her for what she doesn't know."

"But she's got to know, that's the point," said Jimmy miserably.

Angela sat up very straight. Astonishment, anxiety, exasperation broke through the smooth, clever mask. Her voice was a little shrill as she replied to the unheard-of statement.

"Are you out of your mind?" she demanded.

"No, I was, I'm not now. Can't you understand, I can't go back to Sherry — as if things were before — "

"Can't you?" She looked at him with anger. "What about me? I'm Sherry's cousin. We can't avoid meeting. It will cause talk, it's bound to — "

"I thought you didn't care about talk — "

"This is different," she said impatiently. "I know Sherry. She'll put some sort of face on it — provided she remains your wife, which I doubt — but I've always maintained she's no actress. It will be exceedingly awkward."

"What do you mean, provided she remains my wife?"

"Just what I said. She'll probably divorce you," said Angela, "and that's that. Sheila will persuade her not to name me, to save the family." She laughed abruptly. "You hadn't thought of that, had you?"

"No," he replied slowly. "I hadn't. I — it didn't occur to me that she'd feel that way — that anything that mattered so little would — "

"Thanks," interrupted Angela. She could take it, if anyone could, but not too much of it. "Leave me a few illusions. I'd like to think it mattered — for a short time anyway."

He said: "I'm sorry to hurt you. But it didn't, Angela, I didn't realize that — that it could matter so little."

"I was wrong," she said evenly, "about the good average American husband. *He* kisses — but doesn't tell. He keeps it to himself. He sends flowers to his wife and buys her a diamond bracelet. But he keeps his mouth shut — "

"I can't." He looked at her wretchedly. "It isn't possible. Sherry and I — " He broke off and looked away from the woman beside him. "What we had — *have*," he corrected himself strongly, "can't be maintained unless we're honest."

356

"It won't be, if you are. Sherry's no noble creature of a dramatist's brain to rise above a situation like this. You'll see," said Angela, "I'm warning you."

"It doesn't make any difference," he told her. "It can't. It's the way things are with me." His lips twisted, he looked like a man tasting gall. "I couldn't go back to her without telling her — "

"You're a fool," said Angela shortly, "quite apart from me — and your extraordinarily chivalrous attitude!"

She jumped to her feet. She said, standing there:

"I tell you you haven't the brains God gave low-grade morons! You'd wreck Sherry's life and your own — and make me the laughing stock of New York to ease your own conscience."

"Perhaps," said Jimmy. He felt like a fool. He thought that all along his situation had been fantastic. He hadn't an excuse for himself. He thought dimly and with astonishment that if he had felt for Angela some overwhelming, insistent emotion, no matter how forbidden, he would have had more excuse than now. He was not a glorious sinner, the world well lost for his desire, he was a mean, cringing, unwilling, spineless sinner. He thought this, and disliked it exceedingly.

"Oh, get out," cried Angela, her nerves snapping. "I don't believe that even you would do an asinine thing like that — "

Jimmy rose. For a moment they faced each other. He said, awkwardly, "There isn't anything more I can say, is there?"

"You might," she advised mockingly, recovering herself, "tell me you're 'grateful.' That's always a good exit line."

There was no answer to that. He left her and went back to the club. There in his room he sat until dawn patterned the shades and lay, pale and reluctant, on the floor. The room was full of thick blue smoke, the air stale, it hurt his lungs. He rose, knocked out his pipe, opened the windows and undressing went to bed for a little while. But not to sleep.

He was badly frightened. He couldn't believe, as Angela had said, that Sherry would leave him. Surely he could make her understand? Yet he couldn't understand himself.

Two roads were open to him: one, Angela's road; one, his own. Angela's would have him go back to live with Sherry, always provided their previous differences became ironed out, silent, never betraying himself, knowing that Angela was clever at dissembling, counting on rumor to die out for lack of fuel.

The other road meant telling Sherry and risking losing her — perhaps permanently.

He thought, I'm a fool, I suppose; possibly Angela's right, there isn't a man I know, save perhaps Pete, who wouldn't think I was a fit candidate for an asylum . . . but, he told himself, gray with fatigue, I can't do it, I *can't* —

Silence was a lie. Such a lie was a key that would lock a very important door, a door the existence of which Sherry might never guess but which would remain there between them nevertheless, an impassable, an invisible barrier.

Other men had affairs, differing in length of duration, in intensity, born of boredom, of propinquity, of opportunity, of a certain unhappy search after glamour, the curious enchantment of strange flesh. Most of them swore — Jimmy had heard them swear it — that these matters had nothing to do with their love for their wives, their domestic routine — and many of them had far more excuse, were one looking for excuses, than he had had. Many had fallen violently, if briefly, in love, many had suffered, in their legal bed, tolerance or rebellion, indifference or frigidity.

All of them said that, after all, man was, by nature, polygamous.

Was he? Jimmy wondered. Or was that simply a teaching of man, which had borne fruit, a catchword, a cliché, down the ages? Perhaps, if you considered the body alone — but you couldn't consider the body alone. If you did, marriage at once took its place as a tottering institution, exceedingly inconvenient, originated to provide a certain amount of safety for property and inheritance, purity of blood, legality of blood, and originated, too, to provide a minimum of expense for loving.

Sex, he thought, without the spiritual necessity of worship, the mental compulsion of unity, the emotional essentiality of something beyond sex, the outward expression of all that is sex itself, would be absurd. *Was* absurd. He knew that now. There was a twist in mankind's brain which looked on the question of sacred and profane love with blinded eyes. Sacred love, it contended, was decently, if alluringly clad, and profane love went naked.

That was all wrong, he told himself, trying to think it out. The naked body of love, flesh and blood, mind and spirit was its sacerdotal sign. But love's little sister went in garments gilded with glamour and perfumed with romance. Tear off the trappings and you lost all illusion.

These thoughts went with him all the day through. If he could only make Sherry understand.

But on the day she telephoned him that she was back at Little House he knew that he must tell her whether she understood or not. He went home, his heart eager, his brain reluctant. Hurry, and see her, clasp her, hold her close, purge yourself of this burden, cried his heart. But his mind clicked precisely, put it off, don't spoil her homecoming, wait a while . . .

Here were the lights of Little House shining out. He had the car in town with him, he drove up the winding way, past the main house, into his own road. The lights shone from behind drawn blinds. He took the car to the garage and went down the road on foot, in darkness which crackled with frost, in darkness punctuated by the icy shining of blue-white stars.

The door stood open. Sherry said, laughing, "I thought you'd never come!"

Pinch whined and barked, scampering about his feet. Sherry drew him in, the door closed. She looked, he thought instantly, fine-drawn, almost ill. But her eyes were radiant.

She came to his arms with a long sigh, relieved as a patient child at the release from waiting, and he kissed her and hated himself.

Dinner had been planned as an occasion. Sherry chattered throughout it, of the theater, of her mother's invitation — "which I have decided not to accept" — and of a hundred and one things. Watching her across the candleglow he could almost believe that so many things had not happened. She said: "I miss Jocelyn — it seems funny without her — but it's nice to be alone. She must come back to us soon, though. I don't believe she's awfully happy with the Gowans."

Mary beamed, serving; Katie sang a little in the kitchen above the homely clatter of dishes. Pinch lay with his nose on his paws, at the opening between hall and living room and watched and waited, his tail thumping ceaselessly on the polished floor.

After dinner they went to the big couch and sat down there with their coffee and cigarettes. "I told Mary," said Sherry, "not to let anyone in. If anyone comes to call, they can just go away again. The cupboard is bare. So, by the way, quite seriously, is the liquor supply. You must have thrown a lot of parties the little while I was away."

"Not so many," he told her.

When Mary had come to take away the cups again Sherry spoke to her. "You and Katie may go out if you like, after your work is done. You have your keys? Well, lock up then," she told the little maid.

It was good to have her back, Mary murmured.

"Good to be back," Sherry told Jimmy when Mary had left them. She looked around the room. "I don't know why I ever left. These last few months, oh, ever since summer, have been like a dream, part of it nightmarish, part of it exciting. I want you to know I'm never going away again," she told him. "About this — this stage business, Jimmy, can you ever forgive me?"

She leaned her head on his shoulder. He asked uncomfortably, "For what, Sherry?"

"For being such an idiot. For thinking I could act. I can't. You were perfectly right, although I was furious at you. That's why I went to the hotel. Not because of what you said about Holman Benson, not because of — oh, anything. I was — mad, that was all. Like a child. Hurt in my pride and my vanity. But you were right. I knew it all along. I just shut my eyes to it, blamed it on the part, on inexperience, on a hundred things. I was goofy. Only stubbornness kept me at it. Forgive me for that," she said, "and for — for losing the money. It is lost, you know. It was a pretty expensive mistake."

"Forget it, we'll get along. The bank will

reopen one of these days. The depositors will get one hundred cents on the dollar. Think of that money as not really lost." He tried to laugh. "And I've done pretty well. I'll do better. We'll have a talk, soon, and straighten out our accounts. I've been living foolishly. There are a lot of things I can cut out, clubs and such."

"I don't want you to — I wish you'd take my money and use it, Jimmy. After all, why shouldn't you? We're partners. I've said that before, but I'll keep on saying it until you see reason."

He thought of the check he had drawn that day, to Angela. It represented the final payment of his debt to her. If all things were only so simple and could be settled by words and figures scrawled on a slim slip of paper, at nothing more than a material sacrifice!

He said, "I'm sorry for what I said that night — about the acting, about Benson."

"No," she said candidly, "you had a right to say it. About the acting, and — and about Holman too. I did see too much of him. I didn't think anything of it. He — he's really very decent, Jimmy. Don't glower at me. He didn't make passes at me, the way they do in books. He imagined he was in love with me, he wanted me to divorce you, and to marry him — "

Her last words came in a soft little rush. She said, pleadingly, as he was silent: "Don't be angry at me, Jimmy. I suppose it was my fault. I liked him, I was entertained, stimulated. I knew perfectly well where it was leading, I'm not a fool. But I felt so safe, loving you, you see. And we were civilized people, all of us, I knew I could handle it. I hadn't meant it to come to a — a declaration. But it did. It was at Angela's, one time, when he had taken me back there after a party. He had some excuse, I suppose, to think things, to think that perhaps I cared for him and not for you. After all, I'd gone my own way pretty well, and things like that are so — so easily thinkable for the average person. He knew you didn't like my connection with the stage, and he sort of jumped at conclusions. But — he won't, any more. I told him I loved you and that was all there was to it."

Now, he could be sure — sure of her and her loyalty, as one day he had said to himself, If she tells me I'll be sure. She had told him. His arm tightened about her. He said, "As if I'd blame Benson or any other man," lamely enough. But it satisfied her.

Her conscience, never very burdened, was free again. She said, after a moment, "I've been a poor sort of wife, Jimmy, but I'll make it up to you. And to Pinch," she added, laughing, as the dog came in, to settle down at her feet, his head on her slipper. "I did resent him, a little, at first. But things were topsy-turvy. I don't resent him any longer." She hesitated a moment and then she said, "Let's have a baby for Pinch to play with — shan't we? Think of Sheila's annoyance," she said. She looked up at him, her amazing eyes very serious although her lips still preserved their curves. "Let's," she said, "and be a real family . . . I wouldn't have much time for sitting in agents' offices and hunting jobs then, would I? That's all over with."

He thought, I can't stand much of this. He was so still that after a moment she said — "But — I thought perhaps you'd be *glad* — "

He got up so suddenly that she was startled. He stood looking down at her. He said: "I am glad — and ashamed. There's something I must tell you, Sherry. It's this." He swallowed hard, convulsively. His words were torn from him. He stated, painfully, "I love you better than anything in the world, Sherry, and I've been unfaithful to you." He added, in the face of her stunned incredulity, "I suppose people *would* call it that."

She said instantly, "No — *no* — *!*" and

then was silent, the back of her hand caught across her mouth, sitting there, quite still. Then she said, "Who — ? No, I don't want to know!" and then, "Jimmy, if you're *joking* — "

"I'm not joking." He sat down again, away from her, at the extreme end of the couch. He said dully, "I — I've been thinking, for days . . . if I could make you understand. You won't, I'm afraid. It — it didn't mean anything," he said in despair as her face was shut against him, hard as a closed fist, stony, all the color drained from it, "it didn't mean anything — "

"Perhaps it didn't to you," she said after a moment, "but it does to me — "

"Don't you see that it mustn't, Sherry?" He did not dare touch her, he feared repulsion more than anything in the world at that moment. "It mustn't. I — there isn't any excuse — I was lonely, we had become estranged, somehow, I didn't quite know why, — and so, it happened. Just *happened,* that was all — "

"How long has this affair been going on?" she asked in a voice so like Sheila's and in a phrase so banal that he looked at her with astonishment.

"It wasn't an affair — "

"What was it, then?" she demanded.

"I don't know," he admitted miserably, "a brain storm, I suppose — it didn't last. It couldn't. It was over before — before you came back here, before the show closed."

"It was Angela," she stated evenly.

He said nothing. There was nothing to say. She said, "Yes, of course, Angela." She looked at him with a curious cold pity, "That's your real excuse, if any. She's tried hard enough. She got her way, she usually does."

"No one," he muttered, "was to blame but myself — "

"You needn't bother to protect her," she said scornfully. She shook, suddenly, shuddering away from him, pressed close against the arm of the couch. "I — I can't see her again, *ever*." She was suffering all she had once thought to suffer, in imagination. Physical jealousy took her, unendurably, for the first time since his statement had shattered the security of her world. She began to cry, noisily, frighteningly. He begged her, miserably, too cowardly to reach out his hand to her. "Sherry, don't — don't — if you knew how I felt, so abased — so — "

"You didn't stop to think how I might feel," she wept childishly. She controlled herself a little, her words still blurred. She said, "I suppose she wants you to marry her."

Jimmy said gently, "You know that isn't so — "

"She can have you!" said Sherry. With a terrific effort she ceased crying and looked at him with hostile eyes. "I don't want you," she said, "not any more . . ." And then, before he could move or speak, she cried out despairingly, "Why did you tell me, Jimmy — *why?*"

"I had to Sherry. Unless I told you — things couldn't be the same — "

"How can they be the same now?" she asked him. "They can't be. Oh, I suppose telling me has helped you — made you feel — clean — and noble — and — and absolved, in a way. But look what you've done to me! It would have been kinder not to have let me know, to have spent the rest of your life feeling — remorseful or whatever it is you feel — but keeping it from me. It was selfish of you to tell me — "

He said, doggedly, "I had to tell you, Sherry."

She rose suddenly and came close and stood, slender and vibrant, staring down at him. She asked tonelessly, "Did you — love her, Jimmy?"

He flushed, slowly, painfully. He answered, with an effort, "No, Sherry, I've never loved anybody but you."

"Then," she said, bewildered, "I can't understand. I never shall. If you loved me — and didn't love her . . ." She thought of the play which had closed, ringing its changes on this same theme; it had seemed so understandable, so logical, that play, with its written, patterned lines spoken by players. Life was different, it wasn't divided into three acts and a final curtain. It went on, it struck at you when you were absolutely defenseless.

"I have no excuse," he said. "I hoped you'd understand that it had nothing to do with us — that it was like — like insanity. That it didn't even have the excuse of — loving someone else, being attracted."

"No, no excuse," she agreed, sorrowfully. And again, "Oh, why did you tell me, why — ?"

Suddenly she was gone, moving fleetly from the room, running upstairs, gasping a little, the returning tears distorting her face. He followed, on feet that were reluctant to move. She reached the bedroom, shut the door violently. When he turned the knob, it held — the door was locked.

"Sherry?" he said, standing there. "Sherry — please? Let me in, let me talk to you."

She opened the door, so abruptly that he fell back. "No — I — can't, Jimmy. Don't you see that? Perhaps, in the morning." The door was closing, she spoke through it faintly, saying the practical thing, so heartbreaking, because of its triviality, "Your things are in the other room — "

He went to bed, finally, in the guest room next to Jocelyn's empty room. He rose a dozen times in the night and went to the locked door. Once or twice he knocked but there was no response although he knew she did not sleep. He could hear her forlorn and ceaseless weeping.

In the morning the door stood open. Jimmy, dressed since six o'clock, went in. She stood by the windows, looking over the beloved acres of Quaker Hill. She turned and looked at him, not with anger, nor with hostility, but with a certain hard indifference in her sodden eyes. She said "I've been thinking — all night — "

"So have I, Sherry," he said, very haggard in the sunlight.

"I don't know what to do," she cried helplessly, "I want to do what's best, what's right. I suppose I made a fool of myself last night. I thought I was civilized, modern. I didn't know. There are some lines in the play, my lines, you know, where I was supposed to be consoling Norma — remember? I said, 'There are worse disloyalties than infidelity. Other things I couldn't forgive as readily. Nothing was involved in Franklin's

371

disloyalty to you but his man's body; nor his heart or his mind or his soul.' I thought," Sherry went on, "that those were brave words. True ones. Well, they're not, they don't mean a thing — to me. And so, I don't know what to do."

He said, "Sherry, for God's sake — "

"It is for God's sake," she interrupted, "for the sake of the God in me and in you. I've got to get away and see things straight. I'll go, tonight. To Hot Springs and Sheila. And from there to Palm Beach. I'll let you know. You must write me, of course, I don't want her to suspect anything." She began to shake again. "I couldn't bear it, she's the last person in the world who must know now. When I've decided what to do, I'll tell you. I'll come home and tell you. You must see Angela," she said with stiff lips, "and tell her that — that even if Sheila asks her she must not come while I'm down there — "

"I don't intend to see her, ever again," said Jimmy savagely.

"You must. Tell her — to — to stay away from me. — No, don't see her," she cried with a soft, hurried wildness, "don't see her . . . telephone her. Don't see her, Jimmy. I couldn't have that to think about too — "

"I won't," he said. He took a step toward her but halted, remaining where he was as she shrank back, facing him, against the sill. "Sherry," he said brokenly, like a defeated boy, *"don't leave me — "*

Her face softened a little. She spoke, almost gently. She said, "I have to leave you, Jimmy. You see you left me, first. Perhaps if I go away from you I'll find you again. I don't know."

CHAPTER XVII

Little House was empty save for the rather bewildered but loyal presence of Katie and Mary. Jimmy, after Sherry had left for the South, had announced his intention of living in town "until Mrs. Maxwell returns." He mumbled something unveracious to the effect that he expected to join her, if possible, before she came back. He couldn't, however, bear to close Little House. It was an absurd expense to keep it open, but the thought of it silent, deserted, standing darkened and alone through the winter nights, wind in its cold chimney, snow, perhaps, blowing across the windows, banking the roses, was more than he could endure. Besides, with times as they were, the two maids couldn't, he argued, get jobs. So he'd keep them, to look after Pinch and the house.

It was so arranged. He wrote Sherry. He said, inarticulate as always in a letter, "I haven't, I won't give up hope that you'll come back."

He took a room at the Fifth Avenue and went about his business. The last commission given him by Sherry was a difficult one.

374

How did one telephone a woman — specifically how did one telephone Angela and request her to keep out of the states of Virginia and Florida? But he wouldn't see her. He had given his promise to Sherry; moreover, he didn't want to see her.

But he saw her. She walked into the office one bright January morning. Jimmy, with lonely holidays behind him and a Christmas which had been intolerable — he had spent it with Joe McKenzie, in his bachelor apartment, listening while Joe mixed drinks and commiserated with him for not "being able" to join Sherry — he was making up for lost time by hard and successful work. Angela, closing his door behind her, announced, "I won't apologize for this — invasion."

Not his fault that she came, was his instant reaction. She said, standing beside the desk, ignoring his mechanical murmur: "No, I won't sit down. I'm sailing — tonight. I don't know how long I shall be gone. I think I may run into something amusing. Elsie Richardson's divorce is an established fact. She's reversing the usual procedure and buying her trousseau over here in order to return and marry Merry Post, fully caparisoned. I've had a frantic cable from Mrs. Post. People are incredible. She has forgotten how she blamed me for — what didn't happen;

375

how she hated me; how she sent ambassadors to beg me to leave her precious infant alone. Now she wants me in Paris where Merry is awaiting the return of his fiancée. She thinks — I may have influence with him. Entertaining, isn't it?"

Jimmy was not interested. He said, however, "Well, what does that make you — or anyone else?"

"It amounts to just this," Angela responded. "Merry's devoted mamma has come to the conclusion that it is better for Meredith to be involved with a bad woman who wouldn't marry him on a bet than a bad woman who would with or without a wager." She asked, as he was silent, "Sherry's with Sheila, isn't she?"

"Yes."

"Jimmy — ?"

"I told her," Jimmy said.

"So I gathered. Another good reason for me to take a long trek into parts unknown. I'm resigned, I have to be. You are, however, an unmitigated idiot."

"I suppose so — "

"We won't," said Angela reflectively, "be able to indulge in any jolly little family gatherings until we're all old, with long white beards and arthritis. Then it won't matter, of course; and it may even be able to warm our aging blood with the remembrance of how wicked and wild, unhappy and miserable we were, a hundred years ago. She's — coming back?"

"Of course," said Jimmy shortly.

"That means, you aren't sure. I could tell you how to be sure. But I doubt if my conclusions and considered advice would interest you." She turned and walked to the door. Her face was ivory, save for the scarlet mouth, sables were thick and dark and soft at her throat. "Well, old timer, good-by — good luck — And if things don't break for you — there's always Paris."

Angela was gone. The states of Virginia and Florida were safe from her, Sherry was safe. She would read of her departure in the newspapers. He thought briefly of Meredith Post; he thought, Talk about the devil and the deep blue sea . . . but surely Merry wouldn't be such a fool. Yet he wasn't certain.

If Sherry, now at Palm Beach, read of Angela's departure with an emotion of sick relief, Jimmy's reaction was unmitigated sickness when he read that, having succeeded in selling the recent play by Frank Richardson to Superfect Pictures, Holman Benson was flying to Florida. He threw the newspaper on the floor. Sherry would, of course, retrieve something of her vanished money, he supposed he should be glad. But he was not. He was afraid.

Sherry, regarding bright blue water and golden sunlight and the stirred branches of palm trees, looked up from where she sat on the beach and saw Benson coming toward her. He sat down beside her, a very good-looking man in a bathing suit, and said, as if they had parted an hour or so before, "I'm afraid you read of the sale to Superfect Pictures — so my flying down here to tell you about it is the proverbial coals to Newcastle."

She hadn't read it. She congratulated him and herself, smiling, putting her slim tanned hand in his. "I'm awfully glad, Holman."

He told her the price was enough to clear them, to give Richardson a little stake for the future, to repay her a modest sum, to help them all around.

"That's not, really, why I came. I telephoned Rye. I didn't know you'd left town. Has — has anything happened?"

"Why, no," Sherry replied, "what would happen? I was terribly tired. I'm down here for a rest."

"And — your husband?"

"He's living in New York for the present," she explained carelessly. "I expect to stay here until early spring. He may join me."

He knew she lied. Said so, in the face of her hostile silence.

"I don't know what's happened between you. I can guess — there's a lot of talk, bound to be, of course. How any man in his senses could — "

She said coldly, "Let's not discuss Jimmy, please."

"All right. You've left him," he stated rather than asked.

"No."

"Rumor couldn't be quite so far off," he argued. "If you haven't left him, you're planning to leave him. When you get straightened out with the world and yourself, you'll tell me so? You'll tell me there's a chance for me?"

She sifted the golden sand through her brown fingers, watching it idly. She thought, I wonder? Life with Holman Benson would be exciting, it would have the color he had promised. The last fine grains ran through her clasp and mingled with a million other grains, on the beach. She said abruptly: "There'll never be a chance no — no matter what I do. I don't love you, Holman. I never shall. And I — I'm not interested in the theater anymore."

He took that in silence, his jaw a little outthrust. Sheila came up, in an astonishing

379

bathing suit. There was to be a cocktail party. She said, "Sherry, isn't it time we dressed?" She exclaimed, "Oh, good morning, Mr. Benson, when did you arrive?"

He told her briefly.

"You must dine with us." She calculated. "Wednesday?"

"I'm sorry," he answered, "I'm returning almost at once."

"Oh, I see." The farewells were a little awkward. And Sheila didn't see. When she was alone with her daughter at the villa, which wasn't until early afternoon, she asked fretfully, "Why this airplane rush down and back? Why did he come?"

"To tell me he'd sold the play to the movies — "

"That's good," said Sheila absently, "you may save something from the wreck, after all. But writing would have been as fast, and much less expensive." She regarded Sherry closely. "The man's in love with you, of course."

"What of it?" asked her daughter indifferently.

"Is that why you left Jimmy?"

"I haven't left him. How many times must I tell you that?"

"Oh, I know be writes you, and you write — under my eyes, as it were, but — you have all the symptoms of an unhappy wife. You needn't tell me, I don't want to know. I supposed it was Holman Benson. If so, make up your mind. If you have a flair for bad marriages, there is nothing I can do about it. But for heaven's sake decide, one way or another. If you want to go to Reno, I'll go with you. It's an amusing town, they tell me, and one meets all one's best and worse friends there. It would look better, I think, if I went — "

"I don't — I'm not going — " To her own distress, Sherry began to cry. She said, between gasps, "Please leave me alone. I'm nervous, I don't know what I'm saying."

"It *is* Benson," reflected her mother.

"No!"

"Remember," said Sheila, "I came into the dressing room, the night of the opening. I saw you, everyone saw you — sitting there, half dressed, with your producer's strong right arm about you and your head — "

Sherry cried, white, "I don't know what you're talking about."

She didn't. It hadn't mattered. She had forgotten. She had never remembered.

Sheila shrugged. "Have it your own way. *I've* no doubt it was innocent. Not that Jimmy thought so."

"Jimmy?"

"Of course, someone would tell him, wouldn't they?"

Sherry thought swiftly, Who had been in the room? Jocelyn? But Jocelyn would say nothing, would not even interpret the scene as had Sheila. The other women? Sheila herself? She said, after a moment, "I suppose you told him."

"I'm your mother. If I choose to issue a warning — "

Sherry rose and fled. She was now hopelessly irritated by her mother, at all times. There was no common ground on which they might meet. But where could she go? Not home, not yet. She thought, lying upstairs in her great, cool room, Some day I can forgive him, perhaps, but I can't forget. What's the good of forgiving if you don't erase it? And how can you, it's beyond human power. To go through the rest of my life, suspicious, wondering, having to meet her — some time — having to think of them, together — oh, all my life I'll remember —

Her mother had said, of quite a different problem, one which wasn't after all a problem, make up your mind. If only she could.

Back in New York Jocelyn was making up her own. She was lunching with Jimmy, and was displaying to him her father's most recent letter. Jimmy read it. "That means we can expect him back in about six weeks?"

She supposed so, she told him. She linked her hands under her chin and regarded him gravely over the table in the quiet restaurant. "Jimmy," she asked — without warning, "what's wrong between you and Sherry?"

"Why — nothing," he replied uncomfortably, "she was tired, that's all, and decided to join Sheila. It was just what she needed. She'll — she'll be back. Little House is open, of course, but it's simpler for me to stay in town while she is away."

"Yes," said Jocelyn, "she's written me all that. I know I haven't any right to ask, Jimmy." Her voice rose; she said urgently, "But I have to ask, it means so dreadfully much to me . . . what's wrong? Please — please, tell me."

Surrendering, he answered dully. "I can't tell you, Jocelyn. But — it will all come out all right, I'm sure of it."

She ventured, as miserably as a child to whom the expected punishment still comes as a shock. "You've quarreled. Over something big. She's left you, perhaps. You don't — love each other any more."

"I love *her*, Jocelyn, I always shall. And what happened was my fault."

"I don't know what it was," she said, "and perhaps it wasn't all your fault. Perhaps these things must come and no one can prevent them."

"Don't be unhappy about us, youngster. We — maybe it's just the adjustment period you hear so much about, the first year or so of marriage," said Jimmy.

That night Frank Richardson came to the Gowan house where Jocelyn was staying. The Gowans, quite elderly people who knew very little of what went on in the world and had no desire to know, thought him a nice, gifted boy, if rather erratic. They knew nothing about him save that he came to see Jocelyn, and that Jocelyn liked him. They had asked her tentatively, "Would your father approve of this young man?" But that was as far as they had gone.

He said, when they were alone in the stuffy, homelike living room:

"There's nothing to prevent our getting married, Jocelyn — except you. I've my share of the motion picture sale. We can live on it a long time, say, in Italy. Then, there's a good chance of the new play being produced. I've had an advance. We'll go over, spend the rest of the winter in Italy, go somewhere, perhaps Sweden, for the summer, come back for the autumn rehearsals."

She said, looking at him with wide, serious eyes, "Frank, are you sure you need me?"

He was sure. He told her so, a thousand times. He said, "If anyone had told me that a girl — you — could keep me like this — dangling — making these incredible trips to Jersey to plead and beg and abase myself — I wouldn't have believed them."

That night she wrote to Sherry. She said: "I'm going to marry Frank Richardson. His wife has divorced him. He has a little money, we'll live on it, abroad, for a while. There'll be a new play, I think it's really a great one, in the fall. He needs me and I'm fond of him. I'm not in love with him, I don't suppose I'll ever be in love with anyone, I hope not. It does such terrible things to you. I'm afraid Father will be upset. I hate to go behind his back. But you know what he thinks of remarriages and divorces, Sherry. So I thought I'd marry Frank quietly . . . and we'd sail. Father's in Germany. We'll have time to go there, and see him, before he returns. I think that's best. But I can't bear being married without someone of my own. I want you and Jimmy to be there, Sherry — "

When the letter came Sherry read it once, twice. Then she got to her feet and went to her mother's room. She said, without preliminary, "I have to go back. I'm flying, I think — I won't, I suppose, be gone very long."

"You're simply incalculable," said her mother. "What's the matter? Jimmy gone the blond route?"

Sherry winced. "It's Jocelyn. She — she's making a frightful mistake. Frank Richardson. She's marrying him, almost at once, and sailing for Europe. I've got to stop it, if I can."

"Don't be so absurd," her mother replied sharply, "that girl is no concern of yours. Let Jimmy handle it. Better still, keep out of it, both of you. It has nothing to do with you."

"I think it has something to do with me," Sherry said. "I'll be back, I don't know when. I'll take along enough to carry me for a few days. I have the things I wore at Hot Springs, they're warmer."

Her mother said acidly, "I don't know how you expect to engineer Jocelyn's life for her when you're so uncertain about your own."

Sherry arrived in New York after an uneventful flight. It was her first long trip, and ordinarily she would have delighted in it, but it meant nothing to her, she was far too preoccupied. She thought, She hasn't a chance to be happy, she's starting out all wrong, it can mean nothing but misery —

She had wired Jocelyn to meet her in New

York, at the Warwick, and to plan to stay there with her for a few days. Jocelyn was waiting in their rooms when she arrived. Sherry took off her things and looked at the younger girl. Jocelyn sat, her little face serene, her hands relaxed in her lap, by the window. She said:

"It was dear of you, Sherry. I'll always remember it. We — we were to get the license and be married, this week."

Sherry sat down on the edge of a bed. "I didn't really come for that, Jocelyn. I came, frankly, to try and talk you out of this, if I could."

"You can't," said Jocelyn quietly. She looked at Sherry. "I love you and Jimmy and Father more than anything in the world. More than Frank. But none of you separately or combined can change my mind now. I was a long time coming to a decision. Now I won't alter."

Sherry argued desperately.

"Jocelyn, you don't love him, really, you admit it. He — he's erratic and unreliable and selfish. Remember what you told me about — about his wife — "

"She isn't his wife any longer," said Jocelyn slowly.

"Isn't she? I wonder. I think she is," said Sherry. Something was taking shape in her

387

mind, unalterable, a sudden rooted conviction. It had always been there, would always be, she knew that now.

Jocelyn cried out, after a minute:

"No, that's not so, things don't endure like that, nothing endures that is based on — on passion and wanting and — Oh, call it romance, I don't know what it is. He — does feel something for Elsie Richardson, he's one in a million because he still has — has an emotion for her. But what he feels is all wrong, it has destroyed him, it will destroy him again if he isn't helped. I can help. I shall. He has genius, Sherry. You haven't read the new play, I have. It takes your breath away. He'll be great, one day, if he isn't hampered, if he's left free of the things that prisoned him, if he's cured of this — canker. I'll help him to be free. We have every chance for success, we'll build something that will last so much longer than the other thing."

"You can't," said Sherry, "build anything that will last unless you have what you call — the other thing — first, as a foundation."

"That's not true." Jocelyn came to her feet. She went to the dresser and leaned against it, and talked rapidly, her eyes never leaving Sherry's face. "Look at you and Jimmy. I thought you were the most marvelous people in the world, completely in love, nothing else mattering, making yourselves such a secret lovely life. I thought, They'll never fail each other, they'll always be wonderful, they have something that's lasting, immortal almost. But you haven't, had you? I don't know what's happened. I asked Jimmy, I felt I had to know. But it was something. It couldn't have been all superficial, like money or your going on the stage and all, you could have adjusted yourselves to that."

"Jimmy didn't tell you?" asked Sherry, scarlet.

"No, he said it was his fault. That's what nice people say. He is a nice person. I thought once, I'll wait all my life until I can have what they have. But I won't, now. I don't want what you had if nothing comes of it — if everything you've sworn to each other means nothing, at the end. If — even if you hadn't left him but had patched things up, it would alter things. I wouldn't want that, a patched-up happiness. I'd rather marry someone for whom I felt none of what I thought you two felt — for each other. I'd rather marry someone to whom I could go in friendship, without any illusions. Passionate love is an illusion — there's Frank — and — Elsie. They were passionately in love.

What happened to them? Hate and hurt and a horrible sort of clinging to something that couldn't mean anything, after what sanctified it had gone — if it ever existed. Oh, he's told me — told me things that made me crawl with shame for him and for her. At least he's been honest with me."

Sherry said slowly, "Are you trying to tell me that you have decided to marry Frank Richardson because you think that Jimmy and I — ?"

Jocelyn was silent.

Sherry got up and went over to her. She took her by the shoulders. She shook her, very slightly. She said, spacing her words, "You can't — I won't have it — I'll not have that on my conscience — "

"You needn't," said Jocelyn, pale.

"But I shall. Shall I tell you what happened between me and Jimmy?" she asked. "Shall I betray him to you, tell you what I never thought to tell a living soul?"

Jocelyn said, low, "Yes, Sherry — "

"He was unfaithful to me," said Sherry. Jocelyn twisted away from her.

"I thought it was something like that."

"Something? There *isn't* anything like that," said Sherry angrily. "I ran away from it, all the implications of it. It was my fault as much as his. I'll never, of course, understand why it happened — not really, not deep down. You see, Jocelyn, he does love me, I know that now. I've been knowing it, sitting here, listening to you."

"Yes," said Jocelyn, "he does, I know it too. He told me so."

"He did?" Her face lighted with a heartbreakingly lovely smile. "You see, it does last, even when — when — "

Jocelyn moved away from her. She sat down in the chair again and stared out the window. "This isn't an argument — for loving people, is it? To be so vulnerable. So hurt." She said further, "You left him, of course, you couldn't do anything else."

"No," responded Sherry, "I didn't leave him. My body left him, but not anything that really mattered. And I'm going back — home."

Jocelyn cried out at that.

"But to what, Sherry . . . to patching things up, to admitting your marriage was a failure, and that you'll just make the best of it?"

"It isn't a failure," said Sherry, "it's never been a failure."

Jocelyn twisted about to observe her. She said quietly: "But it must be. Can't you see that's just what I'm guarding against? If Frank is ever unfaithful to me" — she shrugged

391

her shoulders — "it won't matter. How can it? I shan't be involved. That's the side of marriage which — "

Sherry went over to her and knelt down beside her.

"Which won't matter? Jocelyn, don't say it. It *has* to matter. It has to come first, a basis, as I told you. If you are sorry for Frank, if you love his mind and his need of you, if you are his friend — and only that — if you love his mind and not his body as well, if you are his friend and not his lover, you will — " She broke off, tears in her throat. She went on helplessly, simply. "You don't know. Nothing I can say will make you know. But it will be hell, Jocelyn."

"No," said Jocelyn. She looked down at Sherry. She added quietly: "And if it is, I can tell myself, it doesn't matter, I can endure it. But I couldn't endure *your* sort of hell, Sherry. You can't make me change my mind. It is as if I had been asleep in some sort of a legend, and am now awake."

There was no more to be said. Frank Richardson came, after a while. He said to Sherry, smiling his twisted smile, "You don't approve, naturally?"

"No, Frank." She took his hand a moment. "For God's sake be good to her."

"I can't promise that," he said slowly, "but

392

she'll be good to me. And so perhaps — "

He was, she thought bitterly, at least candid. They were the strangest pair of lovers she had ever seen. The most pitiful.

When they had gone out to talk to the minister whom Frank had managed to dig up — "She wants it this way, it doesn't matter to me, City Hall's my speed, but — " Sherry went to the telephone. She called the Fifth Avenue. Jimmy, she was informed, was out of town, on business.

The next day she telephoned his office. Mr. Watts, smoothly incurious, gave her the name of the hotel in Cleveland where Jimmy was staying. She wired.

CAN YOU COME HOME JOCELYN TO BE MARRIED DAY AFTER TOMORROW WANTS YOU HERE.

Jocelyn was married in a New York rectory with Jimmy and Sherry as the only witnesses. They were also the only people, save the astonished and expostulatory Gowans, to see them off on a midnight sailing of the *Bremen*. Jimmy said, kissing his niece, "I — if only you'll be happy, Jocelyn." And she told him, after a moment, "I — I don't expect to be happy, Jimmy, but I'll be — interested and excited and perhaps content."

They drove back to the Warwick in silence, in the little roadster. Jimmy looked at Sherry, she was silent and shivering. It was late when they left the Brooklyn pier. They had crossed the bridge and were turning into Seventh Avenue when Sherry said, suddenly:

"Jimmy — take me back to Little House, will you? I — I can get my things tomorrow from the hotel, and you can get yours. It's all a muddle, rather, but I can't bear being alone, somehow."

They had had nothing to say to each other, meeting as they had just in time for the wedding. They had been awkward and constrained, trying to carry it off. He said, "Okay," briefly, over his leaping heart, and the little roadster purred strongly, carrying them out of the silent city toward Rye.

She said, after a long silence: "I wish I could cry for Jocelyn. I can't. I'm past that now." She began to beat her cold hands, one against the other in Jimmy's big fur gloves which he had forced on her. "It was our fault," she said.

"What do you mean, Sherry?"

"We — she relied — she believed in us, and we let her down. That," said Sherry, low, "is a scar I'll carry all my life. She thought, If we couldn't hold love, there isn't any love to hold. She told me so. She's gone into this insane marriage with her eyes open, she thinks, talking, as a child might talk, about friendship and needing people and — other things not mattering. She — she doesn't know, and when she does — Jimmy, I can't think about it, I'm afraid!"

His hands were steady on the wheel, his eyes on the road.

"You mustn't take the blame, Sherry. It — if what you say is true, it's my fault."

"No. I ran away. I could have stayed and faced things and worked out something. You don't get anywhere by running away. Can't you see what's happened to us, Jimmy? It hasn't happened from some lack in us, has it, something inherent in our characters? We had everything, love, youth, trust, belief in life and in ourselves. And we let it all be poisoned, by other people, by casual talk, by smartness and wisecracks and snickerings and whispers. . . . About Angela," she said with difficulty, "I've been seeing that a little, dimly, since I came back. We were always harping on your early friendship, on her being — oh, crazy about you. So that we believed — the people who laughed about it, and myself; and you got to believe it . . . and — And then there were other things, inter-ference all along the line, from quite outside people, from Sheila. We couldn't buck it.

You have to buck it, you have to be two people with your backs against the wall, deaf, blind to everything but what vitally concerns your two selves. You have to build a sort of immunity."

He asked, "Would you be willing to try again, Sherry?"

She did not move closer to him. She sat where she was, huddled in a small but somehow vital heap. "Yes, Jimmy."

Little House was dark, with the darkness just before dawn. They let themselves in and tiptoed up the stairs. But Katie had heard. "Who's there?" said Katie as Pinch, aroused, barked himself hoarse, running into the hall and then stopping, dead, out of his mind with happiness. Lights flashed on.

"It's only us," cried Sherry, between tears and laughter, "we've come home."

CHAPTER XVIII

It was laurel time in the Poconos once more. June, radiant, rosy, and the blue mountains brooding and the flash of bright wings in the sunlight. Jimmy and Sherry Maxwell walked out over the terrace, down the little path, across the rustic bridge and beyond. The falls still flung their singing white waters, the violets still grew in the emerald-green moss, wet with spray. They sat and watched and listened to the calling of the water.

Sherry said, with her hands in his own, "It's just the same."

But it wasn't the same, not really. Things weren't the same, within herself, they altered, they deepened, they progressed. They changed, as the mountains with the seasons, but they did not achieve the recapture of past seasons, as the mountains did.

It's just the same, they told themselves, stopping at the desk to speak to Miss Fisher, red-headed, tall, smiling at them; stopping to exchange a bit of badinage with Sam Packer, as, immaculate in plus fours, he came out of his private office and leaned on the polished surface of the desk to talk to them.

397

Skytop hadn't changed. They had.

If they had thought to recapture the old lovely unwisdom, the new world, discoverable only by themselves, they had failed. Two years had gone by, twenty-four months. They were that much older. You couldn't recapture those flooding, those amazing emotions. It wasn't in human mortality to do so.

Sherry said, "Nothing has changed, except ourselves."

Jimmy had picked up a slender dead branch. A small gray snake slithered away, harmless, repellent. He struck at it idly.

"That's so."

They sat down to rest on some fallen logs. Lady-slippers and laurel were pink in the underbrush, and a delicate white flower grew near by, the name of which they did not know.

"Do you remember that play some seasons back — *Private Lives*, wasn't it? Where they meet on the balcony — isn't that the scene — and he tells her that she holds no mystery for him?"

"I remember," said Sherry.

"It's the same with me," he said unevenly. "Two years ago — you were, just that, a — a mystery, a wonder — I was afraid to touch you, but I couldn't help touching you.

I loved you so terribly it frightened me. I thought, It will always be so, as it is now."

"But it wasn't," she said, low.

"No. Not like that. But it's better, Sherry, isn't it? I believe that. Do you remember the night we came back to Little House, without even a toothbrush between us, after seeing Jocelyn and Frank off — and how we sat up there in our bedroom talking, talking things out, promising, until it was sunrise? Do you remember?"

She remembered. She nodded. "Yes, Jimmy. It seemed to me as if we had never really talked before. I mean, before that we talked about loving each other, and people and happenings and money and — things like that. But that morning we talked about ourselves, you about yourself, I about myself. We came to grips somehow."

He said, after a minute, "Jocelyn will be back in the fall."

They were silent, knowing each other's irremediable regret. Jocelyn would be back, with her husband. They guessed how she would come, very courageous, with a new sort of veneer, a hardness. They had read it from her letters. Elsie Richardson had not remarried. Who had seen to that? Angela, perhaps. But they did not talk about Angela, even now. And once Jocelyn and Frank had left the little place in Italy where they had been stopping, very abruptly. Elsie had come there, with a party. So there had been a flight. It would always be like that for Jocelyn, a flight from reality.

Sherry said, "We can't forgive ourselves, ever."

"No." Pete had forgiven them, not that he knew their deeper culpability. Pete had even liked Richardson, with reservations. But his business was prosperous and they need not fear a hand-to-mouth existence for Jocelyn, that much was certain.

Jimmy said, "And I can't forgive myself — "

She leaned her head against his shoulder in the old way.

"All right. But I've forgiven you."

She had. She had even forgiven him that she couldn't forget. Not yet. Time would blunt the sharp edges, blur the pictures now all too clear, the pictures which sometimes woke her sobbing from her sleep in his arms. She knew that. But this was a second scar they would carry, he and she, in their differing fashions, to the end.

He looked at his watch. "We'd better be getting back for lunch. I'll give you your revenge for yesterday afterwards. Nine holes, and two strokes a hole. How about it?"

They walked back to the club, in the beauty

and peace and the smiling of sunlight. Little by little they would fashion their immunity. She murmured, halting, crossing a field edged with woods, "We'll come back every year, won't we?"

There would be something sorrowful in that pilgrimage, something hopeful and beautiful. They had been married two years. God willing, they would be married for many more. There would be good times ahead, and bad ones. There would be memories and there would be regrets. But something of value, something fine and treasurable belonged to them. There were things which the years would take from them, and other things which the years would bring, in compensation. Or they would believe them compensation.

This was their world, for them created; this world, not of lake and sky and mountain, but of themselves. What they would make of it was in their own hands and was their own grave responsibility.

Thomas Jefferson Library System
214 Adams Street
JEFFERSON CITY, MISSOURI 65101

401

Thomas Jefferson Library System
214 Adams Street
JEFFERSON CITY, MISSOURI 65101

The employees of THORNDIKE PRESS hope you have enjoyed this Large Print book. All our Large Print titles are designed for easy reading, and all our books are made to last. Other Thorndike Large Print books are available at your library, through selected bookstores, or directly from us. For more information about current and upcoming titles, please call or mail your name and address to:

THORNDIKE PRESS
PO Box 159
Thorndike, Maine 04986
800/223-6121
207/948-2962